THE JOURNE...
BE...

The Walker of Two Wo... ...the Seekers in the Hall of Memory. Enter with them now and be seated at one of the four arms of the table of Elements. Lift the goblet before you, drink of the nectar, and follow the Guide who will lead you to such adventures as:

"The Fire of a Found Heart"—His father slain, he was the one who should have assumed the mantle of leadership and brought the fires of vengeance to the enemy of his people, but destiny had chosen a different path for him to walk. . . .

"Family Secrets"—Daughter of the Priest-King of Babylon, the time had come for Shalazar to give herself into the service of her god. But when she stumbled upon the prisoner hidden in the bowels of a long-abandoned temple, she had to choose between duty and compassion. . . .

"Strange Creatures"—Whale Rock was one of those small costal towns where people went to vacation with their kids. But the year-round residents knew that Whale Rock had hidden depths that could trap the unwary and drain the life from them. . . .

EARTH, AIR, FIRE, WATER

TALES OF THE ETERNAL ARCHIVES #2

EDITED BY

MARGARET WEIS

with Robyn McGrew and Janet Pack

DAW BOOKS, INC.

DONALD A. WOLLHEIM, FOUNDER

375 Hudson Street, New York, NY 10014

ELIZABETH R. WOLLHEIM

SHEILA E. GILBERT

PUBLISHERS

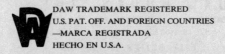

ACKNOWLEDGMENTS

Introduction © 1999 by Robyn McGrew.
Prologue © 1999 by Robyn McGrew.
Burning Bright © 1999 by Tanya Huff.
The Fire of a Found Heart © 1999 by Linda P. Baker.
The Forge of Creation © 1999 by Carrie Channell.
How Golf Shaped Scotland © 1999 by Bruce Holland Rogers.
The Giant's Love © 1999 by Nina Kiriki Hoffman.
Family Secrets © 1999 by Robyn McGrew.
Dvergertal © 1999 by Nancy Varian Berberick.
An Elemental Conversation © 1999 by Donald J. Bingle.
Water Baby © 1999 by Michelle West.
Only As Safe © 1999 by Mark A. Garland and Lawrence Schimel.
Out of Hot Water © 1999 by Jane Lindskold.
Strange Creatures © 1999 by Kristine Kathryn Rusch.
Sons of Thunder © 1999 by Edward Carmien.

CONTENTS

INTRODUCTION
by Robyn McGrew

FROM the dawn of memory, humankind has reached out to the surrounding world, seeking to understand it, to interact with it, and to ultimately control it. Nowhere is this more evident than in the ways we act and react with the Elements.

In the prehistoric world we saw power in the sun and in the sea. As humankind evolved, earth and air came into play, completing the quadrangle. Civilization developed and humankind's conception of the universe grew apace. The Elemental essences became our keystones to understanding ourselves and our world. Out of the crucible of primitive culture evolved the Winged Gods of Babylon and Egypt; the Four Holy Creatures of the Qabalah; the Salamanders, Mermaids, Dwarfs, and Fairies of mythic lore; and the Dragons of the Far East.

According to legend the next evolution of interaction occurred in Egypt when Hermes Trismegistus inscribed the words, "As Above, So Below," on an emerald tablet, launching our world into new realms of thought and possibility. From Egypt, his doctrine spread to Greece, where it eventually helped form the basis of democratic philosophy that shaped the world for centuries to come. While Empedocles, Plato, and Aristotle worked out the nature of humankind, others around the world came to know themselves through

1

their conquering of the Elements and the Elemental essences around them. Fire Walkers braved the hot coals and emerged unscathed. On scattered islands in the many seas, youths dived from great heights, remaining underwater for long periods and emerging as newborn warriors. In the Far East, man-sized kites allowed the monks to become one with the air. In the recesses of earthen hogans and caves, braves and warrior women set out on vision quests.

The Renaissance era brought the birth of Alchemy and the Quest for the Philosopher's Stone. The explorers of this time sought the conversion of base material, both within and without themselves, setting the foundation for the science of chemistry. Renaissance paintings and poetry reflected the integration of Elemental principles into religion, medicine, and social interaction of the times.

Carl Gustav Jung expanded on the thought of Aristotle's and Empedocles' elements within, when he introduced the four basic personality types. These are, the Sanguine (air), the Melancholic (water), the Bilious (fire), and the Phlegmatic (earth), which Jung classified as the Intuitional type, the Thinking type, the Feeling type, and the Sensation type. Jung further expanded this thought and suggested that the Elements in humans gave form to what he called the collective unconscious of humankind and that Elemental legends were expressions of this.

The Elementals have been with us since the dawn of time. Are they simply a part of nature or something more? Who can say? Perhaps, as Jung postulated, they are the reflections of the collective unconscious. Humanity is preparing to surge ahead into a new century. If the ancients were correct, we hold the keystone to a new age within our nature. The Elements, used with wisdom, will propel our world into a bright future and open a new chapter in the Eternal Records.

PROLOGUE

GUIDE and guardian, the incorporeal being waits in the place between time and eternity. He has called to the dreamers, the visionaries, the farseers. These are the Seekers who heard his promise of knowledge and are now in the last steps of their journeys. They come to him by way of the Second Road in dreams, through the byways of mind in meditation, and a very few through the true vision of a mystic. He watches as the Seekers approach the Hall of Memory, walking through the ever present swirling mist that isolates the individuals in cocoons of gray until they enter the great chamber door.

The Walker of Two Worlds watches as the Seekers pass through the portal of dark wood. The mist vanishes, allowing them to see one another and their surroundings. He delights in their wonder: the room he created for them is what they expect of the place known as the Hall of Memory, the Akashic Archives, the Lists of Time, and the Eternal Records. Marble pillars uphold vaulted ceilings. Beautifully arched windows look out upon the Sea of Infinity. Old wood gleams softly in the light, which seems to come from everywhere and nowhere at once.

Several Seekers recognize one another and exchange greetings. The hum of amicable conversation rises as more wayfarers enter the Hall. They are a divergent group—women and men, old and young, dark and fair, wealthy and poor, drawn from the far reaches of the Earth.

The Opener of Ways walks among the Seekers unseen, guiding each to a place at a curiously-shaped table in the midst of the chamber. Their internal queries are clear to him. *Why is the table an equal-armed cross? Why am I drawn a particular arm and not another? Why is each extension a different material?* Silently he promises them answers as the last member of this group enters the chamber and joins the rest.

The Guardian appears to the Seekers, floating above the table at the apex of its arms. He is dressed in a robe, its hood pulled forward so his features cannot be seen. At his waist is a belt of luminescent spheres: one radiates light like a sun seen from a distance; another is the soft blue-green of water. Black, russet, citrine, and olive curl around one another in a third; the fourth gleams with the orange-reds of young fire. Others are partially hidden, their colors unclear. The being studies the group gathered about the table and nods, satisfied.

"Welcome. Be seated and refresh yourselves."

The feet of wooden chairs scrape against the stone floor as the Seekers sink into their comfort. For those seated at the arm of the table made of hardened lava, the Walker of Two Worlds provides ruby chalices. To the Seekers surrounding the arm of living wood he gives tankards of oak. Those at the arm of smoothed coral find aquamarine bowls at their fingertips. The last of the group, seated at the wing made of feathers sealed with bitumen resin, receive golden goblets. The liquid within is nectar imbued with the power to revive body and spirit after a long journey. No matter how much the Seekers drink, their Guide makes certain their vessels remain half full until the time of decision.

The Guardian waits patiently until each is satisfied. One by one, the Seekers look expectantly at him, their hunger for knowledge glowing from their spirits. He turns to those seated at the arm of lava representing the Element of Fire.

"Before time came the spark of life that you think of as elemental fire. It can enhance, or it can destroy. Think well before deciding to continue your journey."

Pivoting a half-turn to his right in the air above the table, the Walker of Two Worlds addresses those gathered about the wooden extension representing Earth. "Creation and the knowledge of its nature always comes at a cost. It can bring you to the heights of joy or plunge you to the darkest depths. Be very sure you want to embrace this energy."

Turning again, he regards the Seekers around the branch of coral representing Water. "The secrets held in the nature of water are more vast than your deepest ocean. To learn them is to know yourself. Ask if you are truly ready to take this journey."

He now faces the individuals at the arm of Air. "There are many levels to air and to wind. Choose well that you do not enter that for which you are unprepared."

Some of the Seekers cast furtive glances at one another. Others look hard at their hands resting on the table. Beneath his covering hood, the Guardian smiles. Their reactions show his warnings have been taken seriously.

"Some of you may wish not to continue your search. Seek the answer within your own hearts. No disparagement will fall on any who choose to leave. It is the sign of one who knows himself. I give you time to decide."

For long moments, the individuals surrounding the four-armed table are silent. Then several rise, nod respectfully to the Guardian, and depart.

"The choice is made. Now your journeys begin anew. You will be guided to what you seek according to the quarter where you are convened: first Fire, then Earth, followed by Water and Air. When your turn comes, drink from your cup and your Guide shall appear."

The being feels nervousness and anticipation flood the Seekers' minds. Those surrounding the table are silent and motionless until a woman finally raises her goblet, salutes the Walker of Two Worlds and her companions, and drinks.

The Guardian smiles within his hood. "The new journeys to knowledge begin."

*The Guardian turns his attention to the Seekers
seated at the quarter of Fire. "Who among you
shall go first?"*

*In answer, a woman with the innate grace of a
bard lifts her chalice and drinks. Behind her a column of sentient Fire appears and takes the form
of a djinn. Rising, the woman follows the Guide
to a door on the South side of the Hall of Memory.
The djinn scribes a sigil before the door with a
finger. The portal opens revealing a cool path cut-
ting through a landscape of fire. The seeker enters
and discovers it leads to the place of:*

BURNING BRIGHT

by Tanya Huff

"MOM?"

Beth Aswith opened her eyes and stared up at the
young woman bending over her. "Good, you made it.
Did you come alone?"

"No, Alynne gave me a lift."

"Alynne?" Beth glanced suspiciously around the
small room as if she expected to see her daughter's
oldest friend hiding behind the curtains or under one
of the ugly, orange plastic chairs. "Where is she?"

"She's waiting for me down in her car. She wouldn't
come in."

"Why not?"

"I think it has something to do with a guy she was dating."

Silver brows dipped down. "She put a date in the hospital?"

Beginning to feel like part of a Three Stooges routine, Carlene dragged a chair over to the bed. "I think he works here, Mom."

"Well, I wouldn't be surprised if she had put a date in the hospital." Thin fingers clutched at the blanket. "She's an eccentric little person."

Circumstances helped Carlene resist the urge to announce, "It takes one to know one." As a child, her mother's eccentricities had been fun. As a teenager, they'd been embarrassing. And as an adult, well, they put Alynne's in perspective. "I don't want to argue with you, Mom. Not here, not now." She caught up her mother's hands in both of hers. "Tell me what's happening?"

"Didn't they tell you? I'm dying."

"Mom, you're not dying." Elbows braced on the mattress, Carlene leaned forward until she could capture her mother's pale gaze with her own. She knew it was a mistake the moment she did it—no argument could stand against that pale stare. When shaking her head failed to dislodge the unwelcome truth, she leaned back. "Oh, my God. You really are."

"I really am. We all have our allotted time and mine has run out. I meant to end this properly, but I thought I had another year. Such a pity because I was so looking forward to seeing how the experiment came out. Let this be a lesson to you." Her fingers returned the pressure of Carlene's grip. "Always check your math."

"Mom, what are you talking about?"

"What do you think?"

"Mother!"

"Sorry, force of habit. That whole answering a question with a question thing; we're all trained to do it." Beth frowned slightly. "It's supposed to make us seem mysterious. Can't see how."

Silently vowing not to lose her temper at her mother's deathbed no matter how surreal things got, Carlene fought to keep from grinding her teeth. "Mysterious, no. Annoying, yes."

"Thought so." She snorted. "Make them work it out for themselves, they told us. Once you start solving their problems, they'll expect you to solve all their problems."

"Mom . . ."

"But enough about me, I'm dying . . ."

"Stop saying that!"

". . . we need to talk about you."

"I'll be fine."

"No, you won't."

Releasing her mother's hand, Carlene pushed back the chair, walked over to the window, counted to ten, and returned. Only her mother could turn what should be a touching moment of resolution into a petty argument. "Yes, I will. I'll miss you very much, but, after a while, I'm sure I'll be fine."

"Fine is a relative term."

"Mother . . ."

"I've enjoyed being your mother." Sagging back against the pillow, Beth seemed faintly surprised by the revelation. "Watching you grow and learn was the most fun I ever had."

"Even when I got suspended for pounding Terry McDonnell's head against the playground?"

"The little snitch deserved what he got."

Carlene returned the smile. "Thank you. I've enjoyed being your daughter."

"You're not human, you know."

"What?"

Her free hand raised to forestall further protest, Beth suddenly struggled to draw a breath. "What time is it?" she gasped as she released it.

"Ten-thirty."

"Oh, bloody hell." The eyes that locked on Carlene's might have been the eyes of a dying woman, but they were also the eyes of a woman who expected to be obeyed. "Stay away from the oxygen tanks."

Carlene waited for the next breath.

There was no next breath.

Barely breathing herself, Carlene slowly stood and backed away from the bed. The too conditioned hospital air had picked up a shimmer, and she could hear nothing through the sudden roaring in her ears.

Her mother was dead.

Beth Aswith was dead.

Bindings began to unwind.

Carlene remembered.

"Oh, crap . . ."

She barely had time to move away from the curtains before she returned to her true form.

The flesh she'd worn for twenty-four years turned to ash so quickly there wasn't smoke enough to register on the alarm over the door. The flooring got a little scorched and the ambient temperature of the room went up about fifteen degrees, but she managed to regain control before she set the whole hospital on fire.

It wasn't easy, and had there been an oxygen tank handy, she wouldn't have been able to resist, but there wasn't and she did, and, eventually, she calmed down.

Burning only enough oxygen to maintain a brilliant white flame barely an inch high, she danced over to the bed and, leaving a scorched line along the blanket, settled in the air above the dead wizard's nose. "See," she said, unable to stop herself from flickering, "I told you I'd be fine."

They'd been together for over a hundred years before the final experiment. Even measured in combustion rates, that amount of time, that kind of companionship, couldn't be burned away as quickly as flesh. Her flame dimmed and she dipped down close enough to temporarily warm cold lips.

"And I miss you very much."

A change in air currents warned her that the door was opening.

"Ms. Aswith?"

She sped past the nurse and out into the hospital corridor. Staying close to the ceiling, where the glare of the fluorescent lights rendered her virtually invisible, she followed the blue line to the elevator, took the elevator to the ground floor with a pair of grumbling orderlies, and finally flew out the front doors.

The sense of freedom was intoxicating. She ignited a dead leaf just because she could, then sped off to rediscover the joys of a world with no boundaries.

A nickel smelter in Sudbury.

Fifteen hundred acres of spruce forest in Siberia.

The marshmallow on the end of a Boy Scout's stick.

A lava flow on Maui.

She was everywhere fire burned and everything burned if the fire was hot enough.

There was only one, small problem. She couldn't burn away Carlene.

She'd gotten into the habit of being human and burning bored her.

* * *

"Tell me again; you're a what?"

"A fire elemental."

"Cool." Feet up on the trunk that served her for a coffee table, Alynne took another swallow of beer. "And Beth wasn't really your mother. She was a wizard who gave you a body so you could see what it was like to be human?"

Resting on the wick of a meditation candle, Carlene flared. "That's right."

"And you liked being human, and now you want my help to get you another body."

"Yes."

"I don't know." Alynne's eyes narrowed as she studied the flame. "You needed my help yesterday afternoon and then you ditched me in a hospital parking lot."

"I said I was sorry!"

"Easy to say." Setting the empty bottle carefully on the frayed arm of the couch, she stood and shrugged a Toronto Maple Leafs hockey jacket on over a faded Grateful Dead T-shirt. "Well, let's go."

"That's it?"

"That's what?"

"You're going to do it?"

"You thought I wouldn't?" One hand beat dramatically at her chest. "You cut to the quick."

"Sorry." Carlene carefully disengaged herself from the wick and followed her friend out into the hall. "I have to say, you're taking this whole thing a lot better than I expected."

"How long have we been best friends?"

"Ever since you bit me in second grade."

"And I should throw all that away?" There were five locks on her door but only one of them worked. "What kind of best friend would that make me? Besides, that whole voice out of a burning bush thing is historically kind of hard to argue with, not that a pot of winter savory counts as much of a bush." She lifted the gate on the freight elevator just high enough to duck under. "Although the next time you show up to tell me you've turned into something weird, you could wait until I'm not holding something breakable." Using the hammer left in the elevator for just such an occasion, she wacked the button for the first floor. "You owe me a Princess Leia *Star Wars* glass."

"Sorry."

"Actually, you're a lot more interesting now than you used to be."

"Thanks a lot," Carlene muttered, lightly charring the two by six bracing the back wall.

Given the gasoline fumes leaking out of Alynne's car, Carlene thought it might be safest if she made her own way home.

To the wizard's house.

It looked different, dark and empty. She'd lived there as a human for twenty-four years and for almost fifty years in her true form before that—had, in fact, helped the wizard decide to buy it—but she felt no more connection to the house now than she did to any other building on the street. Burning a little copper out of the air pollution, the brief blue flare the elemental equivalent of a human sigh, she wondered if everyone who discovered they were adopted felt as disconnected to their past.

The distinctive sound of Alynne parking by Braille pulled her out of her funk and she swooped down to windshield level.

"Swamp gas ahoy." Alynne stepped out onto the sidewalk and hip-checked the driver's side door closed. "You look like one of those will-o'-the-wisp things."

"Sometimes I was."

"Yeah? You ever lure men into swamps to drown them?"

"Once or twice in the old days to protect the wizard." She led the way up the path. "It's not something I could do now."

"Not even to a really bad man?"

"Well, I guess . . ."

"Not even to some guy who like broke your best friend's heart and ripped off her favorite pair of motorcycle boots when he left?"

"I'm not luring Richard into a swamp to drown him."

"Bummer."

"Now be quiet until we get inside. Ever since he retired, Mr. Chou has taken it on himself to be a one man neighborhood watch."

"Was he the guy who found your mom passed out in the garden?"

"Beth wasn't my mother." It was more of a sizzle than a snarl.

"Oh, yeah. Sorry."

The spare key to the side door was inside the hollow body of the hedgehog boot scraper. Alynne fished it out, unlocked the door, and the two of them slipped into the house.

"Don't turn on the lights," Carlene cautioned.

Moving carefully down the basement stairs in the dim glow from her friend, Alynne snorted. "This is your house now. There's no law against breaking into your own house."

"If I don't have a body, I can't have a house."

"But we're here to get you another body."

"And until we do, we shouldn't be here."

Alynne paused and shook her head hard. "Whoa. Paradox. I hate it when this happens."

Carlene decided it might be safest not to ask how often Alynne had found herself in similar situations although she was beginning to realize how much of their friendship seemed to be built on a willing suspension of disbelief.

The workshop door was locked as well but this time, there was no spare key.

"It's a wooden door, can't you burn through it?"

"I can burn one molecule of oxygen at a time and slip through the key hole but I need you in the room with me."

"So burn the whole door down."

"The heat would ignite the rest of the house."

"Not good." Alynne boosted herself up onto the washing machine and sat swinging her legs. "Well, you've always been the smart one."

Carlene settled into the recycling box and absently started burning old newspapers a sheet at a time. She'd always done her best thinking on organics.

"I thought you quit smoking?"

"Ha. Ha." Extending herself a little, she burned the smoke as well.

"So how come you're not igniting the rest of the house now?" Alynne wondered unwrapping a stick of gum.

"Paper burns so quickly it's easy to control."

"You think your mom's cable's still hooked up? 'Cause if we're not accomplishing anything down here, I'd like to go upstairs and watch bull riding."

"Beth wasn't my mother." Rising off the paper, Carlene moved toward the door. "There has to be a way in."

"Fire's not out."

"What?" Adjusting her point of view back the way she'd come, Carlene flared briefly orange. "Crap. Could you throw some water on that . . . ?"

"What's the magic word?"

"Water!"

Alynne shrugged and blew a bubble. "Close enough."

* * *

Burning around the lock did, indeed, set the door on fire but after Carlene had moved up by the ceiling and safely out of the way, a bucket of water put it out again.

"Could I put you out with this?"

"No. I'd just burn the oxygen in the water. I'm not a fire, I am fire."

Alynne shoved the bucket back under the laundry room sink. "Then why'd I have to wait until you moved out of the way?"

"Carlene didn't want to get wet."

"But you're Carlene."

"I know."

"Girlfriend, you need help."

"That's why we're here."

"Right." Shoving the door open with the toe of her boot, Alynne moved cautiously into the workshop.

"You can turn on the light. This room has no windows."

The four banks of fluorescents temporarily blinded human eyes but had no effect on Carlene. She swooped slowly around the cluttered room, lightly touching down on the worn chair pulled up close to the furnace vent, on a coffee mug still holding an inch of cold liquid, and on an old, stained apron.

"You miss your mom, don't you?" Alynne asked softly from the threshold.

"Yeah." This time she didn't protest the relationship. "It's funny but in spite of all the junk in here, this room seems empty without Beth puttering about, or sitting reading, or blowing something up. She summoned me back in 1859, when she needed a really hot and precise burn and we got to talking, you know the way you do, about combustion rates and stuff, and then the next time she summoned me, it was just to talk. I think she was lonely. I was her only companion for over a hundred years before she gave me flesh."

"Why? Was she the last of her kind?"

"No, there're other wizards. They just don't get along." Carlene snorted, a tiny tendril of flame flicking in and out. "A group of wizards together is called an argument."

"Like a flock of geese?"

"Amazingly similar."

Carefully picking her way around stacks of ancient tomes, worn copies of *Reader's Digest,* and piles of boxes labeled *National Geographic*—heavy! Alynne made her way to the stained wooden table in the center of the room. Unlike every other horizontal surface in the workshop, it held only two things; an enormous crystal ball on a gleaming brass base and a bulging loose-leaf binder. "It looks like Beth wrote everything down," she said, flipping the binder open. "Hey, in 1968 you could buy a loaf of bread for twenty-seven cents and you could exchange six ounces of virgin's blood for a quarter pound of dragon's liver. Probably not at the same store . . ."

Picking up one of the loose pages, she squinted at the crabbed handwriting. "So what do you want me to do? Find her original recipe and follow it again?"

"I don't think it's going to be that easy." Discovering that the old steel brazier had been set up for use, Carlene settled into it.

"Why not?"

"First of all, you couldn't follow a recipe unless it led you to Chinese take-out. Secondly, you're not a wizard, and these things are a lot more complicated than they seem."

"Well, duh." Tapping the edges more or less square,

Alynne closed the binder and turned to face the pale flame slowly consuming charcoal briquettes. "So why am I here?"

"I need you to summon the other wizards."

"Cool." She grinned and reached for the crystal ball. "I always wanted to take one of these babies out for a spin."

"Not with that." Carlene flared briefly blue again. "We have to find her address book."

* * *

The metal utility shelves along one wall of the workshop weren't as much crowded as they were stuffed. Old margarine tubs of troll parings were pressed up against tubs of gooseberry jam were pressed up against tubs of . . .

"Whoa! This is not oregano." Pulling a surgical glove from her pocket, Alynne filled it, tied off the wrist, and stuffed it back out of sight. "I always wondered why your mother was so mellow."

"I think it may be more pertinent to wonder why you're wandering around with a pair of surgical gloves."

"Not a pair, just one."

"Oh, well, that's different." Wishing she still had eyes to roll, Carlene continued with her own search.

"Hey, can I have this unicorn horn?"

"If you promise not to use it on Richard."

"Cross my heart."

"Or David, or Amend, or Bruce."

Pouting, Alynne tossed the two-foot-long, spiraled horn back onto the shelf. "Are you even sure the address book is here?"

"It was in 1972."

"That's the last time you saw it?"

"I was never allowed in here as a human child."

"Hate to break it to you, girlfriend, but you haven't been a child for a while now. How'd she keep you out as an adult?"

"She was a wizard."

"Oh, yeah."

Fire saw the world as variations on a fuel source. Magical items, being both highly flammable and completely inflammable gave off a unique signature. In any other room, Carlene could have found the address book in less time than it would take her to initiate pyrolysis. In this room, it could take hours.

Hours passed.

"I am so bored." Sitting on the floor, surrounded by unboxed magazines, Alynne listlessly dumped a Slinky from hand to hand. "You know my mother kept her address book by the telephone."

"Beth wasn't my mother, and she certainly wasn't yours." Irritated enough to be burning almost orange, Carlene blistered paint across the front of a shelf as she tried to work out where the book could be. It had to be in the workshop because there was nothing magical in the rest of the house, but it wasn't on the shelves and it wasn't in the boxes. "Wizards know when they're going to die. She should've been prepared!"

"Anger." Alynne nodded wisely. "Comes after denial, then there's grief, acceptance, and something else."

"Sneezy, Grumpy, or Doc?"

"Just trying to help."

"Then find the address book!"

"Fine." Rolling up onto her feet, Alynne stretched to the limits of the Grateful Dead T-shirt and ambled over toward the armchair. "Why do you want to have a body again anyway? You're fire. You rock!"

"No, that would be earth." Carlene settled back down into the brazier. "And while being fire doesn't totally suck, I'd never be able to eat ice cream again, or have sex, or watch television."

"Sequentially or simultaneously?"

"Does it matter?"

Alynne shrugged. "Just curious."

"I want to be able to walk in the rain, feel clean sheets against my skin, keep doing all the things I took for granted for so long."

"You hated walking in the rain. You said it made your hair frizzy." Kneeling in the armchair, Alynne lifted a tangled pile of dried herbs off the phone, lifted up one end of the old black rotary machine, and pulled a small leather bound book out from under it. "Is this what we've been looking for?"

The steel bowl of the brazier pinged as it expanded in the sudden heat. "You know, you're a really irritating person."

Alynne's smile could only be described as smug. "I'll accept that as the compliment you intended it to be."

*   *   *

The address book updated automatically. All but one of the eight wizards listed had a phone number, six had e-mail accounts, and three had fax numbers. The eighth had only a three word address—New York City.

"Sometimes wizards have trouble fitting in," Carlene explained, hovering over the book and trying not to set her friend's hair on fire. "They can't cope with being so incredibly different and finally they snap."

"We're talking a street wizard here? Eating out of dumpsters, sleeping on vents, freaking out the tourists?" Her lip curled. "That sucks. You've got unimaginable powers and you're eating someone else's spit off used pizza crusts."

"And thank you for that image. Just dial the first number."

"There's no name."

"Of course not. Names have power. Wizards don't give them out to just anyone."

"The number's in Sweden. What if this wizard doesn't speak English?"

"It's a wizard, just dial."

Dialing involved rather a great many numbers, including a few Carlene hadn't seen for the last twenty-four years. Alynne either didn't notice, or didn't care that there were suddenly numbers between eight and nine. But then, in all the years they'd known each other, Carlene could only remember Alynne actually taken aback once—after a grade eight track meet when Tommy Elliot had stripped off his sweaty T-shirt and spontaneously . . .

"Rude bastard didn't even say hello." Alynne's announcement dragged Carlene's attention back to the present. "He's demanding to know who I am and why I'm using this phone. Sexy accent, though." She turned her mouth back to the phone. "Hey, say that you knew our passion was doomed from the start. Why? Because I've always wanted to hear that from a man with a sexy Swedish accent." Her fingers tightened around the receiver. "Yeah? Same to you and your mother!"

"Alynne!"

"Should you be burning that color?"

Carlene got herself under control just as a number of magazine pages began to curl. "Tell him Beth Aswith is dead."

"He says he knows."

"Tell him that while she was alive she gave a fire elemental a body."

"He says he knows. When she died it returned to fire."

"Tell him it's still around and it wants another body."

"He says that's impossible and that you don't exist and then he called me something that probably wasn't an endearment and he hung up." Holding down the button with one finger, she pointed the receiver at the smoldering edge of the worktable. "Should I put that out before I call the next number?"

* * *

Six of the other seven wizards were even less inclined to believe or help. The seventh's line was busy.

Carlene thought over everything she knew about wizards and, had she a mouth, she would have smiled. As it was, she burned a bundle of lavender. "They must be calling each other."

"And that's good?" Alynne asked, waving away the heavily scented smoke.

"Oh, yeah. They know someone's in Beth's workshop."

"That's bad?"

"Well, they can't just leave you here, there's dangerous stuff lying around."

"Oh, yeah, I could really give someone a major hernia with those boxes of *National Geographic*. So one of them's going to show up?"

"No, all of them. They can't leave you here, but they don't trust each other not to try and rip off Beth's spellbook, making the rippee significantly more powerful than the others 'cause he or she would have access to all Beth's spells as well as their own. Wizards maintain a very delicate balance of power."

"And once they're all here, they'll give you a body?"

Carlene burned brighter. "They may not want to, but I'm sure we'll figure out a way to light a fire under them."

* * *

The only uncluttered area in the room was on top of the workbench so that's where all seven wizards appeared—four women and three men of various races. The crowded conditions resulted in a lot of pushing and shoving, and the whole experience didn't seem to put them in a better mood.

Carlene finally ended the bickering by moving just a little too close to a flask of mentholated essence.

The magical resonance of the explosion faded into a stunned silence broken by Alynne's impressed observation. "Cool. Cough drops."

Seven jaws dropped. Seven right hands rose and traced the sign of banishment.

Carlene felt herself flicker, felt the pull of pure burning, and suddenly remembered that in spite of syndication on three networks, she'd still never seen the episode of *Friends* where Rachel moves into Monica's apartment and loses the big hair and she wasn't going anywhere until she had.

Seven sets of silver brows drew down.

"That should have worked," a small Asian woman muttered, staring down at her hand in confusion.

Burning a little more oxygen, Carlene danced forward. "You have to know something before you can banish it."

"We know fire."

"Yeah, but you don't know me."

A tall man in a turban sniffed disdainfully. "It is clear you have been corrupted by human thoughts and feelings."

"Well, duh."

"You should never have been given a body," declared a blond man hiding most of his face behind impressive whiskers. "In creating you, Beth Aswith created a perversion."

"Perversion?"

Alynne leaned away from the sudden heat. "Have you, like really considered the consequences of making her angry?"

One hand clutching the smoking edges of his beard, the blond man added weakly, "And, quite frankly, we have no idea how she did it."

* * *

"We have found the spell." The tall man in the turban moved out of the clump, spellbook open across his hands. "But we still do not understand it."

"No, no, no." The Asian woman snatched the book from him. "We understand it. We just can't repeat it."

"Oh, you understand it, yah?" asked the bearded wizard, grabbing the book in turn. He snapped it shut. "There is nothing to understand, she is leaving out whole sections."

"She leaves out only basics," someone back in the pack announced. "If you study basics . . ."

"Basically, you're an idiot!"

It degenerated into a seven part shouting match fairly quickly after that.

"If you're going to have to blow something up again," Alynne said, tossing another piece of charcoal into the brazier, "could you wait until I cover my pudding cup? The last time you got their attention, you dusted ash over my sandwich."

* * *

"We have decided . . ." An indeterminate noise caused the bearded wizard to pause and glance back at his companions arranged in a semicircle behind him. "We have all decided," he began again, "that since we cannot banish you, we had best might do as you wish and contain you. We have figured out the spell but there is a problem, yah?"

"Yah what?"

"We have no—What do you call them?—raw materials. Usually, we would use straw, or leaves, or other organics. But the wizard you called Beth Aswith used . . ." He looked a little embarrassed. ". . . herself."

"Say what?"

"You were the spark of life added to an inert ovum. Flesh of her flesh, contained by her magical force."

"Wait." Carlene flared, the wizards stepped back in unison, and Alynne covered the mouth of her glass. "Are you saying she really was my mother?"

"In all essential particulars, yah. Your mother. but unless you want to be an infant again, we cannot repeat the spell."

"We?" the Asian wizard muttered, her eyes boring holes in the reindeer knit into the back of his sweater.

He ignored her. "We know how to build a body from organic matter and we even know how to animate it, creating a golem of flesh as it were, but none of us . . ." One hand waved in the general direction of the wizards behind him. ". . . know how to keep it together more than a few days. It would not hold the magic necessary to hold you and to truly live."

"She really was my mother." Burning couldn't express what she was feeling. Grief. Joy. Loss. Confusion. Overwhelmed, Carlene burned up a bundle of sage, Alynne's two sugar cookies, and Beth's old apron.

"Fire should not have emotion," the bearded wizard

observed as Alynne smothered a spark that had fallen from the apron onto the chair.

"So give her a body."

"I have explained why . . ."

"Use Beth's."

Carlene flickered and nearly went out before she remembered to begin combustion again. "What?"

Alynne settled back into the chair and took a deep breath. "Look, she died two days ago right? But because Carlene disappeared, they don't know where to send the body, so it's still in the hospital morgue. Beth isn't using it anymore so you guys use it as the organic matter to build another body. Wizards hold magic, so this new body made out of an old wizard will hold the magic needed to contain Carlene who does that whole spark of life thing again and voila! That's French for bride of Frankenstein lives," she added when all seven wizards reacted by staring at her in confusion.

Seven pairs of eyes blinked.

"But I don't want to be the Bride of Frankenstein," Carlene protested as the wizards went into a huddle.

"You won't be, they'll make you a new body."

"Out of a dead body! That's just gross! How can you even think of something like that!"

"Oh, yeah, that's fine talk from someone who crispy crittered the body she was in."

"That was different! I am fire!"

"Yeah. And you don't want to be!"

Carlene could see herself reflected in Alynne's eyes—a yellow-white flame, four inches high. Magical. Elemental. She turned away first. "You're right. I don't want to be."

"All right. It might work." Once again the bearded wizard spoke for the group. "But how do we get the body out of the morgue?"

Alynne snorted. "Well, you all poofed in here without any trouble."

"This is a wizard's workshop. We cannot poof in, as you say, just anywhere."

"Figures. If I can get you into the morgue, can you poof the body out?"

"It will need two of us."

"Whatever." She checked her watch. "Oh, look. Mickey's little hand is almost on the seven. Day shift'll be on in an hour. I'm heading upstairs to shower and borrow some clothes from Carlene's closet and that ought to give you time to decide which two are going with us."

Fitting actions to words, she pushed past the wizards who watched her go, openmouthed. Except for the bearded wizard who moved back out of her reach.

"But how she into morgue?" asked one of the less fluent English speakers.

"She used to date one of the morgue attendants."

"Somehow, I am not surprised," the bearded wizard muttered.

Carlene burned blue. "Look, if she keeps pinching you, just tell her to stop."

* * *

"Was that Mr. Chou you were talking to?"

Alynne sat down on the bottom step and watched Carlene burn slowly up a broom handle. "Yeah. I told him you were crashing at my place, and I just came by for some of your stuff. He says if you need anything let him know. He's a sweet old guy. Those two turkeys get back with the body okay?"

"Yeah. I just didn't want to watch. I mean, it's just organic matter to them, but it used to be my mother." She sped up a strip of varnish to the top then back down another strip to bare wood. "Doesn't it just weird you right out?"

"After my best friend turned out to be fire and I gave a wizard a wedgie? No, not really. Besides, dead bodies are cool. You know what Gordon told me? If you catch them at the right time, you can pose them and they'll stay that way."

"That didn't help."

Alynne shrugged. "Sorry."

"So, how was Gordon?"

"I led him on, I left him hanging. Same old, same old."

The workshop door opened. Unable to maintain a steady combustion, Carlene flared.

"We are ready now, yah?"

"You go ahead," Alynne told her. "I'll put out the broom."

* * *

The organic matter no longer looked anything like Beth Aswith. That helped. The seven wizards had taken it down to its component molecules and totally rebuilt it. It didn't look like she remembered Carlene Aswith as looking either—probably because she'd never looked at herself from a fire's point of view. The hair seemed a little dry and she had to remind herself that wasn't necessarily a good thing.

"We will use the spell that inserts the spark of life, which is you," the turbaned wizard told her. "When you are conscious of it picking you up, do not resist."

"I'm ready."

The words of the spell were eerily familiar—seven voices with seven accents overlaid a memory of a single voice and a single pair of hands holding her cupped in power.

"I've enjoyed being your mother. Watching you grow and learn was the most fun I ever had."

"I've enjoyed being your daughter."

It was happening. She could feel it happening. Feel herself settling into the body. Arms. Legs. Head. Heart.

"You're not human, you know."

Doubt.

The chanting grew louder. A little frantic.

Not human.

She could smell something burning. A horrible, final, smell.

Then cool fingers slipped into hers.

"You're not going nowhere, girlfriend. You never gave them two weeks notice at work, you have a dentist appointment next Tuesday, your winter coat's at the dry cleaners, and you still owe me a Princess Leia *Star Wars* glass."

You couldn't get much more human than that.

"Alynne?" Carlene opened her eyes. "Where'd all the smoke come from?"

"You burned your hair off. Looks like hell. But don't worry, we'll tell people it's some weird mourning ritual."

"We have done it, yah?"

Cautiously, not wanting to shake herself loose, she moved all the bits that were supposed to move. "You have done it. Yeah."

As Alynne helped her to sit up, the wizards cheered. By the time she was standing, the mutual admiration they'd built by rebuilding her had begun to fade. By the time she'd walked carefully over to the chair and sat down, they'd begun fighting again.

The small explosion took them totally by surprise. Shocked into silence, they turned to face Carlene who blew out the match and tossed the rest of the firecrackers back on the shelf. "Thank you for what you've done. With your help, my mother has given birth to me twice. It's been a long night, you're probably all very tired. Go home and rest."

"That is all, then?"

She looked down at her hands, then up at seven identical expressions. "Unless you want to stay for breakfast."

They had to fight about which time zone left which wizard the most tired but eventually they left—simultaneously as they'd come, unwilling to allow any one of them to have the last word.

When the workshop was quiet, Alynne sat down and picked up the Slinky. "Can I ask you a question? What happens when this new body grows old and dies? Do you become fire again?"

"I don't know," Carlene admitted, running her fingers through the ragged remains of her hair. "But then, you don't know what happens to you when your body grows old and dies either. No one does."

". . . I was so looking forward to seeing how the experiment came out."

The Slinky whispered from hand to hand. "I'm having myself frozen so I can come back to a better world."

"Better?"

"Well, George Lucas'll have the Star Wars movies done anyway."

Which reminded her. "You know, the wizards didn't bring me back. You did."

Alynne looked up and grinned. "Yeah, I know, but let them have their moment."

"You've been great right from the beginning of this."

"Why not? Your whole problem was that in spite of being fire, you were still Carlene."

"Well, yeah, but . . ."

"If you were still Carlene, then the only thing that changed was your appearance."

"True, but . . ."

"You were still you and I was still me and I'd be pretty small if I dumped you because you looked different. If I was going to do that, I'd do it now. At least until your hair grows back in."

"I guess if you put it that way, it's elementary."

The Slinky stilled. "You've been waiting to say that all night, haven't you?"

Carlene grinned. "Hey, I'm only human."

The Walker of Two Worlds waits, studying the faces of the Seekers still seated at the Fire Arm of the Elemental table. A quiet woman with calm clear eyes and noble bearing takes up the chalice before her. She regards it as one who has tasted of its nectar on previous occasions. Nodding her respect to the Guardian, she drinks the liquid in one long quaff. The djinn escorts her to the Southern door, opening it to reveal a view of a desert at night. The woman crosses alone, entering a world where she will learn the meaning of:

THE FIRE OF A FOUND HEART

by Linda P. Baker

THEY will tell you a thousand tales of how the borders were opened.

Of the battles that I fought and won. Of vengeance achieved. Of my bravery and my cunning and my wisdom and how I changed the world forever. They will tell you I burned brighter than the midday sun.

I can speak of it now, without burning. It is the way of old men, for memories of the past to be lukewarm, instead of fiery. But even then, I think, I did not burn. Not at first . . .

I should have burned. I should have burned with the fury of a warrior, with the anger of a son whose father has been taken from him, with the fire that is the gift of the gods.

In the night, blinded by the ceremonial death torches that were the only light in the silent village, I should have burned. My father was dead. The man who had raised me, told me who I was and who I would be. The leader of my tribe. He who led us all. My tribe had been attacked. Our holiest of holy places desecrated.

I should have burned. But all I felt was . . . tired. Drained. Annoyed that the rhythm of my days might never again be smooth and easy. And something else. Something so small and unworthy, something so small and evil that I pushed it away into the darkness. Made it fizzle away to nothing like the dying of fire in the rain.

I didn't even hear my youngest sister until she was at my elbow, speaking. "Asha, are you going to take up our father's spear?"

One of the torches leaped. Sparks, tiny living evidence of our salamander god, escaped into the indigo of the night sky. I watched them dance before I turned toward the empty, dark tent that had been our father's. The mound of earth beside it, upon which my father would have sat, was empty. His hearth fire had been allowed to die. The spear, festooned with red feathers and decorated with the sacred runes of the leader, stained with my father's blood, had been thrust into the mound, waiting for the next leader to take it up. A light, hot breeze stirred the feathers.

"Asha?" Linnan stepped closer.

I was surprised she was outside. I thought all the adults of our tribe were already in the meeting hut. "Aren't you going to the council?" I asked.

"Aren't you?" she countered. "And you didn't answer my question."

Quick and sharp-tongued was our Linnan, and had been ever since she was a baby, spitting out her first words. All my sisters were quick-witted and sharp-tongued, but she was my favorite amongst all four of them. We made an unlikely pair, she tiny and thin-boned and quick, I tall and broad and clumsily muscled.

"No-o-o . . ." I said slowly, thinking she wouldn't realize I was answering both her questions, but she did.

"Why not, Asha? You know Father wanted you to."

I turned away from the forlorn tent, and looked into the night. None of the salamander tribes like the open darkness. We all prefer the bright burning of the mid-day sun. Yet it drew me, that velvety empty black, as if it was trying to tell me something.

"Pauli would be a better leader," I mused.

Closest to me in age, Pauli was my least favorite sister. She was everything I was not, bright and brave and quick and strong-minded. Determined and clear in her goals. And mated already. She had found her anamca, her soulmate, before she even reached womanhood.

But it wasn't for those reasons that we bickered. It was because she was so bossy that I didn't like her. She was so quick to tell others what to do, and she was, annoyingly, seldom wrong in her instructions. It was because she saw the path so clearly and was so unafraid to speak it that she would be a good leader. And her anamca was also her mate and would be her shaman. Since the leader and the shaman were strength and heart of the tribe, they would make an unbeatable combination.

She and her mate, and my other two sisters were already in the meeting hut, in their rightful places among the council members seated cross-legged on the dais. My mother, silent and numb with grief, shaman of the tribe, mediator in the absence of a leader, was there, too, her gleaming skin reflecting the flickering red fire, her dull eyes reflecting nothing.

"Father wanted you to become leader," Linnan reminded me once more.

Yes, my father had wanted it, but not because I was the logical choice. It was because I had not yet found my anamca, and, therefore, one of my sisters would sit as my shaman. If Pauli stepped up, her mate would become shaman, and leadership would be split between two families. Even in death, my father reached out to grasp greedily for power and control.

He had trained me and coaxed me, even though I clearly was not nearly as interested in learning the ways of a warrior as I was in working at manual labor in the mud fields or the kiln or dabbling with the pottery. Now, I supposed, I would have to be a warrior, though the very idea chilled me to the bone and made my stomach churn and knot.

I had no doubt that the council would decide on retaliation for the death of their leader and the desecration of our holy mountain. Skirmishes with the elves were nothing new, although mostly, we kept to our side of the world and they kept to theirs. There was some rare trade—we exchanged glass and pottery for the things they fashioned of wood.

But this time, we had surprised a party of them walking the slopes of Fire Mountain, attempting to approach the consecrated slopes where liquid fire ran in ribbons of scarlet and orange, blessing everything in its path.

The border between our lands, which had once been the site of much bloodshed but since my childhood had been quiet, would once again ring with death shrieks. There would be no trade, no keeping to ourselves. There would be bloodshed and war.

Giving up after so long a silence, Linnan asked, "Aren't you coming in?" She started toward the hut without looking back at me, assuming I would follow.

I watched her long, brown, sun-streaked hair sail out and down as she tossed it over her shoulder. And I surprised her. I surprised myself. "No."

She turned to me, her round face a pale oval surrounding the dark oval of her open mouth.

I had already been inside. Even standing in the shadows at the back, I had felt the heat of the god on my face. I had studied the leaping flame in the center of the lodge. Watched the shaman's circling dance around the fire, her dark red skin painted with ashes of mourning, her fingers clutching the rattles painted with the salamander, symbol of our god of fire.

I had stood in the back, my too-wide shoulders jammed between the beams, my head bowed beneath the too-low eaves. Even hidden in the back, among the flickering shadows, the avid, vengeance-ready gazes of my people had found me. Such scrutiny. So many expectations.

The meeting hut, the only permanent building of our summer encampment, was too close. Too full and too loud. It brimmed with the scents of sweating bodies and sweet perfumes and burning incense and simmering anger. And demands I would never be ready to meet.

Linnan came back to me, laying a hand on my forearm. Her fingers were cool and callused from long hours at the potter's wheel. "Asha . . . you must."

The camp was unnaturally silent this night. Waiting. Even the children's tent, normally filled with shouts and running and laughter, was quiet. I held my breath. I think, for a moment, even my heartbeat slowed.

Only the breeze hastened, brushing my shoulders with coolness.

It seemed a portent that the air had changed so unseasonably, at the same time that the attack had come. "No. I'm going to walk."

Linnan gasped. "A spirit walk! Oh, Asha . . ." Her voice was as breathless and awed as when she was only five and I'd found a nest of baby salamanders at the edge of the camp. "Tonight . . . ?"

Spirit walks were never begun at night, for how could a soul hear the gods when the fire must give its attention to staving off the darkness? When the sun was hidden behind the mountains?

I hesitated, but the lie of accepting her assumption fell easily from my lips. Turning away from danger had always come easily to me. As had allowing others to assume strength and gallant reasons where there were none. "Yes. Tonight." I leaned down to kiss her forehead.

"Pauli will claim leadership if you leave."

Exactly. The decision I didn't want to be forced to make would be made for me. But Linnan assumed it was a problem, instead of the easy solution that I saw.

"If the gods will it," I said with strained piety and turned away from her, knowing that it was not the gods who willed it, but I. Surely the gods would not mind this one, small lie. This one small use of their names for my own purposes.

"But— But— Let me get you some things. Supplies. Water. A torch."

I was already turning toward the night. I was wearing my strongest sandals. I had my fire glass in my pocket, and I knew the light waterskin that hung from my belt was full. "The gods will provide."

Linnan walked with me to the edge of the camp.

She hugged me fiercely and whispered, "The gods be with you."

Then I was alone in the darkness, with only the pale light of the moon to light the way, and the flame of the lie I had told to keep me warm. I did not look back.

For all my talk of the gods looking after me, it was strange to be walking at night. I'd never been outside the confines of our oasis camp alone. My people moved in the heat of day, the bright sunlight, the noontime burn when our fire gods were at their strongest. My people traveled always in groups. We were not loners by nature, as some of the other races were. It was frightening, but not as much as staying in the camp and facing my people.

I wished now, navigating by the eerie pale light of the moon, that I'd accepted the offered gift of a torch from Linnan. I could see perfectly the outlines of the dunes on the far horizon and the looming of the huge boulders that rimmed the valley and set it apart from the mountain lands. I didn't trust what the moon revealed. It was the symbol and power of the water people. Nixsa, the water god, could just as easily be sending a false vision on the beams of silvery light.

Still . . . the land felt right beneath my sandals. Surely the gods could not make me mistake that. The mudflats, which were not really mud at all, but dried cracked earth, crunched and broke noisily in the silence. The smell of raw, dry earth wafted up, carried on puffs of pale dust that moved clumsily in the heavy air.

In the wet season, we moved our tents into the desert sands and made our homes there. We only returned after the waters had receded to harvest the creamy mud for our kilns. When the sun gods began to dry the mud into marbled, cracked ground, then we moved to our summer oasis in the middle of the mud flats. The salamander people were known throughout the world for our clay work, and my tribe in particular for the pale white pots that came from this valley's dried, broken skin.

I realized I had turned without conscious choice toward Fire Mountain. Far away on the horizon, I could see a faint, sullen, reddish glow. I started to change my direction, actually turning my toes toward the east, but the mountain called to me. Perhaps the gods willed it. Perhaps the blood of my father, spilled there, willed it. To both, I owed a debt, so I did not fight the urging, though I wished to.

I put my head down, the hood of my cloak up so that it hung down over my forehead. I didn't want to see or think of the pallid, insensate globe that climbed steadily in the sky. It seemed so much larger than it did from the security of the village. It bore down on me, gilded the crackled earth silver blue. I longed for the warm light and the soothing heat of my sun.

I tried not to think of it. I tried the breathing exercises my mother had taught me, drawing in the damp, cool air deeply and slowly. I played the litany in my head. "Purge your lungs and mind. Invite the fire spirits to touch. To speak."

The way of the shaman was a difficult thing to understand, curtained as it was with mystery and ceremony, with secret spirits and contradictions. Trying to understand it made my head hurt. My mother said her eyes were open in two worlds, the spirit and the living. Mine barely fathomed what was next to me. But the breathing helped. If nothing else, it focused my steps, helped me to put my feet down evenly on the uneven ground. It helped me think only of the brightness of midday sun. Of the beauty of sparks leaping from a fire, of the salamander spirit that lived within the flame.

I stumbled, so caught up in the rhythm of breath in, step, breath out, step, that the sudden lack of visibility was a surprise. It had come upon me so gradually that I hadn't noticed until I put my foot down in the wrong place. The silver light that had been guiding my steps had turned gray and dim.

I stopped and disentangled my sandal from a wide crack in the ground. The moon was barely visible. Thick, dark clouds were sliding across it, pouring across the frozen surface like honey wrapping itself around bread. Ghostly tendrils extinguished the wan light.

The slight cool breeze had strengthened, blowing from the east, and it carried fat drops of rain with it. One splatted on my cheek. Another on my shoulder. It soaked through the thin cloth easily, making me shiver. It was cold, and the next drop was colder.

Early rain! I would have to go back. The rains were not due for at least another two months, which meant we were nowhere prepared to move into the desert. The village would need to move as soon as there was enough light. Else the thick mud that followed a heavy rain would make the move miserable, even dangerous if the rain was heavy enough.

I turned to retrace my steps and realized I didn't know how. The light was gone, drowned by the growing raindrops. There was no horizon or landmarks to steer by. No undulating dunes to the west, or the ragged edging of boulders to the north.

My lungs didn't like the wet air. It was hard to draw it in. I refused to let myself labor for it. I opened my mouth, and the air that grazed my tongue tasted strange and metallic and muddy.

The clouds gathered tighter, crowding each other until not even a sliver of the cold moonlight was visible. They obscured my vision, and just for hatefulness, turned upside down and dumped handfuls of chilling rain. Had my gods any dominion over water, I would have thought perhaps my little lie was not so small a thing.

I remembered that I had passed a boulder, not more than an hour back. I would be miserable and soaked to the skin before I could reach it, but it would offer a small shelter until the morning.

I pulled my hood up tighter, though it offered scant protection, and set about retracing my steps, or as near to them as I could manage with no light to guide me. Funny how circumstance can alter perspective. Only minutes ago, I'd disliked the moon. Now I wished I had just a sliver of its sickly light. This time, when I put my head down, it was to protect my eyes from the sting of the rain.

My light clothing offered scant shelter against the driving rain. Within moments, the layers of tunic and cloak were soaked, the ends heavy and dragging on the wet ground. It was miserable. The cloth was cold, plastered to my skin, tugging with every step. Where my arms and the backs of my legs and my throat were free of the clinging linen, water trickled down. Cold and slithering, like slick worms crawling. Like fat little bugs tumbling, head over tail, down my flesh. The rain dripped into my eyes and my mouth and my ears.

In the space of a few steps, the ground became a slick dangerous place to walk. It sucked at my sandals, grabbing at them. Mud slipped between the heavy leather and the soles of my feet, squished between my toes, and ground at my ankles beneath the knotted ties. I longed for the solid desert boots that were packed away in my tent.

Still, I pushed on. What other choice did I have? I could stand still and be miserable and wet and cold, or walk and be miserable and wet and cold. Peering at the gray wall of water that enveloped me was no help. I could barely see my own feet beneath me. What hope had I of gaining a glimpse of the boulder?

It would be so good to crawl up under the over-hanging edge of it and be sheltered from the rain, even if it meant that I had to crouch in mud. Oh, for just a few moments of not feeling the slithering soft-ness of water washing down my neck . . .

Time passed differently in the storm. I was sure I'd been walking long enough to have found the boulder. But I was also realistic enough to know that I could easily have missed it. Just a few steps in the wrong direction would be enough to take me completely past it.

Lightning flashed overhead, filling the rain with the scent of flame and sword. Fire overhead in the clouds! It set my heart to tripping, fluttering in my chest like the dance of flames in the wind. The quick, hot light illuminated the pouring rain for only a few feet, but it was a sign. The defeat of the cold and dark by the light.

I stopped long enough to remove my sandals. They were heavy as the bricks used to build kilns, coated with mud that washed clean as soon as I held them up to the rain. Walking without them was easier, even though the mud now sucked at my bare feet and the hem of my robe. I gathered the long, heavy folds up over my arm.

The cold rain attacked my knees, but what matter if I was immodest? There was no one to see but the fire gods, playing above my head in the dense clouds. Even so, walking was still difficult. The rain still pelted at my head and shoulders. The roaring of it still ac-costed my hearing. But the fleshes of lightning lifted my spirits. Led me on in the darkness.

On and on, until I was stumbling with exhaustion.

Numb with cold. I couldn't feel my fingers or my feet, or the glide of rain on my face, although I knew it still fell in blinding sheets. And I was too tired to care for anything save the possibility of shelter. Just shelter.

The word throbbed over and over in my head, a prayer, a wish, a promise that the gods set before me, but held another few stumbling steps from my feet. No matter how many steps I stumbled, another few steps from my feet.

Mumbling, now, perhaps raving, I blundered on. My guard was down, as I had been taught to never be, when something hit me! A sharp, solid blow to my face. I reeled back from it and fell, and the fear, the fire, roared up in my chest so that my heart hurt as badly as the blow on my temple.

There was no mud beneath my bare knees, just something rough and slippery. Vaguely, I thought perhaps there had been no mud for several minutes, and my mind was only just now catching up with my senses. I fell back, scrabbled at the slick ground for purchase.

Overhead, my attacker wavered, leaned closer. A tall, dark shape in the blinding rain. I closed my eyes, waiting for the killing blow. And sank into a darkness where no water flowed and no lightning cut jagged lines across the sky.

I woke to sparkling morning sunlight. I sat up so quickly the world spun in strange colors of green and blue and yellow. My muscles were stiff and sore. They protested the sudden movement, and I leaned back against a solid surface that was rough and scratchy against the back of my neck. My forehead throbbed with the memory of a blow, and I touched it gingerly. Bruised and scraped skin twinged under my fingers. I reached back and found the roughness that matched the marks on my forehead.

A tree. It was a tree. My ghostly attacker in the night had been a tree. A canopy of leaves whispered overhead, silvery underbellies twisting and turning lazily in the breeze, flipping to show their bright green tops. A dance of laughter for my folly in the night.

All about me was green, the earth showing through in sparse brown patches and lumps of small rocks. A strange yellow vine ran across the ground near my hand, twined upon itself. A bird, not like any bird I'd ever seen, landed on a branch close enough that I could see the reddish feathers on its breast. It chirped an impertinent, cheerful song, seeming to question my presence, chuckling as softly as did the leaves.

Trees, grass, vines, birds . . . I was in a forest! No, at the edge of a forest. Before me, spread out in a rainbow of color, was a small field of tiny multicolored flowers, smaller and more delicate than any I'd ever seen bloom in the sands. Their smell was light and sweeter than honey. Insects even more peculiar than the tiny bird buzzed and dipped and fluttered among the plants. I found the whole thing, color and scent and movement, strangely beautiful and frightening.

I pushed myself up, standing slowly, straining for any sounds of danger. For anything familiar, but, of course, there would be nothing familiar to me in a forest. The salamander tribes lived their lives in the beautifully barren valley, in the desert. I'd never been closer than the edge of the sparsely grassed area that was no-man's-land, the border between the forest and the valley. Even on Fire Mountain there was no vegetation like this, just scrubby bushes and tufts of grass. Green like that, I understood, but this . . . the colors, the movement of the insects . . .

In the far distance, I could make out a line of jagged edges that matched the huge boulders that ringed the valley. Only from here they were tinged bluish, instead of familiar red, as if the sun itself had little power in this place. If that way lay my valley, I was well beyond the border that divided my land from that of the elves.

Still, so long as I could see the boulders, I could navigate. I could not have walked so very far in the wind and rain the night before. There had not been all that many hours of the night left. If I started now, I could be to the strip of scrubby no-man's-land before the afternoon sun dipped toward the horizon.

I leaned against the tree to re-strap my sandals to my feet. The leather was still damp, as were my clothes, but both would dry in the warm sunlight. I faced the rising sun and offered up thanks for my safety, a prayer that I might find my way back to the blessed heat of my valley and out of this strange land.

The field before me was small, but surrounded as it was by forest on all sides, it seemed too exposed. Insects' wings whirred and buzzed as if warning me away from their rainbow domain. Strange shadows danced at the edges of the trees, slithering and leaping to the music of the wind. I skirted the edge of the field, staying just outside the shade of the forest, analyzing every strange sound, all the pops and creaks of the forest, all the unbelievable sights. The weak sun and my own quick strides warmed me as I walked, keeping the ragged horizon always in my vision.

That was when I discovered that I had lost my waterskin. The strings that had fastened it to my belt dangled uselessly among the folds of my tunic. Of course, its lack made me immediately crave water. But even had I been willing to search for and find it amidst the strangeness of the land, I would not have been willing to drink it.

Once I had circled the field, I had little choice but to enter the forest. I shivered in the shade cast by the trees, but now that I was beneath them, I could see that the trees were not really close together at all. I could still see my destination through their leafy depths. Such tiny leaves, too. They barely seemed worth the effort, compared to the huge fronds that grew near my tribe's encampment. My people constructed walls and roofs and made bowls to carry sand from those leaves.

I couldn't think of anything for which these would be useful, unless they were edible. I plucked a tiny leaf from a bush and tasted it, then promptly spat it out. Bitter and tough. Its juice stung my tongue, and I scrubbed at it with the edge of my sleeve.

That was how they surprised me. I was so busy trying to clear the nasty taste from my mouth that I dropped my guard. I forgot I was in an unfamiliar place that demanded every moment of my attention.

They surrounded me, silent as the soft breeze that stirred the tiny leaves overhead. As alien as the strange, bitter plants. Moving as lightly as the fluttering insects. The only thing that was familiar about them was the way the sunlight sparkled off the shining spear tips. Their faces were pale and angular. So strange, so still and frail, like air, like the fragile clusters of salt crystals that formed in the corner of stagnant pools. Elves.

I swung in a quick circle, crouching and bringing my fists up. I was not a fighter, and there were four of them. But they were elves. Enemies of my tribe, enemies of my ancestors. These might be the very ones who had killed my father, and I would not crumple up with fear before them. Even if it was fear that I felt.

They were dressed like the forest, in close-fitting tunics and pants in browns and greens and tans so mixed the cloth looked like the rain had liquified the dye and made it run. Tall and pale-fleshed. Dark-haired like me, but thinner. So light they looked like the wind would blow them away. Like a slap would break their brittle bones. I was afraid, but I was bigger.

I circled again, gauging which was the weakest link. I moved at the same time they did, choosing the one between me and home.

I hadn't hit anyone since I was a boy. It was a surprise how good it felt. My fist made a satisfying smack as it connected with the stomach of the first one, a thud as I backhanded the one who came to his aid. The first one fell back, grunting with pain, and that sound was even sweeter than the music of my blows. It filled the forest, set the birds to screeching and the trees to blowing overhead as if sending up a silent alarm. The remaining two were eerily silent as they moved in.

I struck out again, and my knuckles skidded along a sharp cheekbone, clipped an elongated ear. The elf beside the one I hit stepped back, caught the flowing edge of my sleeve and used my own weight and the power of my own blow to pitch me forward. I fell, flinging my hands out in front of me, preparing to roll, to kick.

My palms slid along the cushion of grass, and it no longer felt so lush, so soft. It was sharp-edged. It cut into my hands and it gave me no purchase to turn. The smell of it rushed up, green and bitter. One of the elves caught my shoulder, stopping me before my face crashed into the ground.

I flung myself around, flailing out with arms and legs at my attackers. My breath roared out of my lungs, harsh and loud.

The last elf, the only one I hadn't touched so far, stepped past my fists, brought his hand down in a quick chopping motion over my face. The slender fingers stopped just before they smashed into my mouth, wavered above my face. A soft voice, only slightly louder than the whispering leaves, sang out.

My breath stopped. It was not fear or fury. It was not exaggeration. My breath literally stopped. I gasped, but no air entered my lungs. There was no air above my mouth for me to call upon. The pale, fragile elf had stolen it with his strange song.

Pain flashed through my chest. I scrabbled at the damp earth, tearing up clumps of grass and peeling back my fingernails. I arched, expanded my ribs, as if by making more space for my lungs, they might find breath where my mouth had not. Every muscle, every nerve, screamed for air.

None was forthcoming. My last thought, before green and blue and tan melted into black was that the elf had killed me without ever touching me.

For the second time that morning, I regained awareness to a pale gray imitation of the black that had stolen my consciousness. Slowly, much more slowly than they had faded, the colors returned, separating out into slashes of blue and green. The same bright blue sky, but with a difference. It bobbled in my vision, swinging side to side with dizzying monotony, where the ground should have been. And where there should have been blue, the top of my world was filled with green. The trees, with their ridiculously tiny leaves, were upside down.

I twisted, trying to lift my head. It was heavy, too heavy, and aching as if each bobble was slapping it against the upside-down-sky. But pain has a way of clearing the haze, giving back clarity when it is least welcome. I realized I was being carried, ass down, with little care and grace, by the four elves who had attacked me. They each had a rough grip on an arm or leg, allowing my head to dangle free toward the ground.

As I twisted again, the two carrying my legs released me. My body dropped, numb weight, to the ground. The two gripping my arms held on a moment longer, until I almost regained my balance. Then they let go, too, and all of them stepped back. I collapsed clumsily to the ground and climbed to my feet before I should have. The righted landscape whirled before my eyes, and my knees wanted to buckle, but I remained on my feet. I was too angry, too shamed at being so neatly captured, to allow my enemies the victory of seeing me fall.

I wasn't sure how long I'd been carried through the forest, but my clothes and my sandals were dry. As I looked about me, I realized how wrong I'd been to call the glade where I'd first woken a "forest." *This* was a forest. The trees were so close together I couldn't make out a trail. And it was only because I'd been carried upside down that I'd seen the sky. I had to tilt my head far back to see it, now that I was standing.

I took my time getting my bearings. I kept my hands loose and open at my sides as I turned, trying to determine from which direction they'd carried me. I tasted the air, drawing in deep breaths, opening my mouth. The air was different, heavier and damp. It smelled . . . wet. Thick.

It was all . . . unpleasant. I had no word for it, other than to know it was neither the dry warm air of my home, nor were the undersounds the normal, sibilant call of wind and sand. Plants rustled against each other, unidentifiable animals called. The wind was there, but high overhead. Unreachable. Hissing in the tall trees, captive of the leaves. It could not reach my face.

The elves stood back and watched me realize I was lost. At their mercy.

Fear rose up in me, like sand rising before a storm. It climbed my chest, clogged my tongue. It made my breath come out in harsh, tight gasps. It made my heart thump against the paralyzed bones of my ribs. It made my head thump as if they were still carrying me upside down. I couched it in anger.

"Where are you taking me?" I growled in my own language. I knew they couldn't understand, but I was too frightened, too angry, to dredge up the words in trade. I breathed deeply of their cold, revolting air. Spoke the same words again, haltingly, in the guttural trade language that was a mishmash of all languages.

They didn't answer.

I crouched, cornered, ready to fight again even though I had no hope that I could find my way home.

The four elves stood their ground around me, but this time, they didn't make the mistake of letting me charge. In unison, as if they communicated by thought, they lowered their shining silver spears until the sharp, dangerous tips were pointed at me. And then, by careful prodding and graceful movements, they shifted, showing me the way they wanted me to go.

It took the nudge of a spear tip and a delicately released pearl of my own blood to convince me to heed their urgings. As the warm bead trickled down my neck and soaked into my collar, I allowed them to guide me between the trees. Through the forest. They forced me to follow a winding path only they could see.

The pain in my head eased as I followed one of the elves. The other three walked at my back and sides, guarding me. They slipped in and out amongst the trees, flitting like shadows. Like the barest of breezes.

But always guarding me. Leading me. Herding me. They were relaxed, watching, spears ready. At ease. They walked with such lightness, I found myself checking to see if their feet touched the ground.

I grew less fearful, more angry, as we walked. Angry at the loss of my father and the loss of my freedom, at being held captive by these strange people and angry at myself for allowing it. It would have been easier to find my way home had I escaped them sooner. The farther we walked, the farther I was from my mud valley. I held my anger, my fear, close to me. Banking it in my soul until it glowed like coals in the darkness. A fire to light my way, and I watched now for a way to escape.

We moved up, the land sloping so much that my legs protested and I struggled for breath. The long walk took on the dreamlike, striving quality of my walk through the storm. The variety of colors was noisy and confusing, the strange forest sounds like music played out of tune and rhythm, the scents both nauseating and intriguing. How did they find their way, with so much to look upon? Without the sameness of the land, how did they mark their place?

How could I mark mine? I watched the sun, flickering weakly through the trees. Surely the sun moved the same here, in this strange place, as it did in mine. Could I not follow the sun home? Or did it change directions, follow a different path once it crossed over the borders?

The land changed, fewer trees, more rocks. Boulders upthrust through the ground, rupturing the earth, scattering it with small stones, as if some great force had shoved them from beneath.

We walked a narrow swath of bare dirt and rock that clung to the mountain the way a ribbon clings to a girl's hair. The view down through the narrow trees made my stomach lurch up toward my throat, made the soles of my feet tingle. One tiny slip and I'd roll halfway home, over rocks and trees and bushes.

Two of my captors walked ahead of me, two behind, while I shrank sideways and clutched at the knifelike edges of the rock face that bordered the path on the other side. The sharp edges scraped and opened up the grass cuts on my fingers, but the sting was a small price to pay for pretending that I would not fall off that steep path.

Then we came out from between the wall of rock and trees, and thinking I might roll down that gentle slope was nothing. Nothing compared to the great expanse of air and earth that dropped away before me. Despite the steady breeze that streamed up from the gaping hole below, I could find no air to breathe. It was as if the earth itself sent its cold breath up from the ground, spewing it out onto the land, and its great lungs had robbed the air of all its life-giving properties. A giant had lopped off a piece of a mountain, and the elves had floated their camp down into the scooped-out bowl. Living there in the dead breath of the world.

There were fluttering, billowing cones of color. Colors I had not even a word to name, all tucked into the side of the mountain, peppered along the ragged edges. And before me was a sight that stole the remainder of my breath away. The same giant had clawed the earth, leaving jagged, torn runnels deep into its bowels. Valleys so deep I could see no bottom to them. An immense hole from which the noxious breath of the earth escaped.

I edged back toward the path we had climbed, feeling suddenly safe to keep my feet upon that which had seemed, only moments ago, so fearful. The sharpness of spears pricked at my back. But better to die pricked full of holes, my blood spilling into the ground, than to be dashed against the rocks on my way into the pits of the earth.

The elfin warriors surrounded me. The one who had touched me before with his choking spell touched me again, prodding me in the small of my back this time. His urging and a gust of air forced me forward. Out onto the slick, slatelike steps of the mountainside.

I reached out, as if the air might catch and hold me, wheeling my arms like a stripling who has drunk too much ale at his first gathering. Surely I would just slip off the face of this rock. Was the air here substantial enough to hold me fastened to the earth?

One of the elves caught my elbow, guided me firmly around the bend in the path, back away from the edge of the cliff. The mountain curved out, over our heads, then resumed its slope away to its peak. All I could see above me was the roof of dirty red rock, but farther down, where the bowl curved around the mountainside, I could see the trees, marching away up the mountain. There must be trees growing above my head. I could smell their green spice, the rot of their roots, digging deep into the soil.

To keep my gaze from being drawn, as an insect to the light, to the expanse of the gorge before us, I concentrated on the elfin encampment. There were many tents, but not so many more than those of my tribe. And they were certainly less substantial. Away from the edge, the air seemed lighter. Breathing it made my head spin.

Watching all the elves moving about their colorful tents, children running and playing on feet sure and steady on their rock floor, made my head hurt. They moved as if they were not aware of the danger of falling away into the sky. And they had no fire. In my camp, every tent had a fire, within and without. The brightly colored tents looked naked without even a cooking fire to warm their doors.

My captors lost their patience with my fear. They surrounded me again and herded me up into the scooped-out hole in which their encampment lay, into the shadow of the mountain. I gawked now, like some stripling child with no manners, at the encampment. Bright tents, male and female elves working at things I could not fathom, children playing.

The elves, adults and children alike, stopped what they were doing and turned their cold, pale faces toward me as I was forced past. My captors led me to the tallest tent in the center of the camp. It was lightest blue, as if its color had been stolen from the pale elfin sky. It was not round, not square, but both. Rounded with sharp edges all about the circle. It looked like a gust of wind would send it sailing away.

The two shoved me inside the tent. The light, airy sides of it brushed my arms as I went through, and it felt like cobwebs, like steam. Too insubstantial to hold shape, to keep out the elements. Yet it was pleasant inside, dry and cool and fresh. And best of all, I need no longer fear that I might forget and look out, away from the mountain. And down.

My newfound bravery came back, even if it was only airy illusion. I snatched my arms loose from the sharp fingers, flicking away the hands as if I were shaking off limbed bugs. I had actually turned to go when the spidery fingers surrounded my wrist, clamped down on my shoulder. The hands were stronger and more substantial than I had given them credit for.

The hands tried to shove me to my knees, but I resisted, lurching sideways. And so I had my first glimpse of the leader of the elves, from the side, a quick blur of light and air, as I twisted free.

The elf stood, tall and regal, upon a dais at the center of the tent. Frowning and still.

The elves worshiped the gods of air and drew their faerie magic from it. Some even believed they could control the very air that encircled the world, but I had never believed it. Until now. Even watching them walk along a cliff's edge and not fall off, I had not believed it. Until I saw this fey creature, who seemed suspended on air. Composed of it. Male or female, I was not sure. Air stirred its shimmering robes and the long hair, obscuring the face.

Then the elf stepped forward, and I saw that he was male and no airy creature of magic. He was real and strong and my enemy. Stormy of countenance and full of anger and hatred. His light eyes were as cold as the desert in winter night.

"Why have you come into our land?" he demanded. His speech was flawless, the language of Trade that all tribes understood. His voice was harsh and sharp, not at all what I had expected from so thin a creature. "Have you come to kill more of my people?"

"I—I . . ." My voice failed me in the face of such hatred. *Stupid Asha,* I cursed myself. *Did you think they would hate you any less than you hate them?* But I had not hated them until I saw my father's broken body borne home. I had been as indifferent to them as to everything else in my life.

I glanced quickly about me. The warriors who had captured me had dropped back, leaving me to stand alone before the dais. There remained three others off to one side of it. Waiting, watching. All as insubstantial as the leader who towered over me. One was obviously female. Not so obviously rounded as salamander women, but still female.

The other two were male. One silver-haired and aged. One black-haired and no older than me. I stared, forgetting the angry leader above me and the spears behind me. I had never seen two such beings. The old one's hair hung across his shoulder in a thick, gray braid. It was plaited with feathers and beads and shells. His face was as cracked and weathered as the floor of my valley. The other one's hair was unbound, floating about him as if it had a life of its own. His eyes were as blue as my sky, as blue as my own.

I felt a shock, as if something tapped inside my skull. He was as hideous and as alien as were all his kind, yet I knew him. I was sure I knew him. Perhaps I had seen him at a trade . . . perhaps the gods were showing me the face of my father's murderer.

"Why have you come here?" roared the leader again. "Do your warriors follow on your heels?"

I found my voice, my fury. It made me foolhardy. I stood straighter. Although I was no taller, I thought I appeared so, because I was so much wider. "Yes," I sneered. "And when they find me, they will attack your people as you have attacked mine." I waved my hand behind me with scorn at the elfin warriors. "I was separated from my group in the storm, but these found me and led me here, and my people will follow."

The leader glanced past me, toward my captors.

The spell-casting one stepped forward. "We saw no others, my Lord. This one was lost in the forest, wandering."

Was that worry on his thin face? It was difficult to read the expression on such an alien countenance.

"Lost in your atrocious forest," I agreed with another sneer. Of course, I had no reason to believe they could read my expressions any better than I could read theirs. For all I knew, I might be smiling at them. I did not stop to question why I was lying so ferociously. I suppose I thought I was dead regardless, and it was better to die loud and obnoxious than quiet and fearful. "But they will find me."

"We left no trail, Lord."

"They will find me," I repeated.

"They will find your corpse," the leader said. "Kill him."

This expression, this tone, I had no trouble understanding. It was cold satisfaction. Before I could gather my courage, my few wits, they were upon me. Three of the warriors grasped my arms and swept me off my feet. I fell to my knees, at last in the subservient position they had wanted. My arms were twisted back and out, but still I struggled, striking out with my feet, my head. They only held me tighter, and sharp pains wrapped outward from underneath my arms, up around my shoulders.

The soft, singsong voice of spell came to me through the burning pain and extinguished my anger and my hurt. Knowing what was coming, I gulped in air. Thinking . . . what? That I might stave off the spell? Keep my lungs from starving?

The bubble of elfin magic closed over my face, my ears. The air went away.

I cannot describe adequately, even now. The burning in throat and lungs that had nothing to do with fire or heat. The cramping of muscles as I opened my mouth and dragged at nothing. The horror of trying not to exhale, knowing that my lungs would collapse once I did. This was worse than in the forest, because this time I didn't lose consciousness.

They were cruel, so cruel, this enemy. Why not just plunge a dagger into my breast and be done with it? Why leave me here, on my knees, gasping and trembling? So cruel, the way there was no air about my face while a soft breeze brushed my skin, stroked my hands and the back of my neck like a lover's fingers.

The elfin warriors released my arms, and I pitched

forward. The pocket of nothingness came with me. I felt my cheek tear on the sharp, lush grass. I felt my lungs wrinkle and begin to sag. I heard my tunic tear along my back, the collar digging painfully into my throat.

Gray sparkled at the edges of my vision. I could see the elfin leader, no longer in focus, turned sideways and warped as if the gods had grasped him at opposing corners and pulled. How cruel, that his would be the last face I would see! With the last of my strength, I twisted my back to him. Let the weight of my body drag my cold, unfeeling face away. The cloth across my back split slowly, loudly, as I slumped, exposing even more of my flesh to the kiss of chill, foreign air.

Now I could see only the blades of grass, so close they were brushing my eyelashes. I could almost imagine they were palm fronds, silhouetted against the desert sky. My vision was so hazy, the pale blue cloth of the tent had dimmed enough to accent the illusion. The sky went black.

Behind me, someone gasped. Horrified, pained, painful sound. Someone shouted. I had only enough consciousness left to wonder at it. To know that I would never know what had alarmed them.

Then there was cool, sweet air in my face. Slipping across my tongue and down my throat, into my lungs, like liquid. Warm milk sweetened with honey could not have been sweeter. Water across parched lips was not more welcome.

I opened my mouth and my ears and my eyes and my pores. I sucked the air in as I had seen men lost in the desert run to an oasis and plunge their heads underwater. I breathed it in through my skin. My lungs screamed. Air erupted into my veins like sand scouring the flesh loose from bone.

Consciousness came back at me with a rush. A slap.

Light and color and sound. And blessed air. At last, I understood why the elves worshiped it. Why they bowed on their knees before their god, Paralda. Why they lived, perched over a gaping, breathing hole in the earth.

Tears stung my eyes so that I could not see, but I could hear. The elfin leader shouting "No!" over and over with all the fury of a churning storm. A voice I did not know screaming back at him, at someone, "Get away! Get away from him!"

Hands were on me. Slender elfin hands, frantic and rough, but not for meanness, not to hurt. They were trying to pull me up. Cool and strong on my bare back. One hand was on the twisted scar of my tribe mark, my birthmark. The other was tugging the torn edges of my tunic up around my shoulders.

My forehead was resting against a muscled thigh, and the scent I was gulping in was strong and salty and strange. My fingers had gone numb, but they worked. I managed to get my hands under me, to push up.

On my knees, I was barely able to stay upright. I was facing the young elf who had stood to the right of the leader. Breathing his breath. The gods had not shown me the face of my father's murderer. They had shown me the face of my savior.

"I have given an order," the leader hissed, coming down off the dais. "And you have interfered. Now you will carry out the sentence." He still spoke perfect Trade, making sure that I knew I was not to live, not even if I had been given this strange reprieve.

The proximity, his stance upon the ground, made him more fierce, more fearsome, rather than diminished. Up close, he clenched his fists, towered over us, grimaced, and I was surprised that he showed no fangs, only straight, even white teeth.

I heard, rather than saw, the others withdrawing under his fury. Even the old one, the shaman. Ghosting away rather than face his anger. Not so the young one who knelt before me.

He rose gracefully to his feet and faced his leader, stepped slightly forward to put his body not quite between us, but enough to offer himself first. "No, Father," he said quietly. "I will not."

The elf raised his fist.

I cringed, but the younger one, the son, did not.

He faced his father's wrath squarely. Only I could see his fingers. He held them hidden behind the folds of his robe, and they were trembling. "I will not. You cannot. You saw."

The fist hesitated in the air, wavered. Dropped. Still clenched, it sought the same anonymity in the folds of cloth as the son's. "I saw nothing," the leader hissed. "He dics."

But instead of striking me dead where I sat, he turned and stalked away. Striding through the loops of cloth at the doorway with such ferocity that the entire tent trembled on its unseen supports.

I was still slumped on the ground. Still gasping for breath. Stunned and confused.

The elf who had gifted me with a few more moments of life turned toward me. He had saved me, only to be given the duty of killing me himself.

I struggled to gain my feet.

He watched me shift and twist. He reached out in the air, wincing as I stiffened back from his hand.

I cringed inside, expecting the spell to spill from his lips.

"I will not harm you," he said, and his voice without anger was lyrical, like music played on stringed instruments. "I will not allow them to harm you." Gracefully, he stood and walked away. He paused at the doorway to look back. "I will return."

He left me, they left me, alone in my cobweb prison. Wondering how long it would be before the father's voice of sanity and reason prevailed and someone came to execute my death sentence.

I stayed where I was, kneeling on the ground, for a very long time, just trying to sort it all out in my mind. But sorting had never been a specialty. It all just went 'round and 'round, the nightmarish trip through the forest, the airless near-death, the light cool touch upon my back that should have felt so alien and instead felt like coming home. Then the aches and pains of my capture began to intrude, one by one, in quick succession, on my thoughts. The grass cuts on my hands and my face, the spear prick on my neck, the bump on my head, and the strain in my shoulders. The hard ground beneath my knees.

To distract myself, I rose and prowled the tent, opening the carved wooden chests, lifting up cushions. I found a thin dagger, carved of wood but wickedly sharp, and I tucked it into my belt, carefully arranging the folds of my tunic to hide it.

I checked all the rounded non-corners of the soft fabric. There was no opening, save the slitted one I had come through. I peered out. Beyond was the busy camp and the open chasm and two guards, one on either side of the folds of cloth. One of them turned and gazed at me with such loathing that I could taste it. It was like the touch of something cold and slimy.

I went back to tearing the interior of the tent apart. I found a wooden jug, finer and thinner than anything I'd ever made, its surface pebbly and knotted but still smoothly glazed over. It was filled with sweet, cool water that tasted like nectar as I slurped it down. It spilled down my chin and wet my shirt. Once I had emptied it, I spent several minutes examining the vessel, trying to figure out how it had been made, how I could copy it using our clay. Then I realized what I was doing. Where I was.

Reality slammed into me and left me, breathless and weak, slumped on the floor with the jug in my hands. I was a captive, sentenced to death. I would never go home and make pots and bowls and beautiful vases, never see my sisters again. Never.

The pale walls were turning indigo by the time someone returned to me. It was him, the young one with the desert eyes and the kind hands. He came in through the cloth strips in a swirl of cold air and flickering lantern light.

He had things balanced in his slender arms. They might have been the instruments of my death, but all I saw was the lantern with its tiny flame.

I stared at it hungrily, the first fire I'd seen in hours. The first evidence that I had not gone so far from my land that my gods could not find me. It shamed me, that I had been sitting there awaiting death. It gave me a hunger I had thought extinguished.

The elf placed the lantern on the ground near my knee while he spread out the other things he'd brought.

I gave them a cursory glance—berries of some kind and cheese, a mug of wine, a bowl of steaming water, white cloths—before returning to my communion with the dancing flame and to the strange thoughts it engendered in me.

Though I feared he would hear my heart pounding, feel my anticipation, I submitted to the strange elf's ministrations, allowing him to cleanse my wounds. I ate his strange food because I would need my strength. The cheese was harder than the kind we made from goat's milk, crumbly and bitter. The fruit was sweeter than any I had ever tasted. And his hands, cleaning the tears in my skin, soothing them with an ointment that smelled of the forest, were as gentle and familiar as my mother's.

When he leaned close enough that I could feel the cool touch of his breath, I caught him by the shoulders, twisted his slender body and pressed the wooden dagger of his tribe to his throat. I didn't take my gaze from the flame, for fear that this sudden courage and strength would fail me.

He was warm against me where I had expected him to be as cool as the air of his mountain. Strong and square where I had expected fragility. And he did not fight me. I could feel his pulse beating, as hard and fast and high as my own, against my thumb, but he allowed me to twist him until surely his back was near to breaking.

"If you don't take me from here, I'll kill you," I whispered in his tapered ear.

"If I do take you from here, you'll kill me," he rasped.

"No," I lied. "Lead me down the mountain, show me the way to my home, and I'll let you go free." I should have felt no guilt at deceiving an enemy, but I did. The words tasted like the dead ash left in the bottom of a kiln after a firing.

I knew he didn't believe me. I knew it didn't matter. Even before he said it, I knew he would do what I demanded. It didn't make sense, and I didn't trust either my instinct or him. But I knew I could stay there and die, or allow him to lead me to my death elsewhere. Dead was dead, no matter the place. My father could attest to that. He had died defending his tribe in the holiest of places, yet his body was just as deflated, just as cold, as if he'd died an ignominious death in the night. Still, I didn't want to die in this strange place.

I wrestled my captive to his feet. He still didn't

struggle against me, and it roused my suspicions. Surely the two guards were still at the door. His strange stillness only served to further my unease, to stoke my fear. To make me so much more determined to escape.

"Take me out of here."

He nodded, barely moving his head, trying not to move his throat against the edge of the dagger. "There is a robe . . . there." He gestured with the sparest of movements toward the pile of white cloths he had brought into the tent.

Sure enough, when I toed the pile over, mixed in was a robe very like the one he wore, except that its blue was so pale it was almost white. "If you call out, you will die before they can reach you," I warned.

He nodded his understanding, and I pushed him far enough away to bend down and get the robe. It was as filmy, as clingy, as the cloth of the tent, yet it was substantial enough that I did not tear it as I stripped off the remnants of my tunic and wrenched it over my head.

The elf was out of my sight for a moment, but he made no move to escape. He only stood, regarding me with a narrow-eyed intensity that I supposed was not so surprising. Probably, he had never seen a human before, any more than I had seen an elf up close and half naked. I was tall for my people, almost as tall as he, and half again as wide in the shoulders. I wondered if he found my bulk and my sun-darkened skin and the hair dusting my chest as fascinatingly ugly as I found his pale, slender beauty.

Once I was robed in the clothing of an elf, with the light hood pulled up over my head, I caught him up again and held the sharpened tip of the dagger in his ribs. "Take me through the camp. Back to the trail."

For answer, he brushed aside the hangings at the door.

I gasped and stepped backward. It was dark outside. The sky was black and blazing with stars. More stars than peppered the sky over my tribe. The brightly colored tents of the elves glowed from within, a pale ghostly flickering that spoke of fire even though I had thought they had it not. The worst, though, was the blackness below the line of the horizon. I had only thought seeing the great chasm in the earth was terrible. Even more terrible was knowing it was there, but seeing only dark where I knew it to be.

The elf turned back to me, and I was forced to step forward, prodding him with the dagger, before he could raise an alarm. His face was visible in the darkness, and he merely nodded his understanding of the sharpness at his back.

The elves had taken themselves inside. There was no one about, not even guards. I could see their flickering shadows on the softly moving walls of their tents, hear their muted laughter and the wooden clunk of their utensils as they took their evening meal.

My captor become my captive led me through the camp. As near I could tell in the darkness, we went back the way I had come. I could feel the breathing of the earth as we neared the edge of the chasm. I stopped more than once on the short trip. I tried to tell myself I was listening for guards, but in truth, I was too frightened to make my legs move. It took all the courage I had, and a little I didn't know I had, to force myself to walk toward that rift in the earth. My feet tingled and burned, the muscles in my back and thighs knotted, and I froze, only to force myself to walk forward again for a few steps before I froze again.

It was the elf who finally mobilized me by whispering, "I will not let you fall."

The hot burn of shame flashed across my face, and

I hissed into his ear. "I do not fear falling. Only your treachery."

He looked at me strangely, as if there were words that needed to be spoken to that proclamation. But he did not speak, and I did not stop again, not when we turned the sharp corner and headed down the mountain path. Not even when I realized I must walk that path in darkness, without even the light of the moon to guide me.

Of that nightmarish journey, I recall darkness, the stumbling descent toward the tomblike forest, the sharp scrape of the mountain against my arm, and the warmth of an enemy's shoulder beneath my palm.

He guided me, silent and surefooted, as if he could see without light, as if he knew the mountain path the way I knew the mudflats in the valley. If he had meant me treachery, it could surely have come at any moment of that walk in the night. I clutched the dagger in my hand, but had he chosen to slip away or turn on me, he could easily have done so. My attention was on clinging to the side of the mountain, staying away from the slope. I knew it was there, and the knowing that one false step would send me plunging and rolling to my death in the forest below made the soles of my feet burn with fear.

Never was an alien landscape more welcome as we gained the level ground of the forest. It was even darker there, amongst the closely packed trees. The air smelled dank and spicy, a scent I was coming to associate with green, growing things. The arms of the trees reached out to snag me with ancient, gnarled hands, grasping at the filmy robe, tearing out tufts of my hair. And yet it was still more welcome than the winding mountain path. It is amazing how the strange can become preferable. It is all a matter of perspective.

The branches did not grab at my elfin guide the way they did me, and in the darkness, I could not tell how he managed such a feat. Was it magic or cunning? Either way, he bore the weight of my hand upon his shoulder. He did not flinch from the slide of the dagger on his shoulder between my palm and his skin, where one false step could have sent his lifeblood spilling onto the ground.

He did not try to twist away. He stayed with me, all through the depths of the forest. Until even I could discern the thinning of the trees, the coming of the morning. The black turned gray, then slowly the forest began to take on its colors of green and yellow and red. I still didn't know where I was, but I could follow the sun now. Eventually, I would come out across the no-man's-land of grassy plain that divided our lands. Across that would be desert or valley, and from either I could find my way home.

Home would not look the same, I knew. Not because it had changed, but because I had. Perhaps I had taken a spirit walk after all. I had gone into the hands of the enemy and come back alive. Recognizing the change in the forest, getting my bearings . . . I felt powerful. Almost brave. I had done something few of my people had done and managed to live to tell of it. I even had a captive to carry home as trophy, if I wished it.

Though that was a strangeness I still had not unraveled. At any point, he could have escaped, could have done me more harm than I could have done him, despite my greater size and strength. It was a point that had not escaped me, even during the most fearful moments of our walk.

In the first bright beam of light from the sun, we paused and he shared the cool water from a pouch that hung from his belt. I had long since left off clinging to his shoulder for guidance, but I still stayed close, dagger ready. "How are you called?" I asked in my ragged Trade. My voice was rough from a night of being abused by elfin spells and of being clenched in fear.

"D'Atrem," he answered so quickly that it was obvious he was glad to converse with me. "And you?"

"Asha."

He tilted his head, gazed at me with his strange eyes. "That is an unusual name, even among humans, isn't it?"

I frowned at him, but it did nothing to quell the eager interest in his gaze. He bounced lightly on the tips of his toes, setting the robe to shifting and shimmering in the morning light. I had thought it merely blue, but in this light, it rippled with all the colors of the rainbow. Like air made substance. Made cloth. His eyes glittered with the same soft fire.

"It's an old name," was all the acknowledgment I granted him. "It means 'burning heart.' My father planned for me to be a great warrior." The last I said with an irony that he could not have understood.

"Your father," he said, without question. The shimmer about him dulled, and I understood that, somehow, he knew about my father.

"Yes, the one you killed."

"We did not—" He stopped the words as quickly as he had begun them, biting them back.

I would have pursued it, had another thought not occurred to me. He knew who I was. "You knew it was my father who was killed on Fire Mountain."

He nodded. "We . . . suspected. The mark on your shoulder . . ." He pointed, watching me closely, for what I could not imagine. "When you fell and your clothing tore, we saw the mark. Is it not the family mark of a chieftain?"

"Leader," I corrected automatically, my mind on other things. As I have said before, the working out of problems was not my strong suit. But I had plenty of time to think, stumbling along in the darkness, and now I had the main clue to the puzzle. "You have let me escape."

"Yes."

"Because I am the Leader's son? Surely that was only more reason to kill me, as you killed my father."

D'Atrem looked away toward the rising of the sun, toward my land, and the early morning light glinted off his black hair. It shimmered like the rest of him, like a dark mirror coated with black and silver and indigo. "Go home to your people," he said.

He turned his back.

This behavior I did not comprehend. He had done it from the beginning, even in the tent when I was still frightened enough to have struck out at half a dozen elves. He turned his back to me and stood there, facing the mountains of his people. His fists were clenched in the folds of his robe, and his shoulders were set, square and determined. As if . . .

It took me a moment, but at last I understood. As if he was waiting for me to kill him. It was not that he was fearless or stupid. He was resigned to his death. He was waiting to die at my hand.

"They let me escape. But why did they let me take you? Why would they let the son of their Leader go, knowing that I would surely kill him when I had found my freedom?"

He turned and looked at me with something like pity. "You truly do not know?"

"It doesn't make any sense. Surely it wasn't because you interfered with my death sentence. Was what you did so wrong that you were sentenced to death?"

"No," he said quietly. "What I did was not so wrong.

It was why I did it." And before my mind could catch up with his words, he loosened the silvery ties down the front of his robe, slipped the pale cloth off his shoulder and turned enough that I might see the markings there.

I gasped and backed up. One step, two, thunked up against a tree. I hated the forest, the trees. Even when I wanted only to back away, it foiled me.

I sank down slowly. The rough skin of the tree tore at my back, prickling through the fine elfin cloth, rucking it up so that it grabbed at my underarms and held me up on my feet. I couldn't even sink to the ground and close my eyes. I had to stay upright. I had to look at his bare shoulder, gleaming sand pale in the clean light.

It was a strong shoulder, more muscular than I had thought it would be. And it was decorated with a birthmark, an anam, just like the ones that marked the children of the salamander tribes when they come into the world.

We all were born with them. Over them, when we were old enough, the shaman inscribed the runes of tribe and the runes of family and rubbed them with oil and ash so that they became as permanent as the birthmark.

D'Atrem had one, too, but his was clear, not marked over with a tribal tattoo. And it was the mirror of mine. If we had backed up, touching shoulder to shoulder, they would have matched perfectly.

We were matched perfectly. Mated. He was my an-amca, my soulmate.

I jerked forward, disentangling my robe from the tree, and sitting down anyway. There were no bones left in my legs. "That's insane . . ." I protested, but the words were weak. The words were only for my own mind, because he had said nothing. Only offered me the view of his bare back and allowed me to draw my own conclusions.

"Then it does mean something to you," D'Atrem said, and he pulled the robe up and joined me on the ground. He sat facing me, his knees almost touching mine. "I thought . . . I *knew*. When I looked into your eyes, but . . ."

He wanted to touch me. I could tell it. And he was horrified by it. I could tell it because I wanted to touch him. And I was horrified by it.

He was that one soul for whom I had searched my whole life. For whom I would have gone on searching. The soul that was the perfect match to mine, as his anam was the match. The soul that would fit to mine the way a perfectly fired lid would fit to a bowl made only for it.

"You're an elf!" I finally choked out, and I was immediately ashamed at the way the word sounded like a curse, as if I had found something dank and damp where soft, dry sand should be.

"Yes," he answered sadly. "And you are human."

Through my horror at his race, understanding flashed. "That's why they let you help me escape!"

Shame filled his fine features, and he hung his head. "Yes."

His people, his own father, had been so horrified that he might be mated to a human, that they had sent him to die. His people had been so sure that I was a murderer that they had thought they sentenced him to death.

"They hate us so much," I said with wonder, once again, struck as I had been when I saw the fury on his father's face. "*You* hate us so much . . ."

"No," he said firmly. "I cannot. Now."

And neither could I, though I wanted to. Fiercely. I wanted to smash his delicate face, hear his bones

snap beneath the pressure of my hands. I wanted to
touch him. To feel the warmth and softness of his skin.
Show him the fire in me.

His was the soul that was meant to fit against mine
for eternity.

"I know it will not matter," he said, sitting straight
and tall and laying his hands, palms up and exposed,
on his knees in the way of traders who wish to show
they have nothing to hide. "But I will tell you. We
did not mean the death of your chief—your father.
Your people attacked us, and we only defended
ourselves."

At last, something that could make me stiffen with
pride and harden my heart against him again. "You
desecrated our holy place! You—"

"We went to the mountain to gather fire, the same
as you do."

I rocked back, wavering between anger and confusion. "Gather fire? We do not *gather* fire. It is always
with us. We worship our gods on the mountain."

"Ah . . ." He nodded.

I frowned. Perhaps he understood. I still did not.

"The rains came early this year," he said.

I nodded, well remembering my surprise at the
quick rainstorm.

"The gods of water caught us by surprise. We had
no protected fire, so the rains extinguished all. My
people went to the mountain to replenish our fire. We
meant no desecration. And we meant no death to your
tribe. We tried to tell your people, but they attacked."

I swallowed. Well could I imagine it, my father leaping into the fray. Unreasoning and unreasonable.
Burning with the joy of battle.

"Five of my people died in the initial attack. We
had no choice but to defend ourselves."

I nodded. After a moment, I set my hands on my

knees in the same position as his. I accepted the trade, the truth, he had given me.

"My father was furious when I stopped your execution. But then he saw a way of putting it all to right. I could not go against him when I knew it would save you and, perhaps, put the spilled blood between our tribes to right."

Tears, hot and salty, clotted in the back of my throat. The rest of it I understood with a swiftness and clarity that was unlike me. His father saw a way of ridding himself of two problems with one blow. "Your people sent you to die by my hand, in exchange for the deaths they thought I had come to avenge."

"Had you not?" he asked, turning his head in that birdlike way I already recognized.

I almost laughed. Dare I tell him that I had lost my way and banged my head on one of his trees, and for that reason alone, I had come to be in his hands? I could not. He would not understand, for he was brave as I had never understood bravery. And his was the mirror of my soul. I could not bear to be any less brave in his eyes. Perhaps the gods would forgive me this one last, little lie. "Yes," I said. "But there were no warriors with me. I came alone. I did not want— I thought to spare my tribe the horrors of war."

He smiled. Rows of even, white teeth, and a glow that rivaled the sun for cheer, that rivaled a hearth fire for the warmth it caused in me. "Then you knew, even as I did. I did not know why it was so important, but I knew that we must not shed more blood."

I shrugged, once again lost.

"If elf and human can be lifemates, it would be like killing our own kind."

I had no answer for that. I had managed to forget that, in the revelations about the battle on Fire Mountain. It slammed back into me, now. Left me dizzy and reeling.

He took a deep breath and reached out. Took my hand in his own.

I gasped. I clung to him in hunger, as I had clung to him in fear through the night. Tasting the weight and texture of his skin, his muscles, his bones. This could not be, yet it was. "What do we do now?" I asked thickly.

He clasped my hand between his two. Tilted his face up to the sky and considered the question as if it carried the weight of the world. Perhaps it did. "Will you kill me now?" he teased.

I shook my head, still finding my tongue too thick to speak.

"Then we must go home, each to our tribes. We must make sure there is no war."

Go home? I gripped him tighter. My other hand joined the clutch of fingers. Leave him and lose this? This thing, this warmth, this burning I had not even known I wanted. Was not sure I wanted, even as it singed me. "But . . . your father. Your people. They sent you to die."

He shrugged. "They will have to learn better." He said it with such surety, such confidence. As if he knew he could influence them, whether they wanted to be influenced or not.

Could I do less?

He eased himself from my grip and rose to his feet, offering a hand that I might lean on him to do the same. He stood, almost touching me, for just a moment. The sky and all the colors of his forest swam in his eyes. "We will see each other again."

I nodded. Before I could say something foolish, I turned away. I took two steps away before I whirled around, digging in the folds of the unfamiliar robe for the entrance to the pocket. "Here," I blurted. "A gift. So that your people will always have fire." It was sacrilege, to give such a thing to an enemy, a nonbeliever, but I thrust the crystal firestone at him.

He accepted it with absolute trust. In his palm, it reflected the colors of the land the way he did. "Is it magic?"

I shrugged. I supposed it was. "I will show you how to use its magic." I gathered up a handful of dead leaves and hunkered down over them, positioning the stone so that the sun's light was reflected into a bright hot spot over the decaying matter.

He knelt beside me, leaning in so close that I could smell his breath. It was sweet, like the air of his home, and foreign.

After only a few moments, the dead leaves began to smoke. They were damp and would make only a pitiful, sulky fire, but he understood the concept.

As we stood, him clutching the firestone, I offered him the wooden dagger. "I suppose you should take this back, too. I stole it from the tent."

He took the heavily carved dagger and turned it in his fineboned fingers. Then he laughed easily and pressed it back into my palm. "Keep it. My gift to you. It is the ceremonial dagger that marked my father's ascension to Chieftain. Only vow that it will never be raised against my people, who are your people now, too."

I put my hand over his, over the dagger. "I promise," I breathed, and I did not let him go. Not for a very long time.

* * *

Such a sight as I my people had never seen as I strode into my camp.

It was that last moment of dusk when the light is murky and the campfires are pale and reaching toward the sky, only just sensing their power over the darkness.

The sparks of the council fire still danced through the roof of the communal hut, but there were signs already of preparations. Campsites being struck and packed. Weapons strung with the red feathers of anger, standing in rows before the empty hut of the leader. Preparations for the moving of the camp. Preparations for war.

"Asha!" Linnan saw me first. "I was so afraid for you, being caught out in the storm last night!"

No wonder she was my favorite sister. I marched into the midst of our camp, dirty, rumpled, bloodied, wearing the robe and the scent of our enemy . . . yet, her first words were gladness at seeing me, not questions about what and where and why.

Those would come soon enough. I smiled down at her though I knew the movement of my mouth did not match the grimness of my face. "We are moving on to winter quarters?" I asked as I headed toward the leader's hut.

The leader's staff was still there, crowning the mound of earth, where it had been the night before. Pauli had not moved yet to claim her heritage.

Linnan trotted along beside me, chattering. "Yes, with the rains coming early, we knew we must move. And the council has voted for war. Pauli is going to claim leadership, as soon as the warriors gather. She . . ."

Her voice trailed away in my hearing, lost in the chaos of my thoughts, in the excitement of movement in the camp. I paused before the hut of my father. My sense of purpose had been so clear, until this moment. I had been so sure of what I would do. Now, my mouth was as dry as if it was filled with sand. My heart was booming in my chest, rivaling a gong for tempo and rhythm. Even recalling D'Atrem's face did not quiet it.

"Asha?" Linnan had stopped talking. She was standing at my side, staring up at me, her large eyes dark and round. Her small fingers plucked at the sleeve of my elfin robe, then rubbed the cloth back and forth, as if she had only just discovered its strangeness. "Asha!"

I could hear others gathering behind us, the same tone of surprise and question in their voices.

Before I was forced to answer unanswerable questions, I smiled down at her and gently eased her grasp. And I stepped up onto the mound of earth where my father would have overseen the preparations of the camp. I turned my back on the dark, empty tent and faced my tribe.

I touched the spear of the leader, set the feathers to dancing in the bare breeze.

"Asha!"

As my fingers circled the carved wood, I heard the hissed whisper. I looked up and met the stony gaze of Pauli. Her eyes were narrowed, dark with disbelief, hot with warning. Once, I had thought her more qualified to lead than me. Once, I would have been cowed by her anger.

I gritted my teeth, tightened my grip on the spear, and pulled it smoothly from the ground. I did not lift it over my head in triumph, but merely held it at my side. At that moment, the last vestiges of the sun spilled away behind the mountains and the sky went black.

The torches set about the camp leaped, suddenly strong and powerful. Sparks escaped into the indigo of the night, rivaling the stars for brightness. Power, hot and strong enough to taste, flowed through me. The power of my father, of our ancestors, of the living,

breathing gods of fire. And as suddenly as the night
had gone black, as brightly as the fires had leaped up,
my fear and uncertainty slipped away, and D'Atrem's
quiet courage flowed into my heart.

"As eldest child of the Leader, I claim leadership,"
I said to my people. "There will be no war."

* * *

*They will tell you a thousand tales of how the bor-
ders were opened. Of how humans and elves began to
build an alliance with one another.*

*They will tell you of battles and darkness and ven-
geance and bravery. They will tell you I burned redder
than the setting sun. But the truth is always both more
and less.*

*They do not know that it was merely the fire of a
found heart.*

The Guardian turns to the last Seeker seated at the quarter of Fire. A young woman, strong of spirit and sure of movement takes her chalice firmly in hand, salutes him, and empties its contents. The djinn leads her to the same door the other women entered, but marks the air with a different sigil. As the portal opens, this Seeker finds a cavern of Fire. Knowing she will come to no harm if her desire for knowledge remains unshaken, she follows the Guide to the center of a large cavern where a stele glows with flaming runes. The lines of flame shimmer and shift until she reads:

THE FORGE OF CREATION

by Carrie Channell

SHE opened the message from her brother, choked with thrill and fear.

Dearest Thien,
  You won't believe what we've found! I've never seen anything like it. The spell protecting it is more ancient than anything, even the existence of our race. It appears to be all natural as well, not created by mages. It's impossible, and yet it is there.
  I haven't told our father yet, and I may not. You know he'll most likely take it away, hide

*it, research it in private, and keep the results
in the Upper Mage Study Hall so that no one
but the mages of Sheba can ever study it. But
I think it's too important for that. I want to
make this marvel known to the world. The
mages are not the only ones with a right to
know of Creation. It created all of us.*

Thien paused. Hakan had used the magic parchment
that could impart tone and emotion as well as words.
He didn't normally doubt himself when rebelling
against family policy. She heard the question in his voice
as she touched the parchment; it wasn't rhetorical.

*Thien, I'm pretty sure the rest of the dig crew
doesn't know what we've found. But I want
you to see it. You know so much about ancient
spells. Besides I think you want to see it.
Come soon, for I sense danger in the air,
although it may well be my own paranoia.
    Your own,
    Hakan*

Typical Hakan! She thought. He always felt the
world would rob him of what he valued deeply. If only
he realized that he never valued such things until he
perceived them as threatened.

Still, a tingle of curiosity tickled her spine, and she
was doing no work of any importance now. Her family, one of the most powerful mage families in the
land serving the Queen of Sheba, might frown on her
running off on the spur of the moment, but they
trusted her enough not to argue. And if they knew
she pursued Hakan, perhaps they would think the
young man had finally gotten some sense.

*   *   *

Thien's powers flew around her like hair whipping in the wind as she viewed her brother's dig site, but she sensed nothing. For the first time in her life she cursed the fact that Hakan had gotten the danger-probe sense and she had not. Her powers were useless here.

Unless . . .

The thought struck suddenly and painfully.

Unless there really was no danger here, no criminal activity.

But it was *gone*. The dig had vanished, and with it Hakan. There wasn't even evidence that it was ever there, that the sandy earth had been violated at all any time in the last several centuries.

Her panicked probing subsided into stark cold fear.

Suppose the danger had evaded even hypersensitive Hakan until it had been too late?

She fingered his message, tied to the inside of her cloak, turned to her horse and cart, and left the site as fast as she dared.

* * *

Strangely, Thien's magelord father appeared unperturbed by Hakan's disappearance. Hakan often overreacted, and Jamnis speculated aloud that he had grown frustrated at finding nothing and transferred the dig elsewhere. Thien did not tell him of the message, fearing his reaction to Hakan's traitorous words about their family. Unfortunately, without the message, she couldn't justify her fears to her father. She left the Stronghold, uncertain and afraid.

She returned to the site of the dig with a small team of trusted magical archaeologists. There lay the key to her brother's disappearance, below the ground. It was nerve-racking work. Her greatest fear was that she would strike a bad spell. A hard, ancient protection spell could destroy the dig, her team, her chance of finding Hakan. It might even kill her.

Her pick struck something soft and yielding. She paused. Unlike the desert dust, it didn't crumble. Her heart raced, afraid she had destroyed something. Even experts made mistakes.

As she clutched her pick, her team cried out all at once. They'd found the same sort of thing she had. Startled, she realized that this . . . thing was huge. A dwelling? An ancient burial plot? Her heart pounded as she brushed dirt and dust away.

"Stop!" she cried. They hurried to her side. She gazed at the uncovered piece before her.

Shining up at her was a spell, more brilliant, more powerful than anything she had ever seen. Slowly, carefully she traced it, following its edge, connecting everyone's discoveries. It was a single huge spell, a giant bubble or egg, covering all the ground of the dig and perhaps more. Its surface was uneven. She backed away, motioning to her crew.

The magic spilling from the spell vibrated enough to shake away the remnants of earth lying upon it. It burst forth in such brilliance that they all cowered and dashed away.

Thien stopped before everyone else and turned again. The spell came forth from the ground, but didn't expand farther. She edged toward it, fighting the feeling that it was reaching for her and that she should run, run as far and fast as possible. It pulsed and throbbed around her, more powerful than any spell she'd ever seen. Gods and planets, was this what Hakan discovered?

As she neared, she realized the spell remained static, emanating no clear waves or warnings. There were no trips that she could identify that would start chain reactions or other troubles. Just the overriding sense in her gut that she should *not go anywhere near it.* And yet that was foolish. She had touched it, struck it with her pick and not felt this. She started, suddenly realizing the fear emanated from the spell itself, and not inside her, though it felt like her own intuition. This was what Hakan had meant when he said it was natural. No mage could have created a more perfect defense: make people go away because of their own fear.

Fiercely determined, Thien reached the edge of the giant spell. Her gut screamed at her to get out of there, and her skin burned from her fear, but she ignored it. Psychosomatic, all of it, she told herself, and grimly pushed on.

As she reached toward it, the spell seemed to draw away from her. She leaned forward farther and farther, but it was always just out of reach. She heard a muffled cry behind her and turned abruptly just as the spell closed its white shining walls around her.

She was startled to realize her panic had gone. None of the terror or urgency overwhelming her outside the bubble affected her here. Inside, she was calm and curious. She couldn't see through the whiteness to her crew, but she waved that it was all right. She hoped they could see her.

Mostly she was surrounded by a protection spell. The heart of the spell was deeper in, toward the middle and down. She stepped forward tentatively, again cursing her lack of sensitivity.

Abruptly, flames circled Thien. Panicking, she turned every which way, but all escape was blocked by the roaring fire. Her chest constricted, and only when she drew a breath did she realize there was no heat and no smoke.

Reaching one hand forward, she leaned through the

flames. It was a simple wall, a ring around her, and she stepped across easily, once again facing the white blankness. She turned again and the ring of fire had closed into a ball, a brilliant orange mound.

Shapes flickered and changed in the fire like clouds drifting. There was a riverflow of red flame swirling at the bottom, and the top of the bonfire waved like wheat fields. She could see pounding seas and grand mountains, rising, falling, changing throughout the fiery ballet. It was as if the entire history of the world shone recorded in the flames.

Then something deep in the center of the spell squirmed, and Thien put her hand to her throat.

She couldn't see it clearly at first. It was a tiny white blur, below the fields and flow and clouds. As it grew, it gained form and definition. Four short legs sprouted, and an elongated head appeared as a tail stretched out. The fire faded and shrank just a little.

Thien gasped as a comet struck the boiling orb, spewing a powerful jet of fire and shooting into space. In the center of the jet squirmed the salamander. With a quick movement, it rolled itself around the flames, quenching them with its body. It slowed and settled, and as Thien watched, amazed, the roaring fire quieted into a familiar picture, as did the body of the salamander. She gazed at a model of the early Earth and moon, predating even Ilumqah. This *was* one of the creation spells!

The entire spell shuddered, the moon drew back into its parent planet, the cold flames dissolved into a dot, and then nothing. Thien felt the tug as the entire spell collapsed around her. Summoning all her strength and will, she pushed away, closing her eyes so as to not be drawn in again. She concentrated, sweat pouring down her face while the ancient spell tried to suck her down as it returned to wherever it lived. She fought and fought, finally swooning with the effort. As she lost consciousness, a lone tear formed in her eye as she realized she would never find Hakan nor see her family again.

* * *

"Thien!"

She heard her name from a distance, but didn't connect it with another voice. She thought it was part of the jumble in her own head.

"Thien! I see your eyes flickering."

It was Garman's voice, her apprentice. With a weak sob she lifted her arms to touch him, her eyes still glued shut. Something soft and wet brushed her forehead, and Garman pushed her arms back down.

"No. Rest," he said. "At least you're alive."

She wanted to ask what he meant, but a sleep spell covered her too quickly and she passed into unconsciousness again.

When she was finally awake and coherent Garman explained what had happened. They had all stood back as she approached the unearthed glowing glob. The moment she disappeared inside, the entire thing flashed once and disappeared. There was a sensation— more than an observation insisted Garman—that tons of earth were falling and then the plain was flat again, as they had originally found it. They blinked, trying to regain their vision after the intensely bright flash, and realized a body lay on the ground on the spot where the center of the strange spell had been.

Thien's face tightened gradually as he described the scene. Clearly she had only barely escaped at the end, during the earthly cataclysm, and that was why they'd found her lying there. But why, and how, had she survived the ordeal?

Most importantly, she knew now what had happened to Hakan. There was no doubt in her mind that her curious and sensitive brother had embraced the beautiful creation spell, diving directly into its center. Which meant the great salamander had him now. She forced herself to look up at the moon, barely less than half an orb, cold and far away.

But Hakan surely wasn't sitting on the moon literally; he was trapped in the amphibian's cold fire spell somewhere. She sat up too quickly, clutched her head, and groaned.

"We have to leave," said Garman softly. She glanced up at him. He was so tense, prepared for an argument. She sighed.

"Yes," she replied. So simple and so difficult. She could do nothing here with these people, could not endanger their lives. Later, she vowed, with her powerful magelord father or alone, she would return for Hakan. If he really was alive, and she didn't believe the salamander had killed him, she would find him and rescue him.

Or die trying.

* * *

Jamnis' reaction startled Thien almost more than her discovery of Hakan's whereabouts. He gazed at her quietly, almost calmly, for a long time until she thought that he had slipped into a trance. His eyes focused on her finally and he spoke.

"We always knew Hakan would do something foolish and lose himself. We did not think it would be to the Fires of Creation. We must go to the temple and pray."

Of the three or four key religions popular in Sheba, the magelords had never followed any one, although they made appearances on all the major holidays. Her family had always quietly believed in the old gods, the ancient pantheon of planets. Ilumqah, the Moon God, was Hakan's personal god. Thien assumed they would pray to him, though she knew in her heart it would do no good. Hakan had prayed to his personal protector before he left, just as her mother had once prayed to the Sun Goddess, both her and Thien's personal protector, before embarking on her last journey for the queen. Since that time Thien had only been in the temple for her uncle's and her cousin's weddings and her mother's funeral. Her faith was weak. If the Sun Goddess, protector of their great queen, couldn't even save that queen's favored mage . . .

"Hakan isn't dead!" she protested, an iron band suddenly constricting her chest.

Jamnis said nothing but led the way to the small, elaborate family temple. Thien followed, her thoughts and feelings screaming after him.

They sat in the temple, Jamnis gazing upward at the dome, his eyes clear and unblinking, his hands folded in his lap. He was definitely praying, but Thien couldn't concentrate. She had forgotten how to pray and had only pretended at her mother's funeral. But even that emptiness was nothing to the sheer fear coursing through her blood.

"Hakan is heir to the magelord title," said Jamnis quietly.

"I know," she replied, wondering what exactly that had to do with rescuing him.

"To be the king's magelord requires good judgment, good sense."

Thien's middle squeezed again. She pressed her hands together, hoping she wouldn't be sick.

"But our land supports women leaders. We follow our queens. And a king would listen to a female magelord."

The words floated through Thien's consciousness, disconnected.

Her father turned to her. "Hakan has the gift, the sensitivity. But that very gift has landed him in this bind. A true creation spell, the Forge Spell, requires sacrifice. In magic, it always does. Nothing is for free, not for a magelord, and not for a king."

Thien shivered but didn't drop her eyes from her father's. He gazed intently at her.

Abruptly Jamnis rose, sweeping out of the temple. He assumed his mantle of authority again, and Thien closed her eyes, forcing back the urge to scream after him. He had a responsibility to his son! But even if her father treated Hakan as dead, she would not abandon her brother. No matter what it took.

*　*　*

Garman found her.

"You can't go back there," he accused her before she could say anything.

She shook her head.

"At least take a crew," he insisted.

She continued to pack.

"Take me," he whispered.

She turned to him then. "I can't. This is now a family matter."

Garman opened his mouth but said nothing. Family matter meant mage matter and as a servant of the mages he could say nothing. But his eyes betrayed his fear and worry. Thien wanted to touch his shoulder, comfort him, but she couldn't. The terror that had formed in the temple while she sat beside her praying father had matured into a cold, hard lump in her middle that never left. She knew now that she would not return from the dig site, but there was still a chance she could save Hakan.

As she thought his name, her face and her determination grew hard and she turned away from Garman. He left, pained.

She did not actually tell Jamnis she was leaving or where she was going, but he knew. As if on cue, he showed himself in her quarters shortly after Garman left.

"So you insist on this," he said quietly. There was no question in his tone.

"Yes."

"He is not dead."

"I know."

"The power is greater than anything you've encountered."

She gazed evenly at him. "Is it greater than anything *you've* encountered?"

They stared at each other a long time, unmoving.

"No," he said finally. Thien let out a breath she didn't realize she'd been holding.

"Which is why I know exactly how dangerous it is," he finished.

"But Hakan . . ." she began.

"Is lost," he said. His eyes were cold. Even in his darkest moments of judgment, Thien had never seen her father so detached, so uncaring. She shuddered.

"Hakan was too sensitive. He always was. There was no way he could withstand a creation spell and survive intact. It's too much for any mage."

Except me, thought Thien, hearing the hidden disappointment in her father's words. She wasn't sensitive enough to become a magelord and Hakan's rebelliousness had taken him to his death.

No. He was not dead. Even Jamnis only said "lost." She would find him.

Jamnis watched the resolution harden in her face. He touched his cloak, just over his heart, then turned and left the room quickly, saying no more.

Thien closed her eyes, her mind roiling with worry and fear. When she opened them again, she started. A tiny glowing light floated in front of her, just where Jamnis' heart had been. She reached for it, and as the light touched her hand, she heard her father's voice in her head:

"It is not a spell, only a prayer. A prayer to the salamander. But remember, it can only be used if you agree in your heart to become the next magelord to our queen." It was her mother's old title, the one she had held before her death. She had always wanted her daughter to follow her, and until her passing Thien had thought she would. But she had turned it over to Hakan, for he desired the position of power more than she.

Quickly she cupped the light in her hands and internalized it. It was a plea and could do nothing unless she agreed first and then the salamander heard it . . . and answered. And even that much wouldn't happen if she didn't believe in the prayer. Prayers only worked for the faithful, and for the first time since her mother's loss, Thien had to find . . .

* * *

Faith was the farthest thing from her mind as she stood once again on the dark plain. Its very emptiness hovered close, and Thien shuddered even though the breeze was warm. The moon rose, a sliver off full. She gazed intently at it, imagining she could see the salamander's limbs and tail curled about itself, forming the shining, cold white ball floating in the star-spattered sky.

The earth rumbled slightly beneath her feet. She stepped backward instinctively, but the movement ceased. The salamander in the sky remained cold, impassive. She placed her hand over her heart and summoned the prayer.

Nothing. No movement, no release. The prayer was trapped inside her, or gone. Fear engulfed her then, fear held at bay until now. The ground rumbled again.

Tearfully, she concentrated, trying to pull out the magic her father had given her, but still there was nothing. She closed her eyes and fought the dark panic that threatened to stop all her thoughts.

"Father, help me," Thien whispered. "O, Fire Salamander, speak to me. Face me tonight."

A moment later the rumbling earth quieted. She slowly released her grip, both hands she'd squeezed into fists and pressed tightly against her chest. She opened her hands. Inside her cupped palms glowed the prayer. It was larger than she remembered it and pulsed slightly. She glanced quickly up at the moon, but it was as before. She gazed, rapt, at the glowing prayer. Inside, flames danced and for a moment she thought she saw a tiny reproduction of the Great Salamander's birth. She put her face near it, but could feel nothing. The flames were ash now.

"No! Come back! Don't turn away!" she cried to the tiny creature she almost could not see. Was this how it would end? The salamander would keep Hakan, and her work and her efforts would be wasted? Worse, she wouldn't even have the chance to plead her cause.

"No," she said again, dropping to her knees and crying.

This time she didn't hear anything, but afterward she remembered the sound of earth roaring up around her. It was an exploding volcano, a bellowing forge, a crashing forest fire all rolled into one monstrous noise. The earth shot up in geysers and cascaded about her, creating mountains and dunes and chasms where only

flatness had been before. Thien was mildly surprised
she wasn't buried as she gazed into the throbbing
prayer-spell in her hands. The noise finished seconds
after it began, and Thien slowly raised her head and
looked around at the changed landscape.

The hills rose in a perfect circular range, completely
encompassing a valley. Lying in the center of the valley, covering layers of earth and clay, was the creation spell.

As she gazed, it seemed to grow and reach out to
her. She felt herself slipping toward it though her body
didn't move at all. The world altered. First, she
seemed huge and the planet around her tiny, too small
to support her size. Then, abruptly, she was tiny herself, lost in the infinity of the atomic level. And always
the creation spell sat there before her, cold. It throbbed
like a heartbeat and after a moment Thien realized
that the prayer in her hands throbbed in time with it.
She focused on the tiny spell, concentrating on it and
avoiding the large glowing blob. Gradually her perspective came back.

Thien took several deep breaths and forced herself
to meditate on the prayer. She felt herself slipping
away and refocused her mind. After a moment the
pull eased and she was inside.

She glanced at her hands. The prayer was still there,
throbbing gently. She turned to the scene in the center, the Salamander Moon being born. Again the rock
from space struck the fiery young Earth, and again
the cold salamander wrapped in the fire of creation
shot off the surface. Once more it curled its huge body
around the flames, quenching them with its cold, shining white light, circling the Earth.

Thien gasped. Across the vivid scene another pair
of eyes gazed at her. Someone else was watching the
creation of the moon. She stared, but the image

slipped away. She concentrated on the prayer again, and her sight cleared. Without raising her eyes, she saw a hand reach for her. Behind it was Hakan's pleading face.

She reached for him, nearly dropping the prayer. The flames shot up and for the first time she could feel their heat. She grasped the prayer tightly to her chest and the burning sensation faded. She stood like that for a long time, staring at Hakan's outstretched hand.

Hakan! She tried to speak his name, but no sound came forth. She stepped forward, but the flames crept up. She stepped back, and they settled again.

Hakan! she thought. *How shall I reach you?*

His hand moved, just a little. Encouraged, Thien concentrated.

Hakan. Can you hear me?

Thien. I almost didn't believe it.

We need to reach each other.

Concentrate. Everything here is magic. Simple walking or talking does no good.

Thien concentrated. She focused on the outstretched hand, the face in the fire-shadow.

And then they were holding hands, above the spell, although Thien couldn't remember floating upward at all. Her left hand still clenched her father's prayer.

I don't understand, she said mentally.

My dig. I uncovered this on the third day of the seventh month, he replied.

Thien stared blankly at him.

Wait! The last full moon . . . the harvest moon?

Hakan nodded miserably. *The sacrificial moon. The salamander sleeps most of the year, but awakens for the harvest.*

Thien started, almost losing her grip on her brother's hand. *Then how is it you're alive?*

I belong to the salamander now. I can't leave. It wasn't my blood it needed, but my life.

Your heat. Your fire, said Thien, understanding settling over her like a damp towel. She shook her head. *Why you?*

My sensitivity led me to this place. I entered of my own free will. I sacrificed myself.

She could hear his pain. *We're leaving.*

No! Thien, you'll get killed.

What about you?

The salamander won't release me.

She looked down at the repeating scene of creation. The salamander burst away from the earthly fire, and suddenly shot her an angry glance.

Suddenly furious, she clenched Hakan's hand tighter. *We're leaving,* she repeated. She forced Jamnis' prayer into their closed hands so they both held it. The fiery spell shot up and engulfed them. Thien thought she screamed, but all other noise was lost in the howling that surged about them. She glared down at the cold salamander, still staring at her with its passive amphibian eyes. In a rage, she dove down at it and suddenly she and Hakan were caught in its frozen aura. The flames continued to lick at them and at the elemental, but all they could feel was numbing cold from the creature's skin. Thien drooped, drifting into unconsciousness. Her hand loosed slightly, the prayer slipping out, Hakan slipping away.

She jerked her head, snapping herself awake. Her face was near the salamander's now, its black eye staring malevolently at her.

You can't have him! The thought filled her entire being, and suddenly the salamander expanded. She stood at the foot of a giant white salamander, glowing with the reflected fires of creation which nearly blinded her. She held fast to her brother and the prayer.

You can't have him!

The salamander's huge tail swung around and slammed into her, knocking her and Hakan across the flaming plain. Still she held her grip.

You can't have him!

Enraged, the salamander scurried, faster than anything she'd ever seen, and lowered its face to hers. The gigantic mouth opened and blew fire and boiling seas at her. Her clothes burned off, her flesh fried in the heat. Her hands dissolved to mere bones, and yet she clung to her brother's bones.

You can't have him!

The wind turned to ice, the frigidity of the salamander's body freezing her bones to broken glass. Her hands crystallized, the fingers falling off.

No! You can't have him! With her last bit of energy, she focused on Jamnis' prayer, clinging desperately to Hakan. In a burst of faith, she finally heard what Jamnis had said and in her heart fulfilled his last wish and her dead mother's. Hakan's face contorted in pain. She thrust the tiny prayer at the great creature.

Listen!

* * *

The sudden silence was deafening. For a moment, Thien thought she had lost all her senses. But then her eyesight came back, and gradually the ringing in her ears abated. She glanced down. Her body was intact, covered in flesh and clothing. She looked at Hakan, still with her, his hand still clutched tightly in her own. His face was stunned. His eyes were open, but he was clearly unconscious.

They were still here, inside the spell. She could see the ancient amphibian in the center as before, but the backdrop of terror was missing. Abruptly, she realized what had happened.

They were inside her father's prayer. The duplicate salamander lay before her, its expression, if she could call it that, quizzical. She sensed no malevolence from it now. It regarded her coolly, studying her. It turned its attention to Hakan and instinctively Thien squeezed his hand. He grunted and she looked at him in wonder. He smiled sheepishly. He was back, all the way.

The tiny salamander squatted close to her now. It nodded at Hakan, then blinked once rapidly.

* * *

They stood on the plain. The earth was in place again, undisturbed. The sun was rising, and the cold moon shone briefly with a golden fire before setting into the violet morning.

"How?" asked Hakan, his voice choked.

"Father's prayer. He offered himself in your place." Thien's voice was barely a whisper.

"Then why the fight?"

Thien stared at the setting moon, the sleeping elemental, for many minutes before she answered.

"Me. I had to have the faith to release the prayer. It was tied to me. If I hadn't, we both would have been lost." And he had to fulfill his last promise to a dying magelord before he was done, she finished mentally.

Saying it this way made it real, including the part she didn't tell Hakan.

The dawn sun shone brightly, its fire striking her face.

The Guardian turns to the Seekers at the Arm of Earth. "Your time has come. Drink and summon your Guide."

A man with a kindly face and eyes that sparkle with a ready wit drains his tankard. The essence of Earth becomes a gnome, who shrinks in size taking on the appearance of the fae of the Earth, which some call the "wee people." The Guide winks at the man and dances toward the Northern door. The man rises and follows him to a village of simple cottages nestled in a lush green but completely flat landscape. The fae, grinning, stops and points at a road sign:

HOW GOLF SHAPED SCOTLAND
by Bruce Holland Rogers

SOME say that the town of St. Andrews in Scotland is the cradle of golf. That much is true. Some also say that the rolling land thereabouts was made for golf, and that is surely wrong. Those sandy hillocks, the links of St. Andrews, were not made *for* golf, but rather *by* golf.

Long ago, when the fairy folk of Scotland were seen more often, a priest called Father Iain lived in a village not far from where St. Andrews is today. Father Iain was the son and grandson of great swordsmen. He had a warrior's strong arm, and his eyes were as sharp as

the finest archer's. But he never wielded sword or
bow, and the only club he ever held was a slender rod
of hazelwood attached to a thick applewood head. A
golf club.

More precisely, the only club Father Iain ever held
was a putter, for at that time, a putter was the only
sort of golf club there was and the ball was a round
white stone. The very shape of Scotland was different,
too. In those days, the margin along the coast was flat.
Sheep cropped the grass so close that the land was
like green felt laid upon a tabletop. Few men played
golf in those days, first because there were always wars
to fight against the English, and second because the
game was so boring. One hole was the same as the
last, and one course of the flat ground was akin to
any other.

But even a boring game was at least something.
After all, a man like Father Iain—a man with a warrior's strong arm and eyes as sharp as the finest archer's—cannot be ever and always indoors, even if he
is a man of peace. Father Iain played often, putting
the white stone from this hole to that, and he played
well. He often wished for something more, however.
A man of his abilities wants a challenge, and golf gave
him but little of that.

None of the villagers who bothered to try could
beat Father Iain. Theirs was a small village and poor.
They had little to be proud of. Is it any wonder, then,
that the villagers bragged about their golfing priest?
"Aye, Father Iain's the best," they boasted to any
who would listen. "There is no finer player on this
Earth nor in it."

That was bragging indeed, for while mortal man
lives *on* the Earth, the wee folk live *in* it. The boulders
are their homes. The great halls of their clans and
kingdoms lie beneath the ground.

Father Iain knew that he was good with his putter, but he also knew not to tempt the powers of the Earth. "Be careful what ye say," the priest cautioned his flock. "Do not seem to challenge the wee folk on my behalf."

Well, it was as true then as it is now that when a priest says not to do something there are those who cannot resist doing it for that reason alone. The villagers began to say to one another, "To be sure, our Father Iain could even beat the fair folk at this game!"

Never let it be said that the fairies do not like a challenge. One moonlit night, when all the village slept, someone rapped insistently on Father Iain's door. When the priest opened wide the door, who did he behold but a wee little man and a wee little woman, both of them dressed in finery and each holding a gnarled stick and a white stone.

"It's a cauld night the night," Father Iain observed and added politely, "Will ye come in by the fire, strangers?"

"Thank ye, no. We are the King and Queen of Faery," said the King. "We've come to take up your challenge."

"Challenge? I made no challenge!"

"Play us, mortal man," said the Queen, "and if ye win, ye shall indeed be the champion golfer of Scotland."

"That is of no import to me," said Father Iain.

"And we shall lift the curse," said the King.

"The curse?" said Father Iain. "What curse?"

"Why, the curse we have just now laid," said the Queen. "That every cow in the village should go dry and every hen cease laying, that every sheep grow sickly and every bit of man-tilled ground go barren."

"Ye must play and beat us both for us to lift the spell," said the King, and he named a time and place three nights hence for the contest.

In the morning, Father Iain slept later than he meant to, and when he awoke, he had to hurry to prepare for the mass. As he bustled about, he thought that the King's and Queen's visit must have been a dream.

When he got to the kirkyard, though, he found his parishioners waiting for him and looking worried.

"Good Father," said one of the women, "my little bairns are lowing for a sup o' milk, but their mothers have none to give!"

"My hens have not laid today," said a man.

"D'ye ken sich a prayer as will lift a curse?" asked another, "for sure it is that cursed we are."

"Let us celebrate the mass and see what prayers can be said," Father Iain told them. But though the villagers followed him in for the mass that morning, and though they gathered the next morning and the next in the pews of the kirk, their prayers did not deliver them. For three days, the cows gave no milk, the hens did not lay, all the sheep trembled with some sickness. Even the turnip leaves began turning brown. Only then did Father Iain tell his parish of the curse that the fair folk had laid.

"To be sure," said he, "these are the wages of boasting, and God will not deliver us from a curse we have earned." He might have said, *a curse that ye have earned,* but he was a kinder and holier man than that.

Father Iain had no choice but to take up his putter on the appointed night and walk out upon the sward to meet the little King and Queen by moonlight.

Now anyone who has heard aught of the wee folk knows that they love to win by trickery. Father Iain did not expect fair play, and sure enough, when they all approached the first hole, the priest found that a little hillock stood between his ball and the hole. In a place so flat as Scotland was in those days, such a feature was rare.

"Strange," said Father Iain. "I do not recall any mound of earth here, and I have played these same holes often."

"There's many a strange thing in the world," said the Queen of Faery with a smile. She and the King putted out. Father Iain putted over the hillock as best he could, but he fell a stroke behind.

When they all approached the second hole, they saw that this time a little hillock stood between the Queen's ball and the hole.

"How very odd," the Queen said, looking at her husband. "I know this ground like I know my own mind, and yet I find a mound here where I'm sure none was before."

"There's many an odd thing in the world," the King of Faery said with a smile.

The Queen gave him a glare that would have set a stick on fire, but the King took no notice. Father Iain and the King of Faery putted out in one stroke, but the Queen lost a stroke getting over the hillock.

Father Iain knew now that he had a chance. "It may be that I cannot win and lift the curse," he said aloud, "for though the Queen is no better than I, the King is a stroke ahead. Clearly he is the better golfer."

But at the third hole, the King's ball rolled into a patch of sand that he swore had not existed before he hit his ball, and then all three were tied.

The rest of the game, for nine holes out and nine holes back, continued in this way. The King and Queen used their powers against each other as much as against Father Iain. They took turns pulling a stroke ahead, and then falling a stroke behind. As the three players putted close to the final hole—which was the hole they had started with—all were tied again.

When the King took his turn, the ground rippled and turned his ball aside. He glared at the Queen.

Then it was her turn. She hit her ball right toward the hole, but again the ground shook and shifted, forming a little gutter that drew her ball away. She glared at the King.

Now it was the priest's turn. His ball was only as far from the hole as a man is tall.

The Queen of Faery said to the King, "However this game falls out between us, we mustn't let this mortal man win!"

And the King said, "Agreed."

What hope could the priest have now of lifting the curse? The King and Queen of the very Earth were united against him. The ground he must putt across would ripple and roll, dip and rise, and carry his ball astray.

But Father Iain had a warrior's strong arm and eyes as sharp as the finest archer's. He had a warrior's wit, as well, and saw the path his ball must take. By the light of the moon, he found a sharp stone, and he split the head of his putter at an angle so that the bottom was thicker than the top, like a wedge.

"Hit the ball," said the King, "or we will be at this all night!"

"As ye wish," said Father Iain. And though the powers of Faery were united against Father Iain, though the earth bubbled and wiggled like a pot of boiling porridge, he hit the ball with his damaged putter, which was a putter no longer, but the very first niblick ever made. And no Earthly powers could do aught to alter its course, for the ball went not along the ground, but through the air, and did not meet the earth until it struck the bottom of the hole.

"This would not have happened if ye'd played better!" said the King of Faery to his Queen.

"It would not have happened if *ye* had played better!" she answered.

"And what of the curse?" said Father Iain. "Is it lifted?"

If the King and Queen heard him at all, they gave no sign. Glowering at one another, they turned their backs on Father Iain and began to play again. As they played through the night, they made the ground hump and drop all the more. Dunes great and small rose up. Brooks and burns flowed where none had flowed before, and pools and mires appeared.

In the morning, the villagers were astonished to see how the shape of the land had changed. Over the weeks and months that followed, the land everywhere along the sea changed from flat to rolling. Where before the ground had been level, now there were dunes and hillocks everywhere.

As for Father Iain, he was much relieved to find that the village cows again gave milk, the hens once more laid, the flocks regained their health, and the meager gardens yielded as much as they ever had.

What's more, he found the game of golf was much improved by the altered landscape and by the addition of a few new clubs that lifted the ball into the air.

It would be many years yet before golf was played with a leather ball stuffed with feathers, but it was now a game that could truly hold a man's attention, even a man with a warrior's strong arm and eyes as sharp as the finest archer's. No one could ever match Father Iain, though he played the game till the very end of his days.

The Guardian watches the remaining Seekers in the Arm of Earth. They seem reticent to continue, but he knows this is not true. "Come now, who will seek the answer to their question?"

A woman of powerful presence fingers the edge of her tankard, contemplating the amber fluid within it. Her decision made, she takes in the drink in small sips, savoring each until she has emptied the container. Feeling the Guide's presence behind her, she turns to face it. Silent communication passes between them, and she rises to follow the gnome through the North door. Across the threshold, she finds deep caverns filled with great treasures and secrets. One such treasure is:

THE GIANT'S LOVE

by Nina Kiriki Hoffman

THERE were giants in the Earth in those days, before the Diminishment dwindled them to dwarfs. Earthworkers, metalsmiths, gemcrafters they were, save for Stig, who was a wanderer.

Born as he was in the bowels of the Earth, forged by fire and soot and labor into a darksmith, made also into a miner because of his talent for finding hidden treasure, Stig did not see the sky until he was fifteen.

The day he did, he was in an old tunnel whose dig strikes showed it had been dug more than a hundred

years earlier. Sometimes the movable mining settlement went back into old tunnels, sniffing out things
ancestors had missed.

Something called to Stig behind the granite skin of
the tunnel wall, so he dug up into the rock. It was a
job that lasted hours. Something . . . something made
his great hands tingle as he grew closer, so that he
slowed his strokes. Tink! His handpick made a good
sound. He shone his lantern into the shaft he had
carved. Light glinted on green glass, a columnar crystal broad across as his hand, long as his forearm.

All afternoon he tapped around the crystal with his
hand pick to edge the emerald out of the tunnel wall.
When at last, exhausted and sweaty, he cut the crystal
and its surround of rock loose from its nesting place,
he sat down beside it, drank water from his hip flask,
and looked up, wondering if other crystals waited near
where he had found this one.

Something shone from the shaft, a slice of something bright. He glimpsed a gem so blue the best sap-
phire by ore forge light could not match it: pale,
unflawed, perfect. In that moment a hunger grew in
him to own that jewel, a hunger so powerful it over-
rode all his other appetites. He picked at the wall, at
first cautiously, then frantically, but the jewel would
not fall; it only grew larger. The air tasted different,
too, full of scents he had never smelled before, and a
dampness unconfined or tainted with metal or age.

Finally he poked a hole in the skin of the mountain
large enough to leave through. He crawled out into
the open air.

Light lay everywhere! It came from something in
the sky brighter than molten iron, impossible to look
at for longer than a few seconds. Instead, he glanced
all around him and saw greens brighter than emeralds,
a sky bluer than sapphires, clouds whiter than quartz,

tree trunks as fine and solid a brown as the best jasper, though what he was looking at he did not know. Behind him, he saw the bones of the mountain thrusting up through underbrush and earth, speckled granite, and that he could name.

Beneath that earth and rock was everything he had ever known: tunnels dry and damp, cold and hot, wide and narrow, caverns and cubbyholes, underground streams and lakes and springs, home caves and work caves, fire and dark—always dark that waited beyond the end of every flame. Now, here, with so much air above him that he could not see a ceiling, Stig felt a strange lightness, as though he would float upward and never stop, out into an even wider open than he could imagine.

Frightened, he dived back into his tunnel, into the welcome dark and the sense that he was surrounded on most sides by ever present, ever-pressing Earth. He sat with his back to a wall and stared at the column of light that poured in through the bolt-hole he had carved. How the light sparkled on specks of mineral on the ground. What was that sweet smell, finer than the smell of the scented candles underlanders traded with toplanders for? What were those noises and whistles, sweeter than music stroked from a harp? What creatures lived in that light? He thrust his hand into the light and saw for the first time how soot and earth caked his skin, how hairs grew on the back of his hand, gold as finest wire where not singed.

He sat a long time watching the light as it moved across the tunnel floor. Presently a bell clanged down toward the settlement, calling the miners to supper, its sound muffled up here in this distant and little-used shaft. Stig stuffed the emerald he had collected into his carrysack and watched a little longer as light faded. Where did it go? Had something snuffed the sky torch? What could kill so brilliant a light?

When he turned in the day's find to Kort, the older man made much of it: the largest emerald anyone had found in two lifetimes, he said.

Stig could not stop thinking about the sky, so blue and large no one could put it in a pocket or carrysack.

Mag ladled him up a bowl of stew heavy with tubers and roots and light on meat, all of these things bought from toplanders who craved gems and the giants' metalwork.

He had never seen the toplands before. A whole caste of underlanders, the smallest giants, were the traders; they did not frighten the toplanders so much as the rest. They lived in caverns that opened to the air, and spoke with people from other places in languages strange to underlander ears, and traded all the craft and treasure of the underlands for what the people needed to keep them alive. Stig ate the same things he had eaten all his life, with no idea of what they were: did the toplanders mine them or make them?

Stig licked the last drop of stew from his spoon and dreamed of light. Emerald leaves and the aquamarine sky he'd seen earlier haunted him.

The next day he went back to the tunnel where he had found the sky, and again crept into the open air.

After two weeks, he could stay out under the sky for half a day without feeling that he would float away.

He learned the sky had moods, and experienced his first rain, which terrified him: it happened when he was far from his hole, and he could not get it to stop. It seemed the sky was striking him. He grew cold and wet without having fallen into water. He learned that trees would shelter him a little.

At suppers, Kort asked him why he had not brought anything new since the big emerald. Had they exhausted these mineworks? Was it time to move on?

No! If they moved on, would Stig ever find the sky again?

To pacify Kort, Stig spent some days in the dark, searching out treasures.

He told Fenja supplywoman he was working in an ice tunnel and needed a warm cloak. She gave him one.

At supper he took extra bread and fruit and stored them in his carrysack. He also took sparking rocks. And he always carried his hand pick.

One day he went out into the world through his tunnel and did not go back.

* * *

Flowers astonished him. He first saw them from afar, dark pink spots floating against a drift of green. He knelt beside them and cupped his hands around one. It was smaller than the nail on his smallest finger. Beautiful, intricate, tiny; it smelled delicious.

He tried to pick it. His touch smashed it.

He moaned. After a moment, he reached for a second flower. It, too, turned to damp powder between his fingers.

He lay full length in the field, crushing more flowers than he could count. Were all topland gems this fragile? A flower still stood near his eye, and he watched it as the wind shivered it, as bees visited it. One of the most beautiful things he had ever seen, he thought drowsily, as long as he didn't try to touch it.

* * *

He wandered for weeks before he met any toplanders, and then they screamed and ran away. He would have liked to talk to them; he had run out of home

food and now ate things he found in the forest, some
of which tasted good and some of which didn't. He
had seen smaller animals, glimpsed them as they ran
away, but only occasionally; he made a great deal of
noise just walking everywhere, as things crunched and
smashed beneath his feet no matter where he stepped.

Only in the mornings, when he woke, did he see
forest creatures up close, for then they ventured
near, sniffing at him. Some of the winged ones even
perched on him. He always held as still as he could
for as long as he could, treasuring their nearness and
studying them. He found them wonderful. But eventually Nature made him move, and he lost them for
another day.

If he had known where he came from, he might
have gone back belowground, but he got lost soon
after he emerged. He loved the day, when he could
see colors for miles, and he loved the stars at night,
which fluoresced like the underground gems that woke
from noise or shaking or spellcrafting. He loved the
sound the wind made moving through trees and
grasses. But he missed warm food, the talk of others,
the sense that he knew what to expect and what he
had to do to stay alive.

The toplanders were less than half his size. It occurred to him that if he saw something twice as tall
as he was, he, too, would have been frightened. No
wonder they screamed and ran at his approach. How
could he get close to these little people when every
step he took announced his presence?

He came then to ordered lands, fields made square
as salt crystals, with ribbons of road running through,
and in the distance structures that did not look like
forest things, but made things. More toplanders ran
from him here.

He did not step onto the fields or the roads. He

could see they had been worked as a tunnel shaft was worked, but he feared their fragility.

He could not go where these small people went without alarming them.

He sat at the edge of the forest and waited for them to come to him.

First to come was a toplander riding on an animal, a sight that filled Stig with delight. The little man glinted in sunlight: he wore chain mail, a helmet, and a sword, all things Stig had himself forged, but for larger-sized people. The horse glinted, too: his hide gleamed brown and bronze. Together, horse and rider looked like some marvelous mechanical toy.

The toplander yelled at Stig, and Stig only smiled. "I can't understand you," he murmured in his softest voice. He kept his hands on his knees.

The toplander yelled some more, waved his sword, forced his horse forward.

"I can't understand you," Stig said again, "but I wish I could. Do you know where I can find tubers? Roots? Nuts? Bread? I am so hungry! I will work for food. Have you any digging that needs doing?"

The toplander charged him, struck at Stig's knee with the sword. Stig blocked the blow, pushing the sword away. The toplander tumbled from his horse, and the horse ran away. Other toplanders who had been watching from the road screamed and cried, and most ran away, too.

"I am sorry," Stig told the fallen toplander, hoping he had not hurt him. Stig sat and watched. Presently the little man climbed to his feet, shaking his head. He picked up his sword. Halfheartedly, he pointed it at Stig. Stig did nothing.

The small warrior took off his helmet and shook out his long black hair, then turned back to call to the few men who remained on the road. He sheathed his sword and walked to Stig, stood looking up at him.

"Hello," Stig said.

The warrior nodded, his face frowning. "Herro," he said.

Slowly, Stig reached behind him for his carrysack, watching the toplander the whole time. He put the sack in his lap, opened an outside pocket, and fetched forth some eight-sided metal crystals he had found once. They were small in his hand. Kort had told him they had no use, but Stig had always liked them. He held three out to the toplander.

The toplander came to him and stared at the crystals. He reached out, his eyes shifting from the crystals to Stig's face and back. He plucked a crystal from Stig's hand and studied it.

Stig set the other two crystals on the ground.

The toplander picked them up. He spoke to Stig a moment, then walked off down the road toward the others. Some of the ones who had screamed and run had crept back. They watched. When the warrior reached them, they all examined the crystals and broke into torrents of talk.

After a while the warrior returned, and brought three others with him.

* * *

Stig stayed at the village for three years. The villagers taught him much: how they raised things to eat, how to speak their language, how toplanders worked together and fought with each other, and what they worried over. Stig taught their smith many things, and did any work asked of him. Much of what he did early on was lifting, carrying, plowing. He could pull better than any horse they had. They taught him to build with wood, too; indeed, together he and the villagers built Stig a house just in time for the winter, which brought many sky events he did not understand, such as snow and frost. He learned to chop wood and bring it back to the village; and the people gave him food and clothing in exchange for his work, and companionship different from the kind he had had underland, but still satisfying.

In spring one of the village maidens brought him a red flower, and he held it a while without crushing it, but it wilted anyway.

He watched the sky day and night, and in the autumn, he watched the leaves flame and then fall. The brilliance of color, its lavish use in sunsets and sunrises, forests and fields, brought him joy almost every day. Sometimes he paused in the middle of a task just to stare at sky or distance. His heart grew light at these times, floating up until it touched the back of his throat with something deep and wide, a hunger that satisfied itself and then cried for more.

At the end of three years, in the spring, the warrior Rowan, first to greet Stig, grew restless and wanted to wander. He invited Stig to come along.

With Rowan, Stig wandered the toplands, through deserts, forests, mountains. Everywhere he went, he collected sights he had never imagined while he lived down in the dark.

He saw, heard, and smelled the ocean, and even swam in it, loving its immeasurable width.

He and Rowan found a place of waking mountains, where mountains breathed steam and sometimes erupted.

They found an uncut forest in the north where the trees were so big around Stig could not encompass them in his arms, so tall he could barely see their tops.

They found a quaking land where hot, stinking waters lay steaming under winter skies.

Waterfalls, canyons, even an iceland to the far north; they saw many things and met many people.

Sometimes Stig saw toplanders wearing jewels or armor of underlander work, and it made him long a little for his days underground; but never enough for him to seek out the trading caves. He could not give up the sky.

Came a day when Rowan found a lady he wished to spend the rest of his life with. The night before Rowan's marriage, Rowan and Stig made camp in the forest outside the village where the maiden lived. "Do you ever long for someone to lie and live with in a way beyond fellowship?" Rowan asked Stig as they stared into their fire following their evening meal.

"No," said Stig. For a moment his heart ailed, giving his words the lie. He had Rowan for a friend, and with Rowan as his ambassador, he had made many other friends; people liked anybody who worked cheerfully with them, Rowan said, and it usually proved true.

When he thought of dim dark suppers underground, the grunts of other giants, minimal conversation as they planned the next day's work, contact with the women only for food or clothing, rarely bathing, and never seeing the sky, he did not miss that life or long for it.

And yet, to find an Other . . .

Heartsickness turned Stig's stomach sour for a little while. At last he said, "Yes" to Rowan. For the first time he let longing inside him. It hurt.

Rowan, lost the moment before in reveries of the life ahead of him, woke and looked at his friend. Who was there for Stig to love, unless he returned to his people? Women liked Stig, but they were not made to mate with him. Why had Rowan even asked such a question?

They said no more that night. In the morning Rowan handfasted with his love and said farewell to his wandering ways.

Stig stayed a while in the village where Rowan had settled, making himself useful and watching Rowan's joy in his new wife. The wanderlust came over Stig in midsummer. One of the village boys wished to see the world, too, and he and Stig set off on a morning when the world was still wet with dew.

For forty years Stig wandered the world, usually with one companion or another.

Once he wandered with a wizard, and then he learned more about his own seek gift than he had before, and more about beings of the third world, the invisible, than he cared to know.

Mostly he traveled with knights errant or bards or restless peasants, and sometimes with several people at once. Always he searched for new sights.

He loved the life, and yet his heart still hungered.

One day he sat on a grassy hill and watched a sunset flame across a clouded western sky, saw how its reflection in the lake below made it double. He thought: *I have found the one I love.*

He lay facedown on the Earth then, smelled grass and darkness and loam, his heart large in him as colors shifted across the sky, deepened, called. It was the Earth he loved, in all her glory. Sometimes he did not love people, especially those who feared or hurt him; sometimes he did not love life, especially when he was cold, wet, and hungry; but always he loved the Earth.

How could he show her?

The lake, the sky, fire above and below . . .

* * *

In the end, Stig went back underland.

He used his gift to find a rich vein of silver ore, and then he mined it. He mined it until he had enough for his project, which took him ten years; then he went

to the trading caves of his people and hired five silversmiths to help him work.

He had to train them to walk under the sky. They
did not leave the shelter of the underlands easily, but
in the end he convinced them.

First they worked the silver free of the ore and
made it into ingots, and then they hauled it to the
desert; Stig had to hire many carts and carters for that.
Then he built his mold where the sands lay flat. At
the last, he and the five silversmiths each set up a
workstation around the edge of his mold, armed each
with a sixth of the ingots they had made; they built
forgefires, melted the silver, and all poured it molten
and white hot into the mold so that it ran together in
the middle, a round silver plate as big as a lake.

When the metal cooled, Stig and his smiths took
their hammers and polishing cloths and crawled out
to the middle of the plate, then worked their ways
outward to the edges, buffing, hammering, smoothing,
shining the surface of the silver to mirror brightness.

For this was what Stig built for his love: a mirror.
He could think of no finer tribute to the Earth than
to show her how beautiful she was.

At the last, Stig found his old traveling companion,
the wizard, who cut the mirror's ties to Earth and sent
it aloft where Earth could see it best. This wizard built
into the mirror ties that let it travel but always kept
it a certain distance from the earth, always facing
down so Earth's faces shone in it.

For as long as Stig lived—and he lived a very long
time—he and the Earth could look up at Stig's Moon
and see Earth reflected, her wild places and her well-
traveled ones, her wonders and her resting places. At
last his heart knew peace.

When he died, the Moon mourned and shrouded its
face with a yellow-white veil that only sunlight reflected from; and so it has been ever since.

The Opener of the Ways considers those still awaiting an opportunity. He focuses on a small woman, whose every movement belies her anticipation. She smiles at the being floating above the table and drinks the nectar. The gnome scurries to her chair, reaches up, and takes her hand—leading her to the North door and beyond it to deep recesses of the Earth. At one juncture, two marble pillars stand sentry to a dark tunnel. Passing between them, the Seeker learns of:

FAMILY SECRETS
by Robyn McGrew

BLACK smoke disappeared into the reaches above her head from the small lamp she carried. Shalazar pulled the leather strip at the side of the lamp, and the circle of light around her diminished to an arm's length. Footsteps and the unmistakable sound of leather rubbing against metal sounded from the corridors ahead of her. Guards! If they found her, they would take her to her father, Lord Sargon, Priest-King of Babylon. Gods only knew what he would do if he found his daughter had disobeyed him. She looked ahead for a place to hide. A small hollow set into the wall for a likeness of the Winged God would have to serve. Shalazar pressed herself into it and pulled her dark blue cloak around her white gown. The lamp still

116

gave off too much light. With no means to relight it, though, she did not dare snuff it. Facing the wall, she held the lamp close and huddled into her cloak.

The footfalls grew nearer. Now only a turn away from her, she could see light from a torch. Shalazar held her breath and remained motionless. Closing her eyes she prayed, *"Winged Lord, please don't let them see me."* The lamp threatened to burn her, but she didn't dare move. Her heart pounded, and her lungs felt as though they would burst for want of air. The guard's measured steps sounded near. She opened her eyes, pressed her lips together, and dared a glance at the wall. Flickering torchlight lit the area with an amber glow. It receded with the footsteps as the guards continued their rounds. When they seemed far enough away not to hear, Shalazar allowed herself to breathe normally again. Her heart, however, refused to slow to its usual pace.

Stepping from the alcove, Shalazar wondered at the strange old place. How could anyone have used it for a temple? It seemed so lost in the earth, like a long-forsaken cavern. Perhaps if it were filled with light, she might see it differently. Lit only by her small bed lamp, it made the prickles rise on her skin.

Her breath and her heart slowed to normal. Shalazar continued her quest until a last twisting turn brought her to a huge stone archway. Like a Cimmerian sentry, a foreboding door, massive and dark with age, blocked her way. The panel bore an etching that had been dimmed by the passage of time. Shalazar traced the outline of wings, spread to full span as if to protect or to take flight. She had once seen a seal similar to it in the great temple. Why would her father use the seal of the Winged God here? It didn't make sense—he served Inanna-Ishtar, the Goddess of the Moon and of Water. This temple looked very old—perhaps the carving had nothing to do with her father.

A heavy plank set into precious iron braces, speckled with rust, barred the door. Shalazar's free hand rolled into a fist, a reflection of her frustration. She came here to discover what her father withheld from her.

Setting the lamp on the floor, Shalazar braced her feet against the stone arch, grasped the bar, and pulled. Her muscles strained against the unaccustomed task and promised retribution. Flakes of rust floated to the floor, but the bar did not move. Grimacing, she braced and repeated her effort. It still did not move. Refusing to give up, she gathered her strength and gave the bar a hard jerk. It groaned and moved a hand's span. Shalazar held her breath and listened for guards. The sound of her heart pounding in her ears made it hard to listen. She waited. At length she allowed herself to breathe again and returned to the task. Nine more jerks and the bar cleared the iron guard.

She leaned against the door, wondering for the first time what horrible thing would cause her father to take such precautions. Sargon, the Great Warrior, Lord of Babylon, never showed fear. Shalazar doubted he ever experienced it, which made her feel all the worse. She had seen her father face down both wild beasts and fierce warriors. Shalazar forced her mind away from the destructive train of thought. She had come too far already to back away now.

Opening the door enough to slip through took all her waning strength. A stench like rotting meat and worse pushed at the edge of her will, weakening it. Tearing a piece of fabric from the bottom of her gauzy night shift, Shalazar covered her lower face. She retrieved her lamp, raising it overhead to see better.

The air felt cold and moist against the exposed parts of her skin. Olive-green moss gave off weak light,

making long shadows that retreated from the light of
her lamp. Shalazar reviewed the image of her father's
scroll in her memory and started down the nearest
passage. Her bare feet padding against the smooth stone
floor produced soft echoes down the unseen reaches.
What had he concealed here?

Steps led her down to the next level. They were
worn in the center as though they had once known
much traffic, but the layers of undisturbed dirt told
her they had seen little use for some time. Her skirt
brushed a trail through the muck. Setting down the
lamp, she rolled her skirt to her knees and tied it out
of the way. Retrieving her light, Shalazar eased down
the steep decline, using her free hand as a brace
against the all too close walls.

With depth, the cave acquired a humid, closed-in
aspect. She removed her cloak and left it in the muck
on the stair. The stench increased with the heat, forcing her to breathe with care to avoid gagging. Near
the bottom, she detected an open door leading to a
better lit area. Setting the lamp on the stair, Shalazar
steadied herself with both arms. No sense announcing
her arrival to whatever Sargon kept down here. The
short time she'd spent with her father inspecting the
army had taught her that much of tactics.

The next few stairs dropped off steeply, worn down
to almost nonexistence. Testing each step before putting her weight on it, she moved into the depths. Without warning, stone crumbled beneath her feet. Shalazar
fell forward through the opening, yelping in pain.
Gravel cut into her knees and palms as she skidded
to a stop. The makeshift scarf fell from her face, the
rancid smell assailed her nostrils. The stench, pain,
and disorientation destroyed what was left of her concentration. She gagged and nearly retched.

From the opposite side of the cavern a cry sounded,

a groan of pain. Freezing in place, Shalazar searched the darkness about her for an indication of what hid in the recesses. Only the reflection of her own shortened breathing came back to her. Shalazar's jaw tightened and her persistent fear brought clarity to her thought. What made that sound? Captives? Why would her father keep them here instead of the prison? Could this echo come from the structure of the cave?

Only one way she could know for certain—go look. Her knees and palms burned even after she brushed the dirt and gravel from them. Tiny holes sprinkled with blood marked the gravel cuts. Her throat constricted, making it hard to breathe, and her stomach roiled from the stench raised by her movements.

Deep shadows pocked the vast cavern despite the luminescent moss. If someone or something wanted to hide, it would find many places. She edged forward, searching for the source of the noise. There! Turning right, she focused on the odd shape and took another step. The creature let loose a pathetic cry and darted past her. Moving to follow it, she all but tripped on the long, blackened silver chain rattling behind the creature.

Shalazar's heart constricted in grief. Was this poor creature her father's secret? How could a man of such wisdom and caring do such a thing? Surely the Great Sargon could have made some provision better than this? Was this captive why her father had forbidden her to come to the old temple? Did shame make him hide his atrocity?

She followed the taut chain. The creature clambered at the broken stones, trying to scuttle up the steps. His bonds prevented him—yes, a him. Now that she could see it, the creature possessed the body of a young man except for his head. That looked like a bull. Tears welled up in Shalazar's eyes for his sad state. So thin his ribs protruded through his skin. Running sores covered his exposed flesh and vile, putrid-smelling dirt clung to his legs and elbows. Despite his condition, he did not cower before her. Rather, he stood and cast furtive glances between her and his restraints, hoping for release.

Shalazar traced the chain visually to where it connected at his waist. The man-bull stood quite still as she moved cautiously toward him. On closer inspection she discovered the girdle of black leather to be a band of tarnished silver. In back, a locking device similar to the winged emblem on the cavern's door prevented the band's removal.

She moved in small steps trying to edge around him, all the while talking in smooth soft tones. "It's all right . . . I won't hurt you . . . don't pull away . . . that's right."

He looked at her and then with undisguised hope at the stairs. She felt certain that given the chance he would bolt and take his freedom. What would the guards do to him? They would doubtless capture him.

Shalazar pressed her lips together until they tingled. She couldn't leave him here, nor could she just let him go. What should she do? The sad brown eyes caught hers, and she felt certain she saw the sparkle of intelligence behind them. She would take the risk.

"You must trust me. I'm going to help you, but you must wait to leave. Do you understand?"

The creature's eyes closed in an extended blink, and he heaved what sounded to her like a relieved sigh. Standing, he shuffled back into the cavern, allowing Shalazar room to climb the stairs.

She turned, looking a final time at the strange sad creature and debated what he most needed. Everything, or so it seemed to her. Still deep in thought, she picked up the lamp and wrapped her cloak over her soiled dress.

* * *

Sneaking back to the labyrinth's entrance proved harder work for Shalazar than she expected. Somehow she managed to get past the guards, who seemed more numerous than before and made straight for the food stores. She jumped and came near to fleeing when Barnell, the old wizened manservant who knew no greater joy in life but to serve the royal family, spoke from behind her.

"Lady Shalazar, you should not have come to the servants' area. I would bring all you wished. Why didn't you call me?"

He didn't see her flinch, or if he did, he at least didn't mention it. Heart pounding loudly in her ears, Shalazar turned to face the old servant. "I felt restless and decided to take a walk. After a while I got hungry, so I came here." Winged Lord, how she hated lying to her faithful retainer. She did not dare tell him the truth, or he would run straight to her father.

Aided, or rather hindered by Barnell, Shalazar harvested barley cakes, goat cheese, and a skin of goat's milk. She wanted strips of dried mutton, but Barnell would not hear of it.

"You have more here than you need for two nights, my Lady. Now, off to bed with you." He placed a pale hand firmly on her back and prodded her in the direction of her room. She made a show of obedience, but once away from Barnell she circled back to the old temple.

The bag of food seemed to grow in weight the farther she walked, making her wonder if she attempted too much. The memory of the thin, sore body of the man-bull chased away that thought. Voices ahead in the passage alerted her to the approach of the guard. She ducked into another alcove and covered herself

as before, watching them pass by through a slit in
her cloak.

"Three nights left. I'm going to miss this detail."
The larger of the guards glanced casually around him
as he and a younger new guard walked their circuit.

"What do you mean?" the youth asked, his tone
indicating an almost awed respect for the older man's
experience and knowledge.

"Lord Sargon's ordered these passages sealed after
the next full moon; no need to keep a guard, they'll
reassign us. I've walked these passages from the time
I signed on. I'll miss the quiet." Shalazar heard sadness in the man's rough voice.

"Who told you?" The younger man's voice cracked
on the last word and Shalazar could almost feel him
blush.

"Oh, I keep my ears open. A good habit to develop
if you want to get anywhere in the guard."

The conversation faded as the guards moved away
from her. She had heard enough however to know her
father planned more unpleasant things for her new
friend than she'd first thought. Her challenge had increased. The man-bull must not only recover his
health and strength soon, but she must also find a way
to free him. No longer noticing the weight of the
leather food bag, Shalazar eased out of the niche and
hurried to the etched door. It didn't seem so heavy
this time, or perhaps her purpose gave her strength.
She pulled it closed behind her and prayed to the
Winged God that the guards would not notice that the
door was not barred.

She tied her cloak around her waist. The weight of
the food forced her to leave the lamp on the landing
at the top of the stairs. With her hands full, she had
to take the stairs one at a time and almost slipped
twice. Once in the cavern she looked for the man-bull.

He had retreated to the far wall, but came out of the shadows when he saw her.

"I brought you something to eat." Setting down the bag, she used her foot to clear a circle of refuse, rat carcasses, and other things on whose origins she'd rather not speculate. She made a space large enough for the man-bull to sleep in if he so chose.

"Come on . . . here." Shalazar removed her cloak and spread it on the ground. Taking the food out of the bag she set it out like a feast. "It's all yours."

The man-bull took a few tentative steps toward the treasure. He sniffed first at the goat cheese and then at the barley cakes. Suddenly, with a swiftness she would not have attributed to one in such a frail state, he leaped forward. Thinking herself under attack, Shalazar pivoted and sprinted for the stairs. After a few steps, she realized the man-bull was not behind her and stopped. She turned to see the starving creature eating with both hands.

"Eat slowly! You'll make yourself sick if you gorge like that. I'll try to bring you more tomorrow."

He paused, tilted his head, and examined the food in both hands. With reluctance he set the half-eaten barley cake on the ground and returned to consuming the round of goat cheese he held in his other dirt-encrusted hand. Satisfied, Shalazar climbed the stairs and returned to her room, wondering the whole time how she could save the man-bull.

* * *

The next morning she woke to aches and stiffness in her hands and knees. The cuts proved that she had not dreamed the incident in the old temple. The sun nearing its zenith meant she had missed first meal. Wanting to avoid as much suspicion as possible, Shalazar ordered the midday meal brought to her private garden. When served, she picked over it as if not entirely satisfied with the variety. She sent her servant Yani back to the food stores for smoked lamb strips, a jug of water, and some figs. When Shalazar felt certain Yani was far enough away, she scooped the breads and a fowl into a gardener's bag, plate and all. The servant would wonder at its absence, but wouldn't say anything about it. When Yani returned with the food, Shalazar dismissed her.

Alone again, she secreted her stash behind a golden rosebush close to the wall of her small garden. Throughout the day she made several more trips adding things to the growing pile. Just before dinner she reviewed the results—besides the food and drying cloths, she had collected a scrubbing rock, some herbs, and the soft rag her father bought from the sea people. To this she added as many candles as she could take without their absence becoming obvious. The man-bull had lived in a dark place for so long, he would need the candles to adjust to more light. Satisfied, she covered the pile with the heavy sacks the gardener used to cart away dead leaves and branches.

Dinner was an ordeal. Her mother kept stealing glances at the long-sleeved tunic she had donned to hide the abrasions from her foray. Shalazar forced herself to eat, even though she didn't feel like it. Her father would notice. Sargon noted everything, even if he didn't mention it. Did he suspect? She controlled a shudder. If he did, would she find him waiting for her when she went to see the man-bull tonight? May the Winged Lord forbid it. Even if her father didn't interfere, how could she free the pitiful creature?

She closed her eyes and offered a silent prayer. *Winged Lord, guide me. Show me what I must do to save my new friend.*

Begging fatigue, she retired to her rooms. When Inanna-Ishtar drew a cloud over the face of the nearly full moon, Shalazar stole out to the garden and gathered as much of her hoard as she could carry. It took three trips to get it all to just inside the door of the cave.

He must have heard her coming and waited at the bottom of the stairs. The chain rattled behind him as he reached toward her in a gracious civilized gesture, offering to take the bag from her. Shalazar wondered if her father used to come here and visit this creature even as she did now. She released the bag of food to him and returned for another armload, again finding him waiting at base of the stairs.

Sitting together in the cleared circle, they shared some of the water. He reached toward her. She fought not to withdraw as he stroked her cheek with the back of his dry cracked hand. It felt rough to her soft skin and smelled like a camp pit, but the gesture touched her deeply. She smiled and fought the tears forming in her eyes.

"Than . . . you." His voice sounded raspy as if he had not spoken for a long time.

"You are welcome. I am happy to help. I did not know you could speak."

"No reason. Nothing to say until you came." A rumble like rocks grinding together marked his words.

Shalazar smiled and stared down at the floor, ashamed that such a wondrous creature had known such neglect and abuse. She looked at him again, noticing for the first time the magnificent horns that shone, despite the encrusted dirt. "Do you have a name?"

The man-bull nodded, but seemed hesitant to speak it.

"My name is Shalazar."

"Shal . a . . zar," he said it like tasting something sweet. "Call me Minoa."

"Minoa." His name seemed familiar, both in flavor and in texture, but she couldn't think where she'd heard it. "Minoa, I brought water and some herbs to wash your sores. It will make them feel better."

He nodded permission. She mixed the herbs into the water, adding some of her own favorite ambergris oil. Minoa submitted to her attentions, holding still even when she scraped off encrusted dirt with the sandstone. The tarnished silver belt made her work difficult, especially where it had rubbed scars into calluses. When she finished, she examined her handiwork. Despite the ragged kilt and the thinness of his body, he had a magnificent natural beauty. A tear fled down her cheek. How could her father? How could he?

The creature raised his hand and gently lifted the tear from her skin. "Why?"

Her anger flared. "Because of the cruelty you endure. Because I know my father will seal this place three days from now, after the full moon, and you are too noble to die in such a manner."

"I will leave. You will free me." The last statement sounded almost like a plea.

"The guards would stop you. You're not strong enough to fight them."

The man-bull closed his eyes and seemed to think for a long time. At length, he opened them and suggested, "We wait for an opportunity, but first you free me." He touched the black band on his waist.

Shalazar opened her mouth to object, but Minoa placed his fingers on her mouth to prevent the words. Drawing her to her feet, he locked soft brown eyes on hers. "I trusted you. Now you must trust me."

Pressing her lips together she nodded. His broad

mouth twisted into what she took for a smile and he turned to expose the back of the belt to her. Shalazar studied the intricate work, looking for the catch. The tarnished pins did not want to release. She pulled at them with her fingers until she felt they'd break. Then, with a high-pitched moan, one pin and then another came loose. The band remained in place, frozen there by tarnish and dirt. Shalazar gripped the band on either side of the locking device and pulled. It didn't move. Pouring all her strength into the effort, she pulled again. The band, heavier than she had expected twisted in her hands and fell, hitting the stone floor with a loud metallic crash.

Minoa inhaled a deep breath of air and with it the freedom it represented. He kicked the band away and placed his hands on her shoulders. "Thank you. Go now, before someone misses you. Please bring more candles tomorrow night."

At the stairs, Shalazar looked over her shoulder at him. She had to get him out of here two nights from now, or the stonemasons would seal him here forever. He seemed stronger from the food and attention she'd given him, but would it be enough to allow his escape?

The next night Shalazar brought Minoa food and more candles. He met her at the great door, accepted the bundle with thanks, and asked her for privacy. She acquiesced with reluctance. Turning away, she retraced her steps to her room and spent the night in troubled sleep.

On the day of the full moon, Shalazar woke in the morning to find her father sitting beside her bed. Dressed in his gold-fringed kilt and golden cloak, he looked ready to give judgment. Next to him the soiled night shift and cloak from her early visits lay in a neat pile. Her breath caught in her throat.

"Inanna-Ishtar's blessing on you, my daughter."

Pulling herself into a sitting position, she answered in the calmest tone she could manage. "The Winged God guide and keep you, my father."

Her father, by nature a direct man, picked up the soiled linen and ran his fingers over the torn places. "Have you something to tell me?"

The flame of fear ignited in her heart. What did he know? If he knew, how much had he discerned? Should she remain silent? Her throat felt constricted and dry, like she had swallowed a portion of desert.

"I await your answer, Shalazar."

Icy fear joined the flame of fear, spinning together like twin serpents. She felt as if they had frozen her heart between beats as well as her voice. She had to say something. Her father was an implacable man, he would wait for her answer. He also owned an uncanny ability to know when somebody lied to him. Her mother had told her the gift of the Goddess made it so.

"I have felt restless at night of late." Better a vague truth than a lie, maybe then he would not see through her deception.

"Where did you go, that you so soiled your clothing and sliced your skin in such a manner?" He lifted her arm and traced the long red mark the rosebush cut into it. In placing Minoa's store of food under the fragrant yellow flowers, the bush had extracted a payment—her blood for its protection. What would her father ask in payment if he knew of her disobedience?

"I visited the rose garden and several of the other gardens."

Sargon frowned, deep lines making his bronze face appear even darker. He nodded, encouraging her to continue.

Sweat glistened in the palms of her hands and made the backs of her knees sticky. "I know I will not be allowed to leave the Temple of the Winged God until I finish my training. I wanted to enjoy the things I must leave behind."

Her father still looked dissatisfied. He fixed his dark eyes on her face. "You feel you must do this in the dead of night, wearing only your night shift and a cloak?"

Despite the tightness of her throat, Shalazar forced herself to swallow and answer. "Father, you know how it is for us. Even at night the servants follow, wanting to serve me. I need time to myself."

This he could understand. "Tell me, my daughter," the king asked softly. "What is it you fear about entering the service of the Winged One?"

"What makes you think I fear it?"

He laughed. Heat rose in her cheeks. She didn't know whether to feel relieved or angry. "Sweet child, none save the fool knows no fear when he or she enters the unknown. Warriors know this fear. The best of them greet their fear and walk with firm steps and head held high to meet it."

Shalazar studied the man before her, intrigued. He had never before shared this side of himself with her. "Did you feel fear when it came time for you to go to Inanna?"

His smile faded and he looked over her shoulder, seeing memories in the early light. "I feared I would lose my manhood. In submitting to the Goddess, I thought I would have to surrender something of great value to me. I discovered instead that in Her I became greater than before and knew fulfillment."

He pulled Shalazar into a fierce embrace and whispered in her hair, "Trust your instincts, child. Don't let your mind or fear get in the way, and you will do the right thing."

He released her, departing the room briskly, gold

fringe on his kilt swishing in rhythm to his steps. She
did not see him the rest of the day.

* * *

Shalazar waited for her father to leave for the great
dining hall. She waited a few extra minutes in case he
had forgotten something, then slipped into his rooms.
What Minoa needed Shalazar could have with much
greater ease gathered from the palace's general stores.
The man-bull deserved linen and not the harsher wool
she would find among the warrior's garb. She chose a
white linen kilt from the many gold-fringed ones in
her father's cedar clothes chest and chose a cloak of
green and gold to go with it. To these she added a
pair of sturdy leather sandals. Shalazar looked around
to see if she should bring anything else. The familiar
room and the thought she might not be able to return
made her stomach twist in on itself. Still, her father
had instructed Shalazar to trust her instincts. A coincidence? Perhaps. He had told her once that the idea
of coincidence came from the imagination of man; in
truth, the events came as the result of magic. Would
he still say so if he knew that her instincts told her to
release his secret prisoner?

Shalazar felt so nervous about her upcoming Rite
of Dedication and Minoa's release that she didn't feel
like eating. So she begged off dinner, stating that she
wanted to begin her fast early. Images of what she
would do played and replayed in her thoughts. After
an eternity all went quiet save for the measured footfalls of the night watch. She slipped down the corridors that led from her rooms to the great door of the
old temple, the bundle of borrowed clothing tucked
beneath her arm.

For the final time Shalazar entered the cave. Minoa

met her halfway down the stairs. "Please," he reached for the clothing. "Allow me time to change. I will call you."

"If you wish." Something seemed different about him, but in the near dark she could not tell what. His voice seemed different, stronger somehow, but it had gained strength each day she brought him food and fresh water. His speech had improved as well, but this also could have come from their recent conversations.

"Shalazar, please come down now." The man-bull's rumble sounded happy. He had good reason, knowing he would have his freedom soon.

She moved down the stairs, wary of the broken treads, instead she found a hand-packed ramp, formed of the dirt once strewn about the pit. Soft beeswax candles provided a path to the center of the cavern. Minoa stood within a circle of candles, hooded and hidden in the cloak she had provided. All she could see of him were his horns, the leather sandals, and a hand holding the cloak together. She hoped he had gained enough strength to survive in the outside world. At his feet, spread out on empty food bags, were the sweet bread and the bag of cider she had brought him as a special treat the previous night.

"Please join me."

Shalazar entered the circle of light and sat opposite Minoa. They shared the bread and cider in silence. He served her, although she felt she should attend him. She savored the wholesome nutty flavor of the bread and the sweet tang of the drink. The sharing of the simple meal came as a pleasant communion. During their repast, Shalazar studied Minoa. He sat shrouded in the cloak, more of a mystery than ever before.

Even though they had spent little time together she had found him a gentle creature by nature and suspected he held great depth. She would miss him in the days to come.

He seemed to watch her studying him, but kept his silence. She almost asked what would happen to him and where he planned to go. He placed long slim fingers on her lips. The hood moved from side to side halting her questions.

Finishing their meal, he helped her stand. Shalazar led the way up the stairs. At the top she slipped through the door and looked up and down the corridor. She had studied the guards' habits and knew they took their food break halfway through their shift. Only empty corridors awaited them. She beckoned to Minoa. He joined her and together they closed the great door to the place that had served as his prison. He slid the bolt into place, making all as it had been that first night. Alert, Shalazar led him through the maze of her home to the closest exit. He placed a hand on her head, as if in a parting blessing, then disappeared into the night.

* * *

At dawn, maiden-priestesses from the temple came to fetch Shalazar. Dressed in the green and brown of the Winged God, they looked clad in the vestments of the Earth.

"Is it time?"

One of the maidens placed her hand over Shalazar's mouth. "Lady, you must not speak. This day your voice must serve only the Winged One. Come we will prepare you." Surrounding her, the maidens escorted her to the great temple.

On her arrival, priests of the element of air purified her thoughts in the chamber of winds. They delivered her to the Priestesses of Inanna-Ishtar, who bathed

Shalazar in the element of water. She spent midday in the light of the sun, to purify her spirit in the element of fire. White-robed temple acolytes came to rub protective oils on her skin. Shalazar spent the early evening with the priestesses who had escorted her that morning. They chanted prayers to the Winged Lord while bathing her with scented water and then anointed her with sacred oils.

Throughout the rituals, her mind dwelt on Minoa. Even while she knelt in the intense light of the sun, the man-bull's image played inside her mind. How did he fare? Had he made it out of the city?

Shalazar felt guilty over her musings. The training she had received as a royal daughter of the house of Sargon should have prevented her thoughts from wandering. Hoping the Winged God would not take offense, she offered a silent prayer. *Forgive me, Lord of Earth; I know I should keep my thoughts on You and not Minoa. Please go with him and protect him.*

At moonrise, the priestesses dressed her in a green-fringed silk robe and accompanied her to the door of the Element of Earth. They retreated, inclining their heads in the last gesture of respect she would receive again until she completed her training. She must take the last step alone and of her own will.

Shalazar placed her hand on the panel and pushed it open, noticing vaguely that the amber panels on the door bore the outline of wings, spread to full span as if to protect or to take flight. Within, tall cedar pillars graced with flowered vines stretched upward to an open ceiling. Tiny black-and-white wheat ears, nearly invisible in the leaf-laden trees, twittered in sweet tones. A mother leopard raised her head from cleaning a cub and rumbled a greeting. Shalazar pushed the great door closed behind her. She took one step and then another into the vast enclosure.

At the northern end of the room, ten circular steps surrounded a cubed malachite altar. A hooded priest stood there with his back to her. He stood very tall, and wore a green robe reminding her much of the one she had given to Minoa. Minoa—he would appreciate the beauty of this place. She fought that thought to the back of her mind and continued forward.

She stopped at the stairs and knelt. The priest turned and addressed her in a low voice. "Why do you come?"

"I have come to dedicate myself to the Winged Lord of the Element of Earth; that through my service, the people of this kingdom can know His blessing."

Power cascaded over her, penetrated every aspect of her being. Trembling, she knew the God stood before her in person.

"You gave your dedication already and I accepted it."

His voice sounded so familiar. Where had she heard it before? What did He mean that she had already dedicated herself? Awed by the presence of the God, Shalazar bowed her head and closed her eyes. She waited, both in fear and hope, for the God to do whatever he would with her.

He descended the stairs and placed his hands on her head, then on her shoulders. She felt His power, a living thing surrounding her. He pulled her to her feet, as she could have a child.

"In his youth, your father realized there was something that set him apart from his fellows. In seeking to discover the source of the difference, he came to understand that the world held more than the average man or woman can see. He sought this wisdom, and in doing so found the place of the Elements. We, the essence of the elements, were happy to have one of our own return to us. You see, Shalazar, your father is the child of Inanna-Ishtar. It is now time for you to come into your heritage."

Power entered through His fingers and spread throughout her body. She felt it changing her. Shalazar knew a strength greater than anything she had imaged. This was coupled with gentleness and compassion, yet tempered with the love that allows severity. To her shame, her thoughts returned to Minoa. It would please him to see her now, standing in the grip of her God.

Shame burned her cheeks for she knew the God must have heard her thoughts. "Forgive me, Lord."

"Forgive you for caring for Me? No, I shall not."

He lifted her chin and pushed back His hood. Minoa stood before her. His black-brown hair shone in the light of full moon and the bronzed skin so recently covered with running sores glowed.

"I don't understand."

Minoa released her. "The Gods never take anything without testing it first. Many of Our progeny misuse their gifts. Your dedication had to come of your own free will or it would have no value. I would not have awakened what lies dormant within you had you failed." He caressed her cheek with the back of His hand, just as He had in the cavern.

"We shall talk of this again, Shalazar, but now you must apply yourself to your studies." He stepped away from her, taking on the glory of the power of His element. As she watched, He smiled and turned into the Winged Bull.

Minoa vanished from sight, leaving Shalazar alone and happy in the afterglow of His acceptance.

A woman with a careworn face lit by determined gray eyes drinks next. The gnome is waiting for her when she rises from her chair. Together they approach the chamber's Northern door. She steps through the portal to a world of glaciers and snow-shrouded valleys. The woman strides toward the ruined homestead that holds the memory of:

DVERGERTAL
(Intercourse with a Dwarf)

by Nancy Varian Berberick

I DESPISED him, my brother Burgun.

I despised him for a weakling when he let his wife abuse the servants. The bondwomen fled that woman's approach as light flees darkness, and Old Svein the stableman, who'd been good and willing and kind to Burgun and me all our lives, now went with his head low and eyes shifting left and right, ready to dodge the blows he'd never gotten from my mother. Life had been good for us, my brother and me and our few serving folk, until *she* came to Burgunstead, that woman Astrida Jensdatter, to be Burgun's wife.

I scorned him, my brother.

I scorned him because he let his wife stint on food at table, he let her water the ale and allow us no wine. She dishonored us with her tightfistedness, we who had always been known in the valley as openhanded in even the hardest times. Burgun Niggard they were calling him now in the valley. Ah, the bitter shame! In days of fat calves and plump geese, when the crocks overflowed with milk and the cold house stood floor to rafter with wheels of cheese and eggs filled our baskets, my brother's wife handed out food as though famine sat stark-eyed at table with us. She counted our every bite and regretted our every sip. She railed at me night and day for doing little to earn my keep, though it was I who ran her household for her. All this Burgun let her do.

In his high, grassy barrow, out there in the meadow, just beyond the two streams, the ghost of my father Amund Burgunsen paced and prowled, I know it. Upon her stony bier my mother Nisse Grimnirsdatter wept to see her family so fallen, I am certain. And one night, dark and cold and wind-whipped at the end of autumn, I heard them wailing, the shades of my parents weaving their voices together in shame and rage.

That was the night the dwarf came to our door.

* * *

Wind and the scent of the year's end whipped in past the door when I opened to the small man.

"Don't," *she* muttered under her breath when I rose from the hearth at the sound of knocking heard above even the wind's cry. Don't open the door, don't let in the stranger who will eat our food and spend our wood to warm himself at our fire. Don't.

Of course, I did. Once I was mistress of this house, in the days after my mother and father died. Once I handed out a hospitality as generous as the sea itself is. She called that wastefulness and hated me for it, but I know what is right.

Astrida's fist clenched when I ignored her. "Burgun," she said, her left hand upon her swelling belly. There, there in that womb was all she held over him, the child-wealth he seemed to want more than my regard or his family's reputation. That gesture would get her what she wanted every time she wanted it. It got her my mother's fine lace, bolt after bolt of her lovely weave-work, her gold rings and thick amber necklace. Those things that should have been part of my dowry lay in Astrida's coffers now.

"Herthe!" she called to me. She snapped my name as she would that of a servant.

I ignored her, and I pretended not to hear my brother when he called me back. I know what is right, and it is right to admit the bestormed traveler when he knocks. I opened the great oaken door to a sweep of wind and rain and a small man, one who stood not so high as I do. Hooded and cloaked, he dripped and shivered beneath our eaves. I knew him to be no one of mankind. You can always tell by the way the skin prickles on the back of your neck. Be the creature dwarf or elf or some wayfaring god in disguise, you feel the knowing running on your skin like a whisper to say, *Here is one who is not of our kind.*

"Good even to you, *freyja*," he said, courteously naming me lady. His voice as ugly and rough, like the sound of stone cracking. He was a dwarf, I knew, for lore says they sound so, and I had no reason to doubt lore. "Can you spare a cup and a crust and a place by your fire?"

I told him I could spare that and more. Far as I was from her, I heard my brother's wife grinding her teeth. "Come inside where it is warm and tell us your tale."

He did come in, and he greeted Burgun and his wife as fairly as he had done me. When he flung back his hood, I saw his eyes, and they were the color of fire, of amber. When he threw off his cloak, he stood revealed as the dwarf I'd thought him. A tight silence fell upon those gathered, my brother and Astrida and the few servants still cleaning away the cups and trenchers which had held our too-small supper. It is no unusual thing to find a dwarf abroad in the middle-world, but it is always a thing to be remarked for they are unchancy folk who treat with us according to their own ways, ways not always known until some rough lesson has taught us.

"I am Burgun Amundsen," said my brother, careful to offer his own name and not demand the dwarf's. *Easy as offending a dwarf* is not an old saying because it sounds good, and Burgun, it seemed, still had two wits to rub together despite his wife's best effort to rid him of them. "Be welcome in our home."

That pallid greeting I repaired hastily, offering a place by the fire and food and drink. These the dwarf accepted readily and I went and fetched the meal myself, bread and cheese and thin, watered ale. That last the dwarf tasted first, and my cheeks flushed with shame when the wan drink made him grimace. Astrida, in her place at the head of the table, grimaced as well, not for the poor drink, but for the fact that the dwarf finished his cup and got more from me when he looked for it. My brother had not even the decency to look ashamed. Instead he had his eyes always on her, waiting on her will and whim. I hated him for the boneless *nithing* he'd become.

"I feel your blood burning in you," whispered the dwarf as I reached for his cup to fill it a third time.

He spoke of burning, I shivered. It is one thing to hate secretly, another to imagine the hatred is recognized. And it was, it was. He looked into me deeply with only a glance, and I knew there were no secrets left unturned by the time he glanced away. With shaking hand, I piled up food in his trencher and hoped he'd say nothing more. I got what I hoped for, but I should have hoped he'd lose his knowing smile as well. That he kept upon his lips as he looked around himself at the house where he was guest.

It was no good thing he saw, though maybe one who could look so deeply was able to know what this house had been. Once, when the servants weren't beaten and starved, they'd kept the rushes clean and fragrant with herbs, polished with beeswax the handsome paneling which my father and his father and seven fathers before them had carved with cunning and skill to show the history of our family. Our hearth had been wide and high, though now it lay fallen in so that only a meager fire could be built there. Once—did he see it?—love and regard lay between my brother and me, as it should between close kin. No more.

"I am Mótsognir," said the amber-eyed dwarf at last.

Mótsognir. Well, it was a name, though a byname. We in the middle-world know this about dwarfs: they do not share names down the long, long years. Each one takes a new name for himself, one no other has used. Mótsognir Shaper, the real Mótsognir, could not possibly be sitting here drinking my brother's watery ale. They are not gods, after all, dwarfs. Lore tells us that, too. They do not live forever.

As I thought so, the dwarf wiped ale foam from his lips and looked around for more. The jug was empty. I moved to rise and fetch another, but "Wait!" said my brother's wife, her icy blue eyes narrowing.

"What is it?" I asked, never turning to look at her, certainly never naming her sister.

She sat forward, firelight gleaming on my mother's gold and amber. Beside me the dwarf who named himself Mótsognir grew cold and still. Whatever Astrida was going to say, he'd reckoned before he drew breath to speak.

"You think me mistaken," he said, his lip curling. "About my own name?"

"Mistken?" Astrida matched him curled lip for curled lip. "No, guest. How can a man be mistaken about his own name? I do wonder, though, what your real name is and why you treat my husband, your host, so badly that you cannot tell him the truth of it."

As I say, it was the end of autumn when these things happened. You'd expect to feel the chill wind blowing through the chinks in the walls, you'd expect to shiver and think of winter. Just then, though, such coldness filled the house that I almost heard the hiss of snow blowing in under the door.

The dwarf who named himself Mótsognir put aside his cup and stood. Firelight and shadow spilled over him and it seemed to me—though I heard him breathing—that he was made all of stone.

"Woman," he said, "you misname your husband if you call him 'host.' The food he offers is not fit for swine, the ale too meek for children."

Burgun stood; I thought he would offer apology to his guest so ill-used. He did not, for he'd apparently rubbed his last two wits together and had none left to spark. He put both hands on the table and leaned forward. Anger clouded his eyes like storm in the sky. "I will have you dragged from here, dwarf, and stoned down the road!"

Beside him, Astrida sat smug and still.

Mótsognir said nothing. As though he didn't see my brother's threatening anger, he glanced once at the table. The cream in the pot curdled. Upon the board the last of the cheese separated and spoiled. Astrida gasped. Burgun shouted a curse. If Mótsognir heard, he gave no sign.

Came a feeling of gathering, as though unseen armies rode to answer the call of the battle-horn.

In the corners of the house the shadows moved and flowed. A servingwoman cried out, then another. Rats poured out from the shadows, running and chittering, flowing like a dark river across the rushes. I laughed to see their little green eyes gleaming in the firelight, for I thought Burgun Niggard had earned these filthy guests. My laughter choked me, though, when I saw where next Mótsognir sent his baleful glance.

Astrida cried, "No! For pity! No!" as she felt his amber glance fall on her. In the womb her child writhed—I could see it—and I ran to the dwarf, even put myself between his glare and the woman I so hated.

"Guest, I beg you—don't harm the harmless child!"

His amber eyes shone with the fire of his anger. He heard me, though, I saw that, too, for when I put my hand on him, the fire fell. Ah, it fell, but that rage-fire did not die. The dwarf looked around him at what he'd wrought, and he smiled. A terrible smile, his, and he put his hand on me to move me aside.

"Hear me, Burgun Amundsen," he said. He did not shout, and yet it is true that his voice filled up the house to the rafters.

In her chair my brother's wife sobbed, hunched over her wombed child, wrapping herself 'round with both arms as though that gesture could deflect Mótsognir's rage. Burgun stood still, white to the eyes and trembling.

"You have done me insult, Burgun Amundsen." Mótsognir sneered an ugly smile. "Burgun Niggard. Now you must do what is proper to make amends. I claim the right of reparation."

Burgun drew a breath to speak, and color came creeping back to his face. He looked around him at what he had to offer, goods or gold to make good the damage he'd done. It was right, and even he knew that.

"What will you have?"

Ah, that must have hurt to ask, for I knew it that his wife would not let him lie easy tonight if they must part with the least shaving of gold to mend their fault.

"Only one thing," said the dwarf.

Again I felt a gathering, I looked to the corners, but the rats were long gone. What did he gather, then? Cold in the pit of my belly, I wondered, what did he want?

Amber eyes turned upon me, his sneered smile eased a little. My mouth dried up with fear.

"Give me this one," Mótsognir said, his voice a scratching whisper like old leaves on frosted stone. "Pay for your insult by giving me this woman."

Such silence sat on that house! A deep stillness of man and woman, master and servant, of wind itself fallen quiet around the eaves. In that moment I saw all as clearly as though I stood in sunlight, the neglected panels of my father's handwork, the spoiled food, the shivering light of the fading hearth fire.

Burgun winced. His wife drew an easing breath. In the corner where rats had roiled, one little servant girl sobbed my name.

"Take her," said Astrida, boldly agreeing to what her man did not dare. "Yes! Take her, dwarf. Use her for a slave, use her for a whore! Use her how you like, and don't complain if you get no more of this worthless wretch than nothing!"

I cried, "No!" and I shouted, "Brother, please!"

Mótsognir took my arm and pulled me close. I struggled, but though he was a small wight, he had more strength than I. He spoke one word, and then the whirlwind came down upon me, a roaring and howling, a tearing and ripping as the night wrenched open before me, above me, below me. White writhing fog poured in through those gaps, thick as wool and suffocating.

I screamed, and the sound followed me, thin as a

ghost's keening cry, down into the milky nothingness that lies between all the Nine Worlds.

* * *

I huddled in cold, I huddled in terror. I'd been sent to be a slave and a whore. I would be broken, one way and another, until I lived by no will but my master's I knew it, cowering there in never-ending darkness, smelling stone all around me, feeling the fingers of fog creeping over me. Moist, cold, and searching, they touched my face, my eyes. They crept inside the bodice of my gown, they lay upon my arms and my neck, touching always, everywhere. Countless tears had run down that face of mine since last I saw my brother's hall. Trickles became streams, became rivers, became seas. From that weeping grew the fog, and so I crouched, in stony darkness, surrounded by the ghosts of my tears until at last—a day, a week, a year after I had fallen out of the middle-world and into the unending dark—I heard a voice, his voice:

"Now stop weeping."

And I did. Not because I wanted to stop, not because I was able to stop. I stopped because ceasing had been commanded and my very body must obey that command. Sobbing, the last quaking after the storm, I lifted my hand to wipe at my face, to throw back my hair, fallen and tangled. Had a god spoken, his merest word enough to shape my body's response?

"No," said the voice, and now I knew it. Mótsognir spoke, somewhere in the fog and the darkness he stood and spoke to me. "I am no god." And saying that, he laughed as at a fine joke.

"You are not," I agreed, the words still shuddering with sobbing. "You are a thief."

Well, what more had I to fear that I should shy from angering a dwarf?

He made a soft sound, as one who is thinking. Then he said that he was no thief. "For who steals by accepting what is freely given?"

There he was wrong. I was not freely given, and I told him that. "I am given against my will. My brother—"

"Your brother's wife—"

I ignored his further laughter. "My brother's bitch. She gave me, and not by my will."

Darkness, darkness, Mótsognir was there, somewhere in the darkness. Not far from me, I thought so by the sound of his voice, near, and I thought the fog of my tears stirred a little under his breath. I waited for him to say something more, to dispute or agree. He said nothing. My belly went tight. He would reach out now. My very skin cringed. Just as lore promised, he would put his hand on me and claim me.

Isn't it said, in all the tales, that women of the middle-world are prized among folk of the other worlds?

Soft, like a man talking to himself, Mótsognir said, "Now, you think? Now I will make you whore and a slave?"

I swallowed hard, trying for courage. "Isn't it the way of things?"

Silence, so deep and strong it might have been stone itself. I listened with all my ears and heard nothing. Not his breathing, not the merest scrape of a step. Mótsognir was gone, and I crouched in darkness again, shivering till I thought all my bones would rattle apart. Then, swiftly, a breath out of the blackness, a breath that came all at once from the north, from the east, from the south, and from the west.

Upon that breath, that dreaming breath, I slept as though in the finest of all beds.

* * *

Look, he said, Mótsognir in my dreaming, and I looked upon living lore.

I saw the birth of the Nine Worlds, the lifting of Bifrost, that shining rainbow bridge running between one world and another, and always back to Asgard. I saw gods rise up and inspire life into the fathers of all the beings who would inhabit those worlds. I saw giants born, and elves and men. I saw the birth of the Valkyries, Father Odin's own fierce daughters, and before my dreaming eyes golden Valhalla was built, stern to stand against the enemies of the Aesir. Into that Hall of the Valiant came the bright souls of all those men of the middle-world who died bravely in battle. Odin's Army, gathered against a Darkness to come, heroes awaiting the call to serve All-Father at his greatest need. They shone, those heroes, in the golden hall.

I saw seas rise up and mountains fall, then grow again. I saw gods range out and walk among giants and elves. I saw them go among men as they founded their kingdoms, fought their wars, and mended their truces. I saw all these things and much more.

Never in the dream did I see the making of dwarfs.

Mótsognir, he laughed in my dreaming, and he said, *You see the truth and cannot see. You dream, and you cannot understand.*

That much was clear, and when at last I woke, feeling that I had slept an age away, he was there, standing beside me. This time, he held light, a pale gleam like the sun hidden behind clouds. Thin it was, thin, but I rose to it like a bird rising to the sky. I felt that light in me, sparkling in my blood. Mótsognir shook his head, chewing a little on his bottom lip like he was considering a judgment. Then he left me, in darkness he left me and he said nothing.

I lay upon the stone and I wept for the loss of the light, raising up the fog again. When I slept at last, I dreamed again, and this was the same as the first, the building, the raising up, the going out of gods. And so I existed, in dreams never changing and fog never clearing.

*   *   *

"Listen," said Mótsognir crouching down at my side. He pushed my hair away from my face, and I stiffened to feel his hand on my cheek. "No, don't be afraid. Listen."

I wanted light, not anything more. I hadn't eaten since last I'd been in my brother's hall. I didn't feel the loss, my belly didn't grind against my ribs with hunger. I hadn't had to drink in all that time. It didn't matter, I felt no thirst. But light . . . ah, I longed for it, and got only fog and darkness and dreams of the Shaping of the Worlds.

"Please," I said, "let me feel the light."

"Feel?" He tasted the word, he tested the word, and then he made a sound, deep in his chest, that sounded like stone rolling down a hill. I felt it in me— though I didn't understand how!—that he was somehow pleased. "You want to feel the light. Yes."

I pushed myself up to sit. I tell you, I was sick from the darkness, starved for the light, and all my limbs trembled from the loss. Still, I wouldn't lie there, weak and weary and whining. "Have I become so ugly," I said, "that you can't bear to shine some light on me? Should I be grateful, then, that you will not use me for a whore?"

He said nothing for a long moment, then asked, "Why do you think I want to use you for a whore?"

"It is said in all the lore . . ."

He smiled—knew that I didn't see it, couldn't see it. Knew that I felt it, in me and warm.

"And you trust the lore."

What a question! Of course I did. How do you go about in the world without trusting the lore that has come from father to child? Was it not lore that bade me treat him well in the hall?

Fog swirled around me, cold and clammy, the breath of my sorrow. He said, "Close your eyes."

What point in that? I could see nothing. I told him so and said, "If you want to hide something from me, or whisk out a torch from behind your back to delight me—" He ignored the sarcasm. "—then do so. My eyes are blind."

Ah, he changed like a storm sea! He rose up, and I have said he is a dwarf and not so tall as I, but now I tell you Mótsognir rose up and he might have been a giant standing there. Now I thirsted, aye, I did, for my mouth dried up with fear.

"More than your eyes are blind," he said, his voice hard and rough. "Close your eyes!"

I snapped them shut, and in the doing I felt myself falling. I screamed, I reached out, for Mótsognir or for a wall, for something solid.

There was nothing.

* * *

I fell into light, bright and fierce, fierce as sun on snow. I fell, screaming, and then the screaming turned to laughter. Not mine, not at first. It was as though someone else laughed through me, another voice come out from my mouth. Falling, I felt others going by, past me, behind me, above me and below. Others falling?

No, said Mótsognir in my dream. *No one is falling, not even you. Open your eyes.*

I did, and darkness rushed in like silent screams.

Close your eyes! Feel the light!

I did as he said, I must for the lightlessness was too heavy to bear. And closing my eyes, I felt the light again, aye—felt it, for there was no seeing in this state. I felt it surround me gently, the brightness like that in my mother's own eyes.

"I feel it," I whispered, and my awe awed me, flowing out from me, into me, delight. I felt it, light, and I knew that in reaching for it—

You have made it.

I had made the light, called it, created it. A trembling understanding grew in me, small and frail and hardly credited: Out of tears I had made fog. From darkness and want I had made light.

But who were the beings I felt all around me in that falling light?

Mótsognir, he sighed, a small sound, and I thought it held a burden of weariness. Thinking that, I recalled the meaning of the name this dwarf used: Mótsognir, the Weary One.

"Mótsognir," I said, and saying it, I looked around me. I didn't see him. He didn't speak to me. I was, again, alone in the stony place. My stony place.

This time, there was no fog. This time, I had light to see, and I saw that my stony prison was no prison at all, but a wide, high chamber. Embedded in the walls were jewels of all description—emeralds and amethysts, rubies and diamonds shining so brightly I must look away from them. Silver ran in streams through those walls, veins wide and deep, and where there was not silver, there was gold.

I am in the heart of the world, I thought.

In me, in my bones and in my blood, a voice, his voice, said, *No. You are held within a heart, but it is not the world's. Now rest, but save your sleep for dreaming.*

* * *

In that way, that dreaming way, did Mótsognir begin to teach me magic. He was no gentle teacher, and he didn't answer all my questions. All? He answered none, unless you count sudden plunges into magic a form of answer. He said things to me, though, and he named the magic he was teaching me. He called it seidhr.

"This is the magic of shaping," he said, reaching out to touch the stone wall of my chamber. He caressed the stone, very gently, as you would your sleeping lover, and what had been rough was made smooth, what had been dense was made clear, like glass. I touched, and nothing happened. I caressed, and nothing changed. He laughed, and I fell again into dreaming, into the seidhr where my hands learned to feel with other than nerves and flesh. What was in me learned to flow out, what was outside me learned a way into me.

That flowing out and in, it was no easy feeling. No sound came out of my mouth, but something in me screamed, like birthing screams.

"In this way," he said softly, "it is said that I shaped a race."

Mótsognir, the Weary One, so named because he had spent himself, at the beginning of days, in calling out from the flesh of the world small creatures like maggots which men and gods named dwarfs.

"Maggots," he said, considering the word. "Who says that?"

"Lore," I told him.

"Oh," he said, "well, if it's lore . . ." And he said that the way you'd condescend to smile at some child's lisping attempt to explain things only the grown would know about.

He agreed to hear me understand that, silently, wordlessly, the way he does, and that was the first time I realized that what lay within me, understandings, questions, fears, were his to tap.

"How do you know me so deeply?" I asked him, somewhat angry, mostly curious. "From the first moment I saw you, you knew what was in me."

He nodded. "Your anger, your resentment. Your power."

Ah, power. I didn't know about that, not then. But I knew about the anger, don't doubt it. Magic I learned, and the learning was like flying in joy, but I never forgot the anger—no, the rage!—I raised up against my brother and his wife on that day they gave me in reparation to Mótsognir the dwarf. I nurtured it, fanning it like a fire whose flames must be kept alive. And I never discussed it with Mótsognir, nor did he try to make me do that. This was mine to keep, though he saw it and knew it.

He smiled, a rough grin and a gleam in his amber eyes. "I see what lies in you, Herthe. I feel it, and I watch you at the shaping of it. What will you do with that rage, child?"

Well, that was my rage, and talking about it, he came too close to it, he who dreamed in me, who taught me to shape magic. Something I had to keep of myself, for myself. Rage. And I didn't answer him, for he well knew what I'd do. One day, he would be done with me. One day, I would leave him. And then let my brother watch out for his wife and his hall. I would go back stronger than I had left. I would go back a *volva*, a witch. Let Burgun Nithing get ready to reckon with that when time came for me to claim reparation.

Mótsognir, he knew all that. I didn't have to say it.

"Listen," he said, his voice low and darkening so that I thought of storms. "Now I will teach you something more."

"What more—"

My voice fell dead, my words turned to dust in my mouth as the silver veins chased the gold off the walls and gems fell with the sound of ice tinkling onto the floor. All the colors ran into one, melting and melding, and Mótsognir walked 'round and 'round them, three times from the north, three times from the south, and three times from the north again.

Look, he said, but not aloud. *Look into the colors!*

I looked, and terror gripped me before ever the colors resolved themselves into shapes. Ah, gods! What I saw!

* * *

They fought, the gods of the living against the gods of the dead. They raised up armies, one of golden hue, one of bleached bone. They rose up into the skies above the Nine Worlds and they lifted swords against each other, never minding that they were kin and kind. All the worlds were laid waste, some died in fire, others in cold so terrible no word will ever be shaped to name it. Giants perished in Jotunheim. In our middle-world, men fought each other, brother against brother, as did the gods in the worlds above. They died deaths of rage, maddened, all their wisdom turned to war-cunning, and those who died found no home in Odin's golden hall. How could they? Bifrost, that rainbow-shining bridge between all the Nine Worlds, was down in ruin, the colors bleeding in the skies of nine worlds.

Elves went out from Alfheim to serve in the golden army, fighting back to back with gods and shoulder to shoulder with heroes. They met legions from fiery Muspellheim, hordes riding upon steeds of fire, sailing the skies in Hel-ships crewed by dead men. Wolves from Hel's Hall hunted the gods, Fenrir and his kin, and they tore them limb from limb, rent them flesh from bone. The hallowed blood of gods and heroes poured down into the dark void where once worlds spun, running like rain. The screaming filled up the skies shaking the very halls of Asgard and goddesses in their silks abandoned their gardens to take up weapons, fierce to defend their homes.

They fought, the gods of the living against the gods of the dead, and the thing that always happens when Life stands against Death happened. The best of them to die was the first to live: Odin All Father went down before the great wolf Fenrir. He went in fury, raging. He went fighting. And not one of those gods died a better death than Odin One-Eyed. Not long after did all the Nine Worlds fall, their names to be forgotten.

What? said Mótsognir, deep in my bones, his voice running with the magic in my blood. *Do you think that because they are gods things will change for them? No. Life goes down before Death. You cannot shape a change for that. Has not your lore told you so?*

That last he said in a twisting tone. If I could have seen him, I'd have seen a weary smile. I couldn't see him, though, only gods and men and elves, and the dead.

Only them?

He asked that question gently, and hearing it I knew there was more to see than gods and men and elves and the dead. All around them I sensed what I had once sensed before—other beings, others unseen, before and behind and above and below. They fought no fight, they cried no death cries. They went untouched through the battle, simply existing.

I said, not aloud this time, but into Mótsognir's very bones and blood: *Mótsognir, where are the dwarfs?*

We are here.

And all the dying stopped, the fighting ended, the colors on the floor were no longer the ruin of brave Bifrost. They were only colors, and then they were not even that. Then they were gone.

* * *

"Now," said Mótsognir. "You have learned the last of the seidhr. You have learned how to See."

I sighed, aching, and they gathered close around me, those invisible beings I'd first sensed in my falling and next sensed drifting across the blood-fields of the sky, the battlegrounds of the gods. I held myself tightly, shivering and cold. I could not get warm, and tears poured ceaselessly down my face.

"Who are you?" I asked, them and the dwarf who named himself Mótsognir.

He sat beside me, and when I looked over at him, I saw that the silver and gold now ran in the walls, the gems again studded the stone. I reached within for light and lifted it up so that I could see his face. It was the same face I'd first seen in my brother's hall, rough and brown and unlovely. His amber eyes were those I had first looked into and thought, *Here is one not of my kind.* I had been with him—how long? I didn't know how to count the time in this place of magic and weeping.

He said, "I am Mótsognir. I have told you." But he was playing at word games. I knew it, and he knew it, for a small gleam twinkled in his eyes. "Mótsognir Shaper, Mótsognir Weary."

It was on my tongue to say that he could not be Mótsignir Shaper, Mótsognir Weary. That dwarf was a long time dead, gone away to dust and his bones to feed the earth.

"Do you think so?" he said. "Do you really still

think Mótsognir is a byname, taken, perhaps, to annoy your brother's wife? Who then am I? Dain? Aurvang? Dolgathrasir? What name do you want me to wear, Herthe, if not my own?"

My little seidhr light bobbed round his head, and it seemed to me now that he was part of the stone against which he sat, that he had grown into it, or out from it. Closer came the creatures I could not see, presences, felt the way you feel all the sleepers in the hall even as you yourself sleep.

Mótsognir, he who claimed that name and never blushed to do it, lifted up his hand. I felt it then, that the Unseen went from me and gathered 'round him. How can I tell you the count of them? What is the name of the number for All That There Are?

"The whole of them," Mótsognir said, "is the whole of me. They are my children." He sat forward. In the light his amber eyes grew bright as polished gold. It was a brightness of years uncountable, the age of him showed in that shining depth and all the words and questions fell away from me.

"Listen," he said softly. He took my hand, and that was a strange thing, for he'd never touched me but lightly on shoulder or arm in all the age I'd been with him. He took my hand, he held it, and something flowed out from me to him, and back from him to me.

"We are," he said. "We simply are. You have looked around you and seen those beings your lore names dwarfs. But you have looked in the wrong eyes. You have looked and seen what you were taught to see." He let go my hand and held up his own, broad in the palm and suddenly wearing scars I'd not seen before.

I touched one, and then another. Forge-scars?

He laughed, a little. "Isn't that what lore tells you? That we are forgemen and crafters and seekers after gold and silver?"

Pressing, pressing, the Unseen moved back and forth, from him to me, out and back, around and through. Each time one touched me, I felt a thrill, the kind you feel when the lightning comes near and the hair raises on neck and arm.

"Dwarfs, you call us. But we are not that when we look at ourselves. We look at ourselves with the eyes of truth and so we know we are this: We are *dhvaras,* and that is a very old word. The first man to speak gave us that name, and it means phantom or ghost. He was trying to say *spirit.*"

They came before gods, they came before the Void itself, they came from where they cannot recall. They came, though, and they knew a truth men and elves and giants—and even gods!—had long forgotten: They came to inspire, to breathe life into the unliving.

"We like them, those gods, and we like their creations. We fill up the hearts of the gods with power, and they fill up their creations with life. We hold up the skies of all the Nine Worlds, one of us at each north and east, each south and west. We are, indeed, those makers, those shapers, your lore speaks of. Ours are the gem crafts, and ours are the metal-crafts, and our work is good—magical, aye?—because we breathe our own spirits into the crafting." With one finger he traced the scars of his right hand. "But we don't work to be seen, unless someone is looking."

He stopped a moment, saying nothing, looking down at his hands. "Shapers, we are. And I am Mótsognir Shaper, for when my kindred wanted to come strongly into the Nine Worlds, we needed bodies to wear. One must shape all, and that one is me. From the bones of the world I make their bones, from the waters of the sea I make their tears and their blood. Embodied, or free, I have named them every one."

He looked up, his eyes glinting. "You are right, Herthe. We don't share names down the generations. There are no generations, child. There is only us, and sometime we go dressed in those shapes I make, sometimes we don't."

He rested his head against the stone wall, and now he didn't seem to loom. He only seemed like one who'd earned his name, Mótsognir Weary.

I lifted up my eyes to meet his—and I must, for he was not so small sitting there now—and I said to him, "You have shown me the world's end. I know how giants will die, I know how men and elves will die." I shuddered. "I have seen how gods will perish. What will become of you after then?"

Like a sigh spilling out from the heart, all the Unseen, the *dhvaras* around us, moved away, flowing out into the stone of the walls. Their absence felt like a hole opening to emptiness. I looked at Mótsognir and saw that he felt what I felt, too. Or some of what I felt. Heavy sadness sat on me, I had seen the end of things and if that ending would come in times too far for me to reckon, still it would come. I ached in my heart, my soul moaned quietly in pain.

Mótsognir, though, he didn't ache, and his soul didn't moan. He sat away from the stone wall and he leaned forward, like a man with an eager secret to tell.

"Listen," he said, the very softness of his voice drawing me close. "You have not seen all of what will be. You have seen a shadow of it. Another thing may happen, for Doom is woven upon the looms of the Norns. The pattern they make is reshaped each moment. If all the worlds pass away as you saw—I don't know what will happen to *dhvaras,* for I don't remember a time before. What is life for us without the Nine Worlds? I don't know."

He said no more, and when I drew breath to speak,

he was gone. I let that breath go slowly, inspiring only the darkness.

* * *

How old did I feel, who had been swept from my brother's hall an uncounted time ago? I felt like myself, a maid in her twentieth year of life. Long in the hall, unwed with little chance to mend that unless there came a man who cared nothing for dowries. What man is that? None I've ever heard of. Still, not so old. I thought about this for a long time after Mótsognir told me about the *dhvaras*. I started by weighing my few years against his countless years, then drifted to thinking about the hall I'd left, the brother I still hated, the sister-in-law I'd gladly have killed.

It isn't so strange, is it? I had gained something in the leaving, but I hadn't left willingly. I'd been stolen to magic and that isn't the same thing as walking to it gladly. I thought a lot about what would happen should I ever leave Mótsognir's teaching-grounds. I would shape Astrida into a rat, I would shape all the grain in my brother's barns into mud. He would find that the goats in his pens were but dead fishes, and the cows on his hillsides would wither and die before his eyes.

Feels good, Mótsognir said to me, one night when I lay darkly dreaming. My dreams, this time, not his.

I said it felt very good, vengeance contemplated is much like a fine feast anticipated.

More lore?

More lore, and a trustier one than that old tale about dwarfs being born of maggots.

He said that maybe it was, maybe it wasn't. *Time has come that you will learn about that.*

And the dream turned to stone, the stone turned to walls, the walls grew a door like a mouth.

* * *

I stood in the sun, upon a shining hillside. Below me lay the valley where I'd been born, and the steams running round my parents' barrow caught the light like shining silver. All around me they stood, and above and below, unseen, the *dhvaras*. In the moment I knew that, they were one, and Mótsognir himself stood at my side. Him, as I'd first seen him, cloaked and head cocked and not so tall as I.

He rumbled deep in his chest, and he pointed down at the barrow. "See how it's grown."

The hill loomed twice as large as I recalled, and the pit of my stomach knew what my mind had yet to find words to shape: Time had run swiftly while I was gone, that hall of the dead needed room for all who'd gone to sleep there. I looked down into the valley, and I saw the hall of the living, there where it should be, but it did not stand so proud and tall as I remembered. It looked like a hipshot cow, the roof sagged, the doors torn off. No geese ran in the yard, no cows stood grazing on the hills.

"They are gone," I whispered.

"Gone," Mótsognir said. "And no grain in the barn to turn to mud, no goats to kill or cows to wither." He looked down at the barrow. "No sister-in-law to change into a rat, aye?"

None of that, and oh, I lifted up my hands and saw them still young and white, but in me I felt old as gods. Older.

Old as *dhvaras*.

"But you're not," Mótsognir said, this time speaking gently. "No one is that old, not even gods." He took me by the hand, that white young hand, and he led me down the hill with the grasses sweeping against our legs, the larks swooping in the sky at the end of the day. Out by the sea, gulls flew white against the purpling sky, and before us, around us, the meadow flowers bent under the last breeze of day, the first of night. He led me like a bride, hand in hand, and I laughed to think about that, deep inside myself.

He laughed, too, Mótsognir, and he said no dwarf's whore ever was led so sweetly.

"Stop," I said, using my voice quietly. "Don't say that. I am a whore."

"You are none of that. You are a bride of sorts."

I asked him what he meant by that, but he would say nothing. He led me, and I let him, and we went into the yards of the hall, past the old building, and round to the back by the well-stream. The little stone house where women went to their birthings still stood, whole as the last day I'd seen it.

"It's a place to keep you from the rain."

He said it, and clouds before unguessed came in from the sea, darkening the sky, heavy and hanging. I looked up, at the sky where *dhvaras* stood unseen, pillars of that storm-sky, and then I looked around to say something to him.

Mótsognir put a finger to his lips. "Listen," he said. "One will come tonight looking for shelter. Give it. He will want from you the two things all men want from women. Give them."

My heart jumped hard against my ribs. One thing I could guess. The other?

He read me, like he always did, the way runemasters read the stones. "You will see, and never fear. The one thing women are born knowing how to give. The other, I have taught you."

And he was gone, vanished, or simply shed of his body. Which, I didn't know. The going, though, the going . . . It was like my own heart had gone from me, my own soul.

* * *

I was a long time weeping in that stone house of
women, that place where birthing gets done. I wept
the storm in from the sea, I sobbed the thunder down
from the sky. I grieved my lost kin, the family gone
for so long their names were hardly remembered in
the valley now. I grieved Mótsognir, for I knew it,
lying there in old straw, upon woven blankets long
chewed by rats, that I would not see him again. In my
bones I knew, in my blood where runs the seidhr
magic he gave to me, I knew.

We were gone from each other. There had been a
time I wished for it, but that time was an age ago.

Rain fell hissing, dripping through the cracks in the
stone roof. Thunder hammered the sky, and Odin's
son gone to war against giants. Did he know what fate
he and his kind would meet? Did he have that wisdom? No. He didn't know. The magic in me knew,
Mótsognir himself knew, but no god knew.

In the darkest part of the night the old door gave
voice, someone knocked from without. I rose up from
my tears and pulled the old blanket around me. One
will come, Mótsognir had said. Well and good. Like a
woman in a dream, I went and opened the door.

One had come. A tall man, wrapped up in a thick
blue cloak against the storm, hooded in the night, his
face all shadows.

"Let me in, girl," he said, to me who was nearly as
old as gods. He looked past me and I could hear the
smile in his voice. "I see you've no fire to share."

"None," I said. I stepped back. "Come in and share
the roof and walls."

Ah, you could feel him, that tall man standing. You
could feel the fire in him, a young man's fire that is
seldom banked and rouses always for a woman. You

could feel the excitement in him, the thrill of the storm, and I'd have known one of the things he was looking for here if Mótsognir had said nothing. Here in the birthing house, he was looking for a woman to take him into her arms. He wanted a sweet young body near his, he wanted to rock the night with his loving as the storm rocked the sky with its thunder.

Well and good.

I closed the door behind him, and what burned in him now burned in me, fire leaping from one to the other. Whore, my long-ago sister-in-law had named me, and surely she would now if she could see me. I dropped my blanket, and I dropped my gown. I stood before the hooded stranger in my shift, and then I dropped that, too.

"Ah," he sighed, and he took me in close, wrapping me naked in his arms. "Ah," he said, tasting my lips and tasting my skin, tasting.

It was like fire with him, and flying. He touched me in places no one had touched before, not even Mótsognir who had sung in my blood. He roused me and he ruled the fire in us, and when all the storm was done, all the night had passed, he lay in my arms, his head on my breast, and he said: "Are you the one? Do you know me?"

I shivered in the cold and he covered me against it with his blue cloak. Gray light came in through the cracks, and now I saw his face, the scars there, the one eye gone, its gap hidden behind a patch of black silk. My hands began to shake. My mouth went dry as sand. I knew him. I had seen him die in the jaws of the Wolf. A god lay there in my arms, his head upon my breast.

His face fell into grave lines, that one eye of his looked long into me. Not as Mótsognir could, not so deeply. He looked with greed, hungry and—I will say

it!—frightened. He knew it: I am full of Seeing and
that means I am full of fearsome secrets.

"You do know me," he said, walking past the fear
as, in my Seeing, he had walked past those who would
try to keep him from the Wolf. He fights his own
battles, this one, and if he fears, he sees only another
fight to win.

"You have more names than most remember," I
said, "and the one I know is Odin One-Eyed."

He smiled, but it was a wolfish grin. "That's one.
Another is Wanderer. A third is—"

"—Seeker," I said. And everyone knew that name
of his, for all the gods who walk abroad in the worlds,
he is the one we see most often, Odin Seeker on his
quest for knowledge.

I got to my feet, shivering in his cloak and feeling
around me, not with my hands, but with the Sight
Mótsognir had awakened in me. Three times three I
walked 'round that birthing house, and he sat watching, still and silent as stone.

"Look," I said, walking, and he did, his eyes on
the floor where the dirt and the straw were changing,
arranging themselves into golden shapes and patterns
I knew and he would soon see. "Look, and what you
see you will not like, but what you see you will take
and consider and you will use."

I showed him what now men call the Ragnarok. I
showed him the death of the gods, his own wolf-death.
I showed him all that Mótsognir had taught me to see,
and I wept again, for the gods, the worlds, and now
for a man who had lain as a lover in my arms. It all
fell to ruin, there on the floor of the birthing house.
The golden halls, all the Nine Worlds, gone as though
they had never been.

If I wept, he groaned, and he balled up his fists and
his rage ran across the skies of Nine Worlds.

"This!" he shouted. "This you show me! Why? What good? What gain?"

Worlds died at my feet, shattered before the god, and when all ended as it had in my first Seeing, I sighed and made to turn away. But one more thing caught me, something small in the pattern on the floor, two creatures—gods, they were, he saw them and cried out their names, then whispered, "My children!"—two ran out from the ruin and the devastation of worlds. They hid for a long time, till all the fires burned down, till all the weeping void grew still. And then they came out, standing boldly in the darkness, seen only by me and Odin One-Eyed.

"This," I said, soft. "This is what you have come to see. Not your death, All-Father. That will be in every vision. That is your doom, for in this gods and men and elves are alike."

He said nothing, only sat there, straight and tall.

"Those." I pointed to the images, to his children. "Those are who you came to see. Now go."

Thus I spoke to the god who was not, perhaps, used to being so easily dismissed. In me, in the blood, something laughed, not Mótsognir, but his echo, my magic.

"Go," I said, "and know this: Fight your battles, never give up, for you don't fight for yourself and your Nine Worlds, god-Odin. You fight for the one world to come."

He looked at me, and then at the two small images on the floor. Already their world was changing, growing. From the ashes of the Ragnarok grew something new and vital. On the birthing room floor grew a world unguessed even by gods.

What more must we say to each other, that god and me? Nothing. He got up, and he dressed. I girded on his sword for him, and I gave him back his cloak.

"What more do you know?" he said, touching my cheek, his hand lingering.

"I know a lot."

"What more will you share?"

Outside, the day woke. Birds sang in the meadow. Dawnlight shone on the barrow where all my kin lie sleeping. What more would I share? I didn't know, for I had shown him all I had Seen.

"Come again," I said, wrapping up in old rags. "And we will see."

He went, and he did come again, once each year on the same night, the Hallowed Eve when the world turns to winter and long sleeping. Some things he saw that he liked, some he didn't. Some things he heeded, and others he ignored. He is a god, and that is to say he likes his own will.

One thing he never forgets, though, and that is the way to my house. Another thing he keeps always in mind, and that is his death. And if you ask me why it is that I love him, for I do, I do, I will say to you this: He was given to me as a gift, Mótsognir's gift, and whether or not he knows it, I was given to him as a bride. He goes out in strength, and he goes out knowing how it is he will die. He goes, and he comes back, and never does he waver from what it is he must do: Gather up his golden army of elves and gods and heroes. With them he will finally go into battle, climb upon his pyre, his Ragnarok, and die for the sake of a bit of ash and the two children who will live to light a new world to life.

All this I know, me and my seidhr Sight. And all this, I shape each time he comes and Sees with me again.

And Mótsognir, it is as I said: I have not seen him from that day till this. He has set me upon the path we each need me to walk. Unseen he is, but this is also true: He has not left me, for he sings in my bones, in my blood, ever unseen. *Dhvaras,* in the magic.

The last Seeker seated at the Earth extension of the table is a man with the lines of hard-won wisdom etched in his face. He sits contemplating images in his tankard that only he can see. Coming to a decision, he drinks and waits. The gnome taps him on the arm, but when he turns, the Earth elemental shrinks to a tiny size and climbs up his trousers and shirt to sit on his shoulder. Following instructions that his new companion whispers in his ear, the man crosses the threshold of the Northern door. Beyond a great expanse of dark and light squares stretch in every direction. He must cross them to find answers:

AN ELEMENTAL CONVERSATION
by Donald J. Bingle

REVEREND Francis Pendleton wearily set aside his calculations on next year's budget for the Deacons. He checked his watch and glanced at a chess set on the far edge of his desk. It gleamed invitingly in the orange light of the sunset spilling in from the window. It was time.

He tugged the set to the front edge of the desk, where he could get a better grip on it, and carried it to the coffee table in the middle of his cluttered living room. A stained-glass ceiling lamp was directly overhead, shining down like a soft spotlight and doing the set more justice. And the couch was more comfortable than his desk chair. He eased his lanky frame into it and marveled at the chess set for the hundredth time. He never tired of the beauty of the variegated brown-and-white stone pieces and relished feeling the cool stone beneath his callused fingers.

It was hardly an expensive set; he'd purchased it for fourteen dollars in Tijuana years ago when he visited his sister in San Diego. Well, nineteen dollars, actually. He had felt guilty about bargaining down the street merchant to such a cheap price and had snuck back half an hour later to slip the merchant an extra five while his sister and her children were busy elsewhere.

Even at nineteen dollars, the set was certainly a bargain. Why, he and Randy Jackson had played scores upon scores of matches on it in the past five years. Ignoring the hyperactive blandishments of "Must See TV," they met practically every Thursday at seven PM for coffee, chess, and conversation right here in the parsonage of the Riverton Presbyterian Church—a small church, even by Iowa standards, but home to him for the past fourteen years.

The Reverend supplied the place, the chess set, and the coffee (instant, with some of the hazelnut flavored nondairy creamer). Randy supplied a snack, usually a half-dozen Krispy Kreme doughnuts, and the topic for the evening's conversation. During the years they had talked of current events, politics, music, gardening, tools, cars, sports, their thinning hair and growing wrinkles—even art and science and occasionally religion. Although their views sometimes differed, the conversations were always pleasant enough and generally intellectually stimulating. Except for that one time they discussed whether the Chicago Bulls should renew Dennis Rodman's contract.

Yes, it was time. It was almost seven—Francis had worked on that budget for most of the day. It was time for a break. And it was time to set up the chess set for his Thursday evening entertainment. He sighed deeply, wondering if the millions glued to their television sets for the night really knew what "friends" were actually all about.

The hint of a smile crept to his face when he heard the tires on the gravel drive and the door of Randy's '91 Taurus slam. He patted the edge of the chessboard and headed toward the front door.

"It's open, as always," Francis hollered before Randy could even open the screen door to knock. Although a good bit younger than he—thirty-seven to his fifty-two—Randy had the well-settled, comfortable look that characterized small town folk who were happy with their simple, peaceable lives. The younger man's tanned face wore a broad grin, and his free hand brushed an errant lock of brown hair from his fog-gray eyes.

"Hey there, Revren Frank."

The two exchanged pleasant nods.

Most of the congregation referred to Reverend Francis Pendleton as "Reverend Frank," or just "Rev," excepting, of course, the senior farming set, who were much too traditional in their religion to ever be too familiar with a man of the cloth. To them it was always Reverend Francis Pendleton, shortened very occasionally to Sir.

"Let me grab a plate for these Krispy Kremes and I'll be ready to start the game," Randy called.

Francis gestured toward the kitchen. "No rush. No rush. Take a seat. I was just heading in there to put the water on to boil. I'll get a plate and . . ."

"Heck, Revren, I can get the coffee. You just sit yourself. You've got enough to worry about today without playin' host to me." With that, Randy brushed by Francis, leaving Reverend Frank to settle down on the couch.

Enough to worry? Francis scratched his head. The Deacon's budget was hardly a major problem, and Randy wouldn't have any reason to know he had been working on it most of the day. It had otherwise been a slow week; the sermon was coming along on schedule, there were no funerals and only one premarital counseling session, church funds were close to on target, and the parsonage, though well-worn, was in good repair. True, he worried a bit as he was growing older that the parsonage was not his. He was building no equity in a home to hold him over once he retired. But he had never mentioned his concerns to Randy (or anyone else for that matter), and those concerns were no different today than yesterday.

"Why should I be worried today?"

Randy returned with both the coffee and the Krispy Kremes.

"C'mon, Rev. You know the rules. No startin' the evenin' topic till we're at least five moves into the game. Otherwise, we'd never get to play." Randy placed the food a respectful distance from the board, at the edge of arm's reach, pulled up a worn, overstuffed chair, and contemplated the board. His turn at the white pieces.

White: Pawn to King four.

Perhaps, Francis mused, there is nothing to worry about. Randy has not been winning as often as he used to. It could be he is just trying to distract me from my opening game.

Black: Pawn to Queen's Bishop four.

The opening game was as ordinary as could be, the Reverend observed.

White: Knight to King's Bishop three.

Black: Pawn to Queen three.

White: Pawn to Queen four.

Black: Pawn captures Pawn.

Certainly nothing in this opening gambit would warrant a cheap psychological ploy of making me worry, Francis considered. He waited patiently for his friend to move. The Reverend knew the conversation worked best when you talked during your own move. Then you were not unduly intruding into your opponent's concentration.

White: Knight takes Pawn.

"So, what's tonight's topic and my supposed worry?"

Black: Knight to King's Bishop three.

Randy frowned and sucked his lower lip into his mouth. "Revren, you really should turn on the TV occasionally. CNN has been running it all day. SETI, you know, the Search for Extraterrestrial Intelligence, claims to have picked up an intelligent signal from deep underground—in solid rock. On our very planet. Not somethin' from outer space like you'd expect. Picked up another signal in the middle of the ocean. And they think they got a third inside of some volcano in the Pacific. Looks like there finally is definitive proof of other intelligent life-forms."

White: Knight to Queen's Bishop three.

"I spent all afternoon on the Deacon's budget, although this does explain a brief snippet of conversation I overheard in line when I went to pick up dinner. I simply thought the couple was talking about some science fiction show on cable." He reflected briefly on the game, steepled his long fingers under his chin. "But why should this piece of scientific news worry me? Water sprites haven't splashed in Grover's Corner, New Jersey, or anything, have they? Fire elementals haven't taken over Times Square, I hope. What does the 'intelligent signal' say?"

Black: Knight to Queen's Bishop three.

Randy stared at the board and thrummed his thumb against his knee. "They haven't got a clue. Some Nobel prize winner interviewed on the tube says it could be years, even decades, 'fore they figure it out."

White: Bishop to King three.

"Hmmph. Sounds more like a publicity stunt for some movie coming to the theater than a demonstrated scientific proof of intelligent life other than our own. And exactly why should I be worried about this news report?"

Black: Knight to King's Knight five.

"Gosh, Revren, if they prove the existence of new life-forms, alien creatures livin' in bedrock, in the water, maybe in a volcano, aren't you out of a job?"

"How's that? If people take these reports at face value, I would guess that church attendance would be up slightly. People need reassurance that their world hasn't changed in any fundamental way. It's comforting."

"But proof of another life-form changes the world and religion and all in a pretty basic way, I would figure."

White: Bishop to Queen's Knight five.

"Now, Randy. We touched on this briefly, back in ninety-six, when the space scientists first announced that there were possible signs of bacteria or life of some sort on that Antarctic meteor they think came from Mars. First of all, the signals from underground do not conclusively establish life, much less intelligent life, or even more importantly, sentient alien life." He reached to the plate and snatched up a Krispy Kreme. "And so what if it did?" With his free hand he moved the knight.

Black: Knight takes Bishop.

"Gee, Revren. Meanin' no disrespect or anythin',

but it seems to me that if there's an intelligent new life-form, then science's finally won the battle against religion, and religion is bound to die out. I mean, it might not even be life as we know it. Well, it can't be. Not if somethin' can live without air. Wonder what it would eat?"

White: Pawn takes Knight.

"I've never understood why so many people see science and religion as being in opposition to one another. There's no basic incompatibility, you know."

Randy stuffed a Krispy Kreme in his mouth and thoughtfully chewed. "That's not what those Creationists say, Revren. Why, they've been fussin' about evolution versus creation in the schools for a long time. And the sentiment against evolution is 'bout as strong as it has been since that monkey trial way back when." He brushed the crumbs off his jeans and took a sip of coffee.

"Now, Randy, I've had sermons about the fact that the Bible is not necessarily to be taken literally. The seven days of creation aren't necessarily 'days' in the same sense that we use that word now. They could easily represent epochs—maybe millions of years long—in the process of creating Earth and man. It isn't important whether man was created 'poof' in an instant or through an evolutionary process. What is important is that man at some point first had a soul. Maybe you slept through that talk."

Black: Bishop to Queen two.

"Revren, you know that I work late on Saturdays. 'Sides, I 'member most of your sermons."

White: Bishop takes Knight.

"I was just teasing, Randy. When I was young and paid attention, it was just too depressing. I even knew an intern once who put regular coffee in the decaffeinated pot for the preservice fellowship to try to keep the faithful awake. I care only if the spirit is willing."

Black: Pawn takes Bishop.

"Sure I know that the Bible has a lot of stories and parables and psalms that are there to teach us things, not necessarily to tell us what actually happened. Stuff like Noah's flood. But it still seems to me that the farther along science gets, the harder it is to see a need for God to exist to explain the universe." Randy pushed up the sleeves of his plaid shirt and considered his next move for a while.

White: Rook to King's side.

Francis fingered a pawn thoughtfully before pushing it forward and resting his index finger on it as he considered the wisdom of the move. "Actually, there's a pretty good explanation of the Flood in *Pastwatch: The Redemption of Christopher Columbus.* Yeah, I know it's science fiction, but this portion of it is drawn from some scientific theories and papers. You might want to check it out." His move confirmed, he removed his finger from the pawn and reached for another doughnut. "I also differ on your notion of the direction science is taking. A lot of science convinces me that God is essential to the existence of the universe."

Black: Pawn to King three.

Randy pushed a pawn himself. "Yeah, like what?"

White: Pawn to King five.

Francis knew his next move, but delayed action to pour himself more coffee. "Lots of things. For example, what are the odds that the moon of any planet would be at exactly the right size and distance to let one view the sun's corona during an eclipse? Eclipses are important to more than just ancient mysticism and astrology, you know. Einstein's theories were first scientifically validated by measuring during an eclipse the effect of gravity on light rays from distant stars passing near the sun." The Reverend turned his attention back to the pawn positioning war on the chessboard.

Black: Pawn to Queen four.

The stage had been set for the Queen to come into play, and the game became much more considered and dangerous. Some reflection began to accompany every move.

"Gee, I never thought about eclipses much, but that hardly seems to be the type of scientific proof we were talking about. I mean, look at evolution. If there is this infinite progression from ape to man, when does a soul first appear?"

White: Queen to King's Bishop three.

Things were definitely getting serious.

"Interesting that you should bring that up, Randy. The latest evolutionary theories don't talk about infinitesimal changes, but of sudden evolutionary leaps. The thought is that there is not enough of a survival advantage in small, preliminary steps in the development of a large, complex system or behavior like flight, for existence, to make the preliminary steps evolutionarily favored by natural selection. Instead, larger, sudden changes that are evolutionarily favored by natural selection occur at random intervals. Supposedly, the fossil evidence bears this out. It's easy to see how some supernatural guidance in these leaps could occur and, by the way, how man, with a soul, suddenly could come into being."

Black: Queen to King two.

"I don't know a lot about biology, Revren, but everythin' you just said sounds to me like the scientists are just refinin' their knowledge about how the rules of evolution work. Complex changes could occur naturally, if infrequently. The critters with bad complex changes die off in a generation and, odds are, never leave any fossil evidence to be found. The critters with good ones survive and reproduce like crazy, leaving plenty of fossil evidence."

White: Pawn to Queen's Knight four.

The Reverend reflected in silence.

Black: Pawn to King's Knight three.

Randy pressed the attack. "Besides, let's go even farther back. My niece, Gladys, is taking physics up at Iowa State, and she told me that they have all sorts of papers and math and computer simulations that explain the makeup of the entire universe beginnin' a tiny, tiny, fraction of a second after the Big Bang."

White: Pawn to Queen's Knight five.

Francis wavered, indecisive for a moment. "Let there be light. And what created the Big Bang, according to your niece?"

Black: Bishop to King's Knight two.

"Well, I've got to say I didn't follow everythin' she said about that real close. The gist of it was that the universe probably expands in a Big Bang and contracts in a Big Crunch on a regular basis. She did say it takes billions and billions of years, so not to worry."

White: Pawn takes Pawn.

"And your point, as I understand it, is that if scientists understand all the details of how things work, from the vastness of the cosmos to the quantum mechanics of how things function inside atoms, there is no need for God."

Black: Bishop to Queen's Bishop one.

"Basically. She also said her quantum mechanics course teaches that there is a cloud of possibilities that exist at any given moment and that there is a universe that exists for each choice that can be made. I gotta say that I didn't understand the science of that, but that it made sense. See, if only the universe of the possibilities that occur exists, then it seems to mean that everythin' everywhere every time is predetermined and that strikes me as pretty depressin'. I mean, everyone would have any excuse for anythin' that they ever did: 'It's all fixed beforehand, so why blame me?' "

White: Queen to King's Knight three.

His defenses reinforced, the Reverend pondered a counterattack. "It all depends on how powerful your God is, I guess."

Black: Rook on King's side.

"Huh?" Randy hesitated.

White: Knight in the third row to Queen's Knight five.

"Certainly a God powerful enough to create a universe and powerful enough to allow free choice would need to create and be able to create an infinite number of universes to allow for all possibilities to be chosen."

Black: Bishop to Queen's Rook three.

Randy exhaled slowly, then drained his coffee cup. "But Gladys also says that every particle in the universe seems to know what every other particle is doin' the instant it does it. 'Action at a distance' she called it. She also says that the information seems to travel faster than the speed of light, which is impossible. Right?"

White: Pawn to Queen's Rook four.

"Well, of course, the orthodox Protestant answer for that is that a God powerful enough to create the universe and allow free choice is also powerful enough to know what choices will be made at every juncture. Thus, in quantum mechanical terms, God knows what universe of the realm of possibilities we will exist in."

Black: Bishop takes Knight.

Randy moved, then pondered. "So things aren't predetermined, they're just predestined in the sense that God, but not us, knows what will happen."

White: Pawn takes Bishop.

The Reverend countered rapidly. "So you remember something from those Catechism classes years ago."

Black: Queen to Queen's Bishop two.

"That's comfortin', I guess. But I still don't see why you say science is confirmin' the existence of God. Maybe science doesn't disprove God's existence, but you haven't convinced me that science needs God to exist."

White: Knight to King's Bishop three.

"Well," mused the Reverend, as he considered the situation, "current theories of quantum mechanics do seem to require the universe to have more than the three spatial dimensions that we know as length, breadth, and height. It seems that the math just works out that way. According to this 'hyperspace' theory, the universe has ten spatial dimensions, six of which are curled up in a ball too small to have any practical effect. The other four spatial dimensions affect us in our everyday life, but we only perceive three of these dimensions." The Reverend was beginning to wonder who was distracting whose game with tonight's discussion.

Black: Pawn to Queen's Rook three.

"You lost me there, Revren. How can there be a dimension that we don't notice?"

White: Queen to King's Rook four.

"Imagine for a minute, Randy, a two-dimensional world like the surface of this chessboard. Creatures living in that two-dimensional world could not perceive us or anything in this room, except to the extent that it touched the planar surface of the board. To them, the pieces are just round shapes that rest on the board's surface, but inexplicably disappear and reappear in different places when we pick up the pieces to make a move."

Black: Pawn to King's Rook three.

"Since nothin' that they perceive moves the shapes, it seems supernatural or . . . even miraculous to them, right?"

White: Pawn to Queen's Bishop four.

"Perhaps. Maybe they just call it 'action at a distance' or something similarly scientific sounding. The point is that a force, in this case a sentience that perceives an extra dimension and can manipulate objects in that third dimension causes things to happen that they don't understand and can't fully comprehend. Sometimes a round shape disappears and does not immediately reappear elsewhere. To us, this simply means a chess piece has been captured."

Black: Queen's Pawn takes Pawn.

"So you're sayin' that God resides in the fourth spatial dimension and makes things happen—miracles and such—by manipulatin' things in the fourth dimension?"

White: Queen takes Pawn.

"Certainly there were those who claimed, almost a century ago when higher spatial dimensions first became a subject of significant scientific and literary discussion, that the fourth dimension was a handy explanation for the location of Heaven and Hell. It also gave a plausible explanation for such things as ghosts, angels, and spirits of all kinds. I can't deny that such could be the case."

Black: Pawn takes Pawn.

"Gee, Revren, I'll grant the possibility, but I don't see how that proves that God needs to exist, only that He or some other sentience could exist in the fourth dimension."

White: Queen takes Pawn.

"Patience, Randy. I was getting there. You have to look at another experiment, a kind of wave pool experiment. I read about it in *Newsweek* more than a year ago."

Black: Queen's Rook to Queen's Knight one.

Randy laughed and fixed himself another cup of coffee. "A pretty strange source for the latest in science

or religion. You mean a wave pool experiment like
we did in high school physics class? You know, where
you make waves in a flat tank and see what happens
when you have one or more holes in a barrier?"

White: Queen to Queen's Bishop four.

"Exactly, except this experiment used light waves
and holes in light barriers—black paper or something,
actually something probably a whole lot more sophisticated. As you probably know from high school physics, if you shine a light on a barrier that has a single
pinpoint hole, you get a circle of light opposite the
hole on a detector screen. If you have two holes, you
get a dark-and-light-barred pattern from the interfer-
ence of the waves going through the two holes." Francis paused, both to let Randy visualize the experiment
and to let himself consider his position in the game.

Black: King's Rook to Queen's Bishop one.

Randy hesitated, whether over the game or the discussion. "Okay, so . . ."

White: Rook to Rook six.

"So, the scientists set it up so they could send one
photon—one light particle—at a time at the screen
and so they could tell which of the two holes each
photon went through. I think the purpose of the whole
thing was to help understand that 'action at a distance'
thing we were talking about earlier. When they were
able to detect which of the holes each photon went
through, instead of a light-and-dark-barred pattern,
they got two circles of light on the detection screen
opposite the slitted barrier. When they turned off the
device that let them detect which slit each photon was
going through, the bars reappeared." Reverend Francis let that sink in while he mulled over the board.
"Observing the path of the individual photons
changed whether their waves interfered with one
another."

Black: Rook to Queen's Knight seven.

Randy was ready with his move.

White: Queen to Queen four.

Reverend Frank fingered his rook. "The thing is, when they left the path detector on, but erased the record of the detection before it could be read by anyone, the two circles of light disappeared and the bars appeared. The result was just the same as if the detector was turned off and had never recorded the path of the photons. It wasn't the detection of the photon path that changed the result, it was the perception of that detection by a sentient being that changed the result of the experiment." There was a long silence before the Reverend made his next move.

Black: Rook to Queen's Bishop seven.

Randy was obviously distracted. "So nothing happens unless it's perceived by somethin' sentient? That's like the old 'If a tree falls in the forest, but there's no one there to hear it, does it make a sound' conundrum. I always thought that was a pretty stupid question, but this experiment makes it pretty profound, I guess." Randy pushed his rook to press the attack.

White: Rook to Rook seven.

"Go the next step, Randy, and you'll see where I was going with the extra-dimensional stuff. If the math requires extra dimensions for the universe to work, but we cannot perceive those dimensions, then there must be some sentience that can and does perceive those dimensions—God—or they could not exist."

Black: Queen takes Pawn.

"Maybe. But maybe these newly discovered creatures can perceive, even manipulate, the fourth spatial dimension. Therefore, that dimension can exist."

White: Knight to King one.

"Remember, Randy, what I said before about the

other six spatial dimensions. They're curled up in a ball smaller than the distance between an electron and the nucleus of an atom—tough to imagine these radio-transmitting alien creatures being able to perceive that."

Black: Rook to Queen's Bishop five.

"Fine. I'm not sure I'm convinced that science proves God has to exist, but let's get back to the subject of these creatures. If they exist, Christianity has got some serious explainin' to do . . . I mean, it's just not fair if the only way to be saved is to believe in Christ, and here these creatures maybe existed for millions or billions of years underground or in the water with no way of knowing about Christ and, thus, doomed to hell due to no fault of their own. Religion's just gotta be fair on some elementary level, Revren, or God doesn't look like the nice guy he's made out to be."

White: King's Rook takes Pawn.

" 'Fair' is a pretty odd word, Randy. Christianity isn't 'fair.' It's more than 'fair.' You get saved for believing that Christ died for your sins, whether you 'deserve' it or not. Besides, this is the same issue that theologians have dealt with for some time. What about natives in the deepest jungles of Africa several centuries ago? They had no opportunity to know of Christ, which is why missionary movements have historically been so important to the church."

Black: Rook takes Queen.

"So, that just says that we should be sendin' missionaries to the stars. Is that why so many evangelists want their own radio and TV shows?"

White: King's Rook takes Bishop.

Randy grinned. "Oh, by the way. Check. I think you're gonna be sorry for takin' my Queen."

"Plenty of maneuvering room left, I think, my

friend. Your end game still needs work. As for your point of discussion, perhaps a better comparison is the theological treatment of babies before the age of comprehension, which counts the children of the faithful as being also redeemed in Christ."

Black: King to Rook one.

Randy pressed the advantage.

White: King's Rook to Rook seven.

Black: King to King's Knight one.

White: King's Rook to Knight seven. "Check."

"Randy, you know about the old and new covenant, right?"

"Sure, Revren. The old covenant saved the Jews before Christ arrived if they obeyed a bunch of laws., and the new saves anyone who believes."

"And at exactly what instant did the old covenant end?"

Black: King to King's Bishop one.

Randy stared at Francis and not at the board. "Gee, I don't know."

Francis needled him. "Christ's birth? His death? His resurrection? The coming of the Holy Spirit? Once everyone in Palestine had a chance to hear the news of Christ's resurrection?"

Randy refocused his attention on the game.

White: King's Rook to Bishop seven. "Check. You tell me, Revren."

"Who knows? Maybe it's still in effect. I certainly wouldn't want to limit God's mercy."

Black: King to King's Knight one.

"Holy Moses, Revren, it sounds like you're saying that there might be more than one way to be saved. That's pretty radical stuff from an Iowa preacher!"

White: King's Rook to Knight seven. "Check again."

"Don't get carried away. I just said I wouldn't limit

God's mercy. You've heard of the Parable of the Laborers, haven't you? Matthew 20:1-17."

Black: King to King's Bishop one.

"Boy, I sure don't know how you remember all those numbers, but, yeah, you did a sermon on it last year. This vineyard owner hires a bunch of laborers one mornin' for the day for a penny apiece. They go to work. At noon, he sees some guys just loafin' about in town, so he hires them, too, and says he'll pay them a fair price. As the day gets later and later, he keeps hirin' more guys and, in fact, hires a bunch right before quittin' time. At the end of the day, he pays them each a penny. Is that about the gist of it?"

White: King's Rook to Bishop seven. "You're in check again, by the way."

"Needless to say, the first-hired laborers complained that they should get more, because they had labored all day in the sun and the others had gotten the same reward. But the owner said "You got what we bargained for. Why do you care that I am generous to others with my own money?' This is where the infamous 'and the last shall be first' quote comes from."

Black: King to King one.

"Yeah. It's s'posed to teach us not to be jealous of people who are saved at the last minute."

White: King's Rook to Rook seven.

"It's also a terrific parable for the modern business world. Everyone spends too much effort griping about what somebody else is getting paid, rather than concentrating on doing the job they have at the price they agreed to."

Black: Rook to Queen two.

White: Rook to King's Rook eight. "Check. So, what's this got to do with the old and new covenant and these alien creatures?"

"It all goes back to not limiting God's mercy. Why

should we complain if the aliens have souls which are saved by God through something other than what we know as Christianity?"

Black: King to King two.

Randy was taken aback. "You mean somethin' completely different form Christianity? You'd better not let those old farm traditionalists hear you say somethin' like that, Reverend Francis Pendleton. Hell . . . I mean, heck, Revren, they'd ride you out on a rail and I'd hafta find a new chess partner or somethin' else to do on Thursday night."

White: Rook to King's Rook seven. "Uh, check again."

"Maybe something completely like Christianity, but in a different social context. God's mercy is infinite, as is Christ's sacrifice. Maybe, just maybe, there are infinite acts of redemption which have occurred, or are still occurring, around the universe."

Black: King to Queen one.

Randy's expression suddenly changed as he realized where the game and the discussion were going. Neither was what he had anticipated at mid-session.

White: Rook to King's Rook eight. "Check."

Reverend Francis simply made his move and let his friend reflect.

Black: King to King two.

White: King to Rook seven.

Black: King to King one.

White: Rook to King's Rook eight. "Check. And Christ just goes from world to world suffering torment and death for yet another civilization's sins?"

Black: King to King two. "Draw. You've forced the same board position for the third time. Congratulations. And, yes, Randy. For all we know, what you were just saying could be the case."

"But, gee, Revren, wouldn't that change the Bible a lot?"

"Not necessarily, consider John 3:16. 'For God so loved the world, that he gave His only begotten Son, that whosoever believeth in Him should not perish but have everlasting life.' "

"Well, I'm no match for you when it comes to knowin' the Bible, all them numbers and references and passages and such. Seems like a pretty big thing, infinite acts of redemption, if'n it were the case, though."

"I'm not saying it is, Randy." Francis allowed himself a wry smile and cast a quick glance at the chessboard. The white king winked at him. "Just that it could be. In any case, I sure don't think that getting a confirmation of an intelligent life-form from under the ground, maybe a creature made of stone, or a life-form made from the sea, is going to put me or God out of business."

Randy stuffed another Krispy Kreme in his mouth. He carried the coffee and dirty dishes back into the kitchen, then headed for the door. "See you next week, Revren. Well, and on Sunday, too."

Francis waved to his friend as the Taurus started up and pulled out of the driveway, then went back to his desk and reached for his well-worn King James Version Bible and took out a pen. On the coffee table, the chess pieces fell to devouring the last doughnut.

"It would," the Reverend said to himself, "involve a small change, however." He read aloud as he corrected the passage: "For God so loved the world, that he gave His only begotten Son, that whatsoever believeth in Him should not perish, but have everlasting life—life as we know it, or otherwise."

The Walker of Two Worlds turns his attention to those seated at the coral section of the four-armed table. "Who among you will continue your quest to the Element of Water? A woman with a confident gaze drinks deeply of the nectar. The scent of sea air comes from behind and permeates her senses. To her right a sea eagle lands at the end of the table. It waits for her to come abreast and then flies to the Hall's Western door. She follows, passing through to the world of the:

WATER BABY

by Michelle West

IT was the year of the storms.

Wild storms. Raging in a graceless, terrible freedom across any land they chose. She watched them on the television in the harbor of her father's lap, her mother's pitying murmur accompanied by a tightening of her father's arms. Then, wild child that she was, she would rush outside, seeking the rain.

"Too silly," her father would say, words heavy with affection, his upper body protected by the tented folds of a large umbrella, "to know when to come in out of the rain."

And she would laugh, splash him, throw the water from the folds of her cupped palms into his dry face before it could fall, wasted, to ground.

"Water baby," he said. And because the taste of his affection was so strong and so startling in the word *baby*, she never objected.

* * *

It was the year of the storms.

Later, years later, water lapping the edges of her hair, warming the fringes of her lashes, snow freezing against the weathered layers of skin, she would remember them more clearly than any other event of her early childhood.

Childhood was a wilderness. Close her eyes at any time in her adult life, in crowds, in isolation, during work or play, and she can see, not exact faces—they vanish, like all of her memories under too close a scrutiny, as if they can only be viewed like the faintest of stars, from the sensitive corners of the eyes—but rather the expressions those faces took.

Warmth, turned to her; something darker and lonelier than night when they looked at each other. The details of their faces are lost to their expressions, but if she works hard, hard, hard, she can see the lines around their eyes, dug there by time, worry furrows, smiles' frames.

Only when the loneliness is sharpest, and the hunger of a type that, as a small child, she could never have experienced, can she see her dead clearly, made perfect in memory by longing. But as all things were, the seeds for that longing were laid then: at five years of age.

She remembers the storms more clearly than she can remember her parents.

She tries.

It is raining by the lake.

* * *

She wanted to go to Disney World.

Bombarded by Mickey Mouse and the smiling face and impossible clothing of a real, live Snow White, promised fun, fun, fun, she had turned to her father, her eyes wide, her voice high, the screen of the television so clear she could almost step through it and be right there.

"Next year, I'll be in grades," she told him, toning down her words because serious always worked best. "Next year, I'll be a big girl."

"Big girls can still go to Disney World."

"But they say it's best for kids, Dad."

"Oh, Amy. Grades don't turn you into a big girl."

"Oh." There was a slow pause as she thought about this, as she questioned just how much he actually *did* know about being a little girl and a big girl, given that he was a boy.

And he picked her up. He smelled of tobacco and worn out aftershave, and his chin was stubbly and prickly, which she liked, which even now she retains a fondness for. She tucked her head under his chin, making a chair of him, a chair with heart and breath and promise. He promised to speak to her mother.

Her mother held, as they say, the purse strings. Pinched with the responsibility of making the hard decisions, aged by throwing herself over the brink of childhood as if it were a cliff and not a gently crossed threshold one could linger over, she was their sergeant.

They argued about the money, her father caught between the utter faith of the five-year-old and the harsh reality of the twenty-five-year-old, both costly.

When it rains, she can't see the surface of the ocean; it's broken everywhere by the falling weight of water, absorbed, changed. She used to love the storms.

So much to hide, in the storms.

* * *

Disney World: place of plastic ears and plastic rides and music so distorted by fairground speakers it fights for attention over the shrieking of happy children, the crying of tired ones, and the rumbling of vehicles trapped on their steel frames for the pleasure of the visitors.

She met the future there. At five years old, her father's hand tucked in hers, her mother's frown eased by the freedom from her day-to-day life—at the time, she'd thought that even her mother had to love Disney World—she saw the woman.

She seemed ancient, at that time: older than her father, even. Her hair was streaked white, and tied tight in a funny knot at the back of her neck. Her face was narrow, like the sharp edge of an ax's wedge.

"Hello, Amelia," she said, although no one called her Amelia unless they were angry.

She tightened her grip on her father's hand, but his hand was suddenly too large to hold on to tightly enough. Her father's noticing the tightening of grip looked down and then up, his gaze swooping like a bird. He laughed. "Amy," he said, "don't you recognize who *this* is?"

She shook her head.

"She's the witch," he said. "From the *Wizard of Oz*." He laughed again, held out his hand; the woman took it, her own bone-slender and steady.

What Amy didn't know, couldn't say until years later, was that the *Wizard of Oz* and Disney World had nothing to do with each other. She heard the pleasantries her father exchanged with this terrible, cold woman, this creature of shadows and ice, and then she moved on, attached to his hand, while the old woman's unblinking gaze fastened on to her back like a burr.

*   *   *

The storms came in Florida. They came when Disney World was already becoming a much tidier memory than the fact of days spent in the confines of its huge parks. The car was on the road, the muffler was complaining—her father's word—and the winds were howling across the freeway.

She heard her father swear, and that quieted her and woke her at the same time. He so seldom swore.

"Jack," her mother said.

The rain came. But it didn't fall; it flew, sheeting sideways against the windows of the car.

"Jack," her mother said again, her voice lower.

They slid, spinning into something. The side of the road; the guard. Her father swore again. Cars. She remembered that: although the rain came down in sheets, came sideways, obscured all sight as if it were the heaviest of storybook fogs, she *knew* that cars littered the freeway like wingless flies, helpless, crawling, or stalled. She could feel the water that windows kept from touching her skin, and she could see through it, as if it were some sort of glass that had been washed and polished free of fingerprints for her eyes alone.

The storms; the storms obscured all sun, hid the fire that, from a distance, made the heat in Florida so unbearable for her mother; it washed away the dirt beneath their feet—and their tires, when they once again slid off the road and into the dirt median, stalling there, finally, like a planted spike. Even when they managed to open the doors, the air tasted of water, heavy and wet.

"Jack!" Her mother's voice. Heavy with fear, a fear that Amy had never heard before, but would hear again and again as she grew older.

He walked into the rain.

*   *   *

That's what she remembers as she stands on the pier, the handmade, rough-hewn pier that was her husband's stubborn creation, his proof that he was, like his father before him, a man who could use his hands to create order from chaos. He walked out of the car. Into the rain.

He went for help.

Wilderness. God, it's been so many years since she's heard his voice, and the pier creaks dangerously beneath her feet: storm.

* * *

Help came. But it wasn't her father. It was some men in uniforms that she thought belonged to the army. Her mother said something else: National Guard. She wasn't sure what it meant then, and now it doesn't matter. They had the authority granted them by panic, by uniform, and by law, and the storms that had been gathering in an angry knot over the coast had unleashed enough destruction and enough panic that the Guard had finally been called in.

One town, two towns, half a small city—that was a national disaster. People showed up on your television asking for money and donations and help—or patience if you were a bit too close to the danger.

But this was the *coast*. The worst hurricane in history. One small town was completely lost; rooftops could be seen later, devoid of the things they had once protected. Bodies, thickened and distorted by water, were taken from that element and given to earth; she could almost hear the storm's outrage. The second town followed it, a town that had been split by a river and joined by a bridge. Farmers had loved it for the water when they had first chosen to settle its banks.

The water was all that was left.

The storms howled.

* * *

She never saw her father again. That's the truth. Not even in her dreams, unless one counted the sight of his back, denim shirt and pants, short boots meant more for dress than for water or snow, hair so flat with water he might have been bald if not for its color. She had screamed his name so many, many times she had lost count, but the feel of it leaving her throat in the morning renewed his loss with the start of the day.

She and her mother, car abandoned, were taken to an unused school in a town that was considered at risk. At risk was good. The auditorium was a terrible place. Full of people, many of them weeping, half of them sleeping, some covered in vomit that smelled even from across the room. It seemed to her that they had come here not for safety but to die. She didn't want to die.

"Is Daddy here?" she asked.

"No. No, Amy. But if Daddy can make his way here, he will."

It was meant to be comforting. But Amy knew what it meant: It meant that if he didn't show up, he was dead. She knew better than to howl or scream. But she held on tightly to her mother's hand as the men in uniforms took her to a patch of floor smaller than her old crib and told them to sit down. "Washrooms are there," one man said, wincing. "Food twice a day; we're doing what we can," he added, before her mother could speak.

"But the children—"

He looked at her. Something in his face opened and closed, like window shutters or doors. Amy didn't understand what it meant, this ripple of expression, but her mother did. She said, "God, I'm so sorry—"

But he put up his hand to stem the flow of her words. He didn't want her sympathy. Amy didn't understand it: Her mother's sympathy was like the touch of God; it could heal all pain.

They sat on the floor in the terrible, smelly room, and it was only when the baby started to cry that Amy was distracted at all. She walked in the direction of that cry.

"Amy, you be careful—don't go outside and don't get lost!"

And found the woman she had seen at Disney World. The wicked witch her daddy had said was from Oz, face so sharp she couldn't help but look unkind.

But she was walking the baby, cuddling him into her shoulder the way mothers did. She felt a pang of envy for the strength of those arms; no one let her carry a baby like that, although if she could—if she could, she knew she could make any baby calmer.

"Hello, Amelia," the woman said softly.

"Hello," Amy replied, as polite as she could be. "Is that your baby?"

The woman's face did what the guard's face had done. "No," she said at last. "Not my baby."

"Why're you holding it?"

"Because his mother is sleeping. She's exhausted and terrified. She's like you—she doesn't live here, doesn't know how to get home. I'm helping her."

"Oh." She waited a moment. "Can I hold him?"

"If you think you can carry him without dropping him, yes."

She held out her arms.

It was a lie. To hold out her arms like that. But she wanted to hold the baby.

The woman handed him over, and she staggered with his weight, determined to shoulder it anyhow. The baby started to wail.

"Understand," the woman said, her voice hard as her face looked, "what it is you ask for, when you ask for it. This once, you have a chance, but there's no turning back. There's no turning back, once you make this choice."

"What choice?"

"We've gathered, for you. You're far, far too young—but your—your predecessor failed. Witness it," she added. She took the baby back, pressed him into the warmth of her shoulder—and just how warm that shoulder was, Amy would discover years later, through bitter experience. She motioned Amy toward the door.

"We aren't allowed to go there," the girl said softly.

"No. *They* aren't allowed to go there. But you, Amelia, are already special, and it's important that you see what must be seen."

She loved the words. The words were the ones she most longed to hear and to *be*. To be special. To be important. But she hesitated.

The old woman held out a hand.

Amelia took it.

The witch woman walked, babe in arms, child in hand, to the door the guards stood by. Amy waited for them to speak. They did—but to each other, words of despair and anger. Words that her father would have told her she wasn't allowed to use.

Her father.

"Come, Amelia." No way to disobey that voice. Even her teacher's angry voice didn't have that power of command. She followed.

The doors fell away as if they were curtains, and she and this strange woman had just stepped out onto the stage, into the darkness from which the audience, unseen and unseeable, were watching and judging.

"She should have been stronger," the woman said softly. "But she wasn't. This is what happened."

No beach, this, although the world was a world made of water as far as the eye could see. It wasn't unbroken; houses jutted out of the foam, street posts slanted halfway to ground, tractor trailers, like abandoned toys, lay across what might have been roads.

She wanted to scream.

The woman's hand tightened, and she felt not warmth but heat, a terrible, burning heat. She looked up. The baby was asleep on her shoulder, face turned toward the storm-laden street.

"You don't know who you are," the woman said. "No more did I. Look at me, Amelia. What do you see?"

Amelia swallowed. She took a step back, but the grip on her hand was tight.

"Not yet," the old woman said. *"Look at me, girl."*

She looked.

"What do you see?"

Fire.

Eyes of orange light, white light, blue light. Skin like a vessel for something that couldn't quite be contained.

"Yes," the old woman said, soft voice crackling. "You have the sight. Do you want to stop this?" She turned, her hand still on Amelia. Unlike her father or her mother, this woman did not—would not—let go.

"Yes," Amelia said, without thinking.

"Do you want to go home?"

"Yes."

"Then you must tell it to stop."

"Tell what to stop?"

"The water, child. Tell the water to stop."

Amelia was terrified. Something descended on her, the way the water had upon her father as he left the safety of their car, seeking help.

She tried to pull her hand free, and this time the woman *let go.*

The water rushed in. The rain came in torrents. The lightning and the thunder volleyed across a sky so black with roiling cloud it was like the essence of

storm, undiluted by any experience she had ever had
of rain.

Amy couldn't see anything at all. Liquid filled the
mouth she had opened to scream, silencing her. The
water slapped her harder than her mother had ever
done, even when she was angriest. She was lifted off
her feet, carried away in the current that, she understood suddenly, would destroy the old school that all
those people—and her mother—were shut away in.

Five years old.

The summer of storms.

She shouted wordlessly, fear for and fear of completely separate for just that moment.

No!

And the water stopped.

NO!

Froze a moment, becoming a sculpture that was
somehow still alive. It spoke to her in a voice that
sounded like waves breaking against rocky shore, but
older, deeper, colder. *Who are you? Who are you to
speak to me? We have no covenant. I am unbound.*

"Not true," someone said, and the woman who was
fire appeared by her side. Amy wondeered if she had
ever truly left it. The babe on her shoulder was dry
and quiet. She wondered if he was dead.

*It is true. The price was not paid. The vessel was
broken.*

"No," she said again, and light left her lips like
dragon's breath. "This child is of our blood. If she
were not, you would never have heard her voice."

She cannot command me. I am free.

"You are free," the lady with the sharp face said,
her voice soft. "But what does that mean? You are
eternal. You are the essence of all water, and all
names that accrue to it accrue to you. Who knows
what lies beyond the simple names given you by men

since time began? Who sees the heart of your need? Who speaks to you in a voice you can hear?"

I am free, the storm said, but it grew smaller. Amy wasn't fooled; she had seen hands gathered like that when someone was preparing to strike, bunching, curling, becoming dense and solid.

"You are *alone.*" The fire woman said. "You have only three sisters who are your equals, and the quarters cannot be crossed.

"This child *is* your child; her voice *is* the voice that speaks to your heart."

She is a child.

"Yes." She turned. "Amelia," she said, in a voice that made the babe cry out in terror, although she did not grip him more tightly. "You are a child. But it doesn't matter. The water is lonely, and it will listen to your voice. Speak. Ask it to spare this town and these people. Tell it of the deep oceans, the place where even light doesn't exist without the permission of the ancient depths. Tell it of the falls that thunder like storm gone true, of the lakes that bring life and death."

She was silent.

"Tell the water its name," the woman said, "or you will perish here, and so, too, will the babe."

Five years old.

"I don't know it's name," she whispered, staring into something that the fire lady had given such imperfect and strangely adult words to describe.

"No," the woman said quietly, "and yes. Tell the water what is true: That you love it. Tell the water that you love it."

She should have been afraid. She *was* afraid, but not so afraid as she had been, because she saw in the water something very like arms, like her mother's arms had once been when her mother had been the vastness of all life, all warmth.

She had always loved the rain. Her father had called her water baby. It didn't seem so strange, just for the one second, that his words should be true.

She opened her mouth; her words were carried as far as storm wind could take them. But she spoke and the water understood the word that was not, could never be, simple. Love.

It swallowed her.

And the fire said,

"She has paid the price."

And the water smiled.

*   *   *

Her mother never went to Florida again. Months after their quiet return to a house that was empty of all the right noise, but noisy nonetheless, she finally offered Amy the one thing she had locked tight behind her eyes: tears. Before that there was anger, and after that, anger as well.

Amy didn't understand it, not then, not immediately: Her father was dead. She wondered, for all of the rest of her childhood and the prickly, wild adolescence that followed it, what she had done *wrong*.

Her mother's answer—when she was young and foolish enough to trust her mother with the question—was always the same. "You didn't *do* anything, Amy. Your father didn't leave *you*."

But when she was eight years old, and her mother was speaking on the phone to her aunt, she heard her say, "If we just had the *body*, we'd be certain. I know it would be easier for Amy if she could just *see* that he died, that he didn't desert her."

And she thought that maybe, just maybe, her mother didn't believe it either. Her mother stopped being the source of all comfort.

She had a different one.

* * *

She had always had dreams, of course, and some of them were vivid enough that she bridged the gap between the waking world and the sleeping one with a scream.

But these dreams were different; they were dreams, always, of water; of a world without earth, or air, a world which had never *seen* fire. Sometimes the water would speak to her. It would speak with her father's voice, with what she remembered of her father's voice, that low rumble of play-monster that evoked the shrieks of delight she would hear later, from the children of strangers. She would tumble into its depths, feel the pressure of its vast weight as some kind of textured, stubbled blanket in which she might find both terror and safety, one tumbling after the other, over and over until morning called her back.

Those dreams, it was best when she played at sea; worst when she came to the surface and there was something like air in her lungs, something that took her away from the comfort—and took the comfort away from her.

The storms came after her then.

She would dream of the rage of water, and she learned—even though she would wake to the comfort of her room—that the water that comforted and protected her could fall like the fist of God—if there was a God, and if He chose to strike. She watched, the first time, as a small costal village was destroyed, seeing the smallness of the life that was lost in mere minutes without the grace of air.

It was easy to watch.

Easy until the fire lady came.

That's when she knew it was more than a dream.

Because the fire lady slapped her, hard, and it *hurt*.

The fire lady's hands hissed and burned where they touched her wrists; her grip was tight.

Amy started to say, *You're hurting me,* but the words came out a gurgle and then not at all.

"Come and see," the fire lady said, her face so sharp the expression cut, "come and see what you've done."

Her feet anchored to earth, her face in air, her wrists ringed by fire, Amy went to face death. She didn't realize it of course; not until it was too late.

In Florida, she had seen the dead bob by, flotsam and jetsam, like the roofs of whole houses, something that had once provided warmth or shelter. But the bodies, water-laden, had been distant, almost like elements of some bizarre fishing game, the dark side of the amusement park that had, inadvertently, cost her her father.

"Oh, no, you don't," the fire lady said, catching her chin. "You *look.* You *remember.* You could have prevented this if you'd stopped to *think.*"

She's a child, the wind whispered.

The fire lady's eyes burned. It shouldn't have been a surprise; it was. She cried out at the mark fire's glare left across the back of her hand.

"So," the fire's voice said, "was he."

At Amy's feet, a small body bobbed, facedown, in the water; the water caressed its still flesh, filled its open mouth, tossed it and turned it as if it were a ball. She could feel the playfulness of the tide and the tide's desire.

This child would never fulfill it.

"The storms," the fire said, "must stay *at sea.* When you're older, Amelia, you'll be able to join them. Come."

She's only a child, another voice said, heavy and broken with age, *but she's all we have. Let her see what's been done. Let her understand it.*

Broken glass.

Snapped wood.

Twisted aluminum.

Frames, all, for the bodies that lay broken by the
tide. Sometimes they were tangled, those bodies, father and child, mother and child. The tableau was broken by the living; the long cry—high and pathetic—of
a dog that limped on the flat of a house calling—as
she herself had called—for someone who would never
come home.

"You did this," the fire lady said, as Amy started
to cry.

Careful, the whisper said. *We're too close to the
water. Be careful, Grace.*

"We're too close to too much," the fire lady replied.
She bent, gritting her teeth, her sharpness dulled a
moment by a pain that rippled up the length of her
long face, and shoved her hands into water; kept going
until Amy could see only shoulder.

When she stood, she held a baby in her arms.

Dead baby, but she put it over her shoulder and
cradled it there. "You killed this child."

The water killed the child, the quietest voice said.

"Yes," the lady said, but her eyes never left Amy's
face. "But *you* should have stopped the water. You
know how, girl. I taught you."

Amy wept. "I—I didn't—I didn't know it was *real.*"

"Doesn't matter," the woman said, as she lifted herself out of the waves. "Doesn't matter a damn to the
poor baby what you knew or didn't know. He paid
the price anyway."

She cried; water ran down her cheeks, a curtain.
Armor. But not thick enough, not yet.

When she woke, there was a blister on the back of
her hand; it hurt for days, and when her mother asked
her how she'd burned it, she didn't answer.

She still bears that scar; not the first scar, not the
deepest, but the one she first become aware of for

what it was because the pain was so simple, the lesson so clear.

The rain doesn't wash it away, and it washes away so much else as she stands in its path, arms spread like a cross.

* * *

She stayed at sea in her dreams.

But her life grew colder and clearer, and the ground beneath her feet grew harder, and everywhere she turned, things burned: she entered adolescence by moving from the town she'd grown up in to Clayfield, a steel town in the North.

There was a lake five miles from her house, and a broken-down, thin little thing that the townspeople called a river. Might have been once; the banks to either side of its meager flow were steep and carved out of more than dirt: stone had made way for the water's insistent pressure.

By the riverbanks she made so many mistakes.

She lit fires.

She smoked her first cigarette.

She discovered the difference between romance and sex, the warmth and heat of the former, the pain and the sticky wetness of the latter. Discovered the difference between dreams of love, the reality of small stones, blanket askew, night sky, and the contempt that comes after the game has been won and lost.

Afterward, left alone with a cool, "I'll call you," the pain receding and the wetness reminding her—because of everything it *wasn't*—of the water, she saw the fire lady again.

This time, her face was less sharp. The decade had aged it, thinned it; she looked skeletal, but somehow stronger for the lack of flesh, a bright burning thing that should have been shadow.

Some of that fire was warm, not hot.

"We're flesh," she said sadly.

"Why're you here?" Amy asked, turning away, fumbling for the cigarettes in the fanny pack that lay uncomfortably in the rumpled folds of a full-circle skirt that had been ruined for her, forever, by the act of the afternoon.

"Because you are," she replied, almost gentle. "Here, let me help you with that." She didn't move, but the cigarette was free from the confines of cardboard and paper, lit and glowing, an ember to her bright, bright eyes. "Water," she said, "is the least forgiving of the elements."

Amy frowned. "Water forgives everything," she said.

"Does it?"

"Forgives *me* everything." She hadn't forgotten the storms, and as she spoke, she felt that she'd swallowed them; that the lightning was destroying the fabric of skin from the inside, its bite sharp and terrible.

"Try to remember that," the woman said. "Earth is the patient one. All things return to earth. Fire is the destroyer."

"Water?"

"Takes life, but you knew that," she said. Evasive.

"And gives it," she said, knowing that as well.

"Yes."

"Why are you here?"

"Because the storm is in the air, Amy. It felt what you did; it's growing."

That night, and the next, and the night after that, the storms came in, freak of nature and worse, from the ocean, carried by winds she didn't have a name for because she paid so little attention in school. Heat and cold tangled and neither won. Air and water. Fire and water.

Amy and water.

She didn't want to go home. Didn't want to face her mother's questions. There were things that you didn't share with your mother, things your mother didn't share with you. That was the way of it. Right. Wrong. Didn't matter. Some truths were neither. That night, on the banks of the river, she dreamed of water.

The riverbanks were flooded, the mud melting into the water's grasp. Whole houses were carried away in the torrent. *His* house. His car. His life.

She should have felt triumphant; she did. God help her—if there was one—she did. But it left her in a rush with the rest of the dead. Her best friend, face blue, lips purple, hair tangled in something that looked like kelp, soft and green. Her favorite teacher, the only teacher who had ever been willing to take the time to show her how to fit in, at least in his class, glasses broken, but strapped to his neck by the ridiculous chain he wore because he couldn't remember where he'd put them otherwise. Didn't need them now.

Her own house destroyed.

Her mother.

And the fire's voice hissed as the water doused it: *You have paid the price.*

* * *

The storms stopped as suddenly as they started; Amy swallowed them whole, and let them out as the year progressed. First, in the thunderous silence of guilt. Then, in the howl of anger, the wildness of a fury that had no target but herself. Months later, when all but the most determined of her friends had been blown away, anger gave way to the keening of loss. The tears. She thought the last of the tears would come; they never did. Some part of the storm was hers forever.

She was not quite old enough to live on her own.

She was not quite unrelated enough to become a ward
of the state. Her father's sister, a woman she hadn't
seen in the five years she'd lived in Clayfield, showed
up in a car that defined the words "beat up" and took
her back to a place she would call home for another
few years.

It was a port city, whales for tourists and shipyards
for everyone else, with the requisite fight about dangerous emissions. And the storms *never* touched it.
Not when she felt them. She spoke; they listened.

The dead man had scarred her terribly. Not so terribly that she could abandon the water—might as well
abandon breath—but deeply enough that she carried
an umbrella, held it above her head same as anyone
else when the rain spilled groundward from the height
of rolling clouds.

Only when she was alone, when there was no one
who could be harmed by the wildness, did she sometimes walk into the ocean; where others skimmed surface, she found depths. And she wrapped herself in
them, found comfort there, not certain where her tears
ended and the ocean's great hands began.

Water was mother now, father now; it offered her
a comfort that no one her age was ever offered.

And the water was happy.

*   *   *

Rain is everything she sees. Turn, and the water
falls in sheets at her back; hold out her arms—and
she is, again, she is—and it forms a wall of sorts that
skirts the rounded palm of her hands.

The fire lady—Grace, she thinks, but the fire was
never graceful—came to her when she was ready for
college. God, she'd seemed so old then.

"I was wrong, you know," she said, her voice sharp
and crackling.

"About what?" It was summer, and she had taken a job on the boats that carried tourists to where the whales were. She had no qualifications; that had started out as a problem. But she had made a beat with the man who owned the boat when he'd come to the restaurant she worked at on weekends. "I can bring you whales," she'd said. He was sheepish about the bet when she showed up the next day, but good-natured enough to let her make a fool of herself. Or him.

They came. And when she left the boat, they left. He made her do it three times—three times, the number of so many superstitions—and then he let her join his crew.

The fire lady came as a tourist. "I was wrong about you, Amelia. I thought you'd fail early."

"I did."

"No. You had a tantrum."

"People *died*," Amy said.

"Yes. But everybody mistakes their power at one time or another. Doesn't make them evil. Doesn't make them a failure forever, but it does mean they did fail. Learn from a failure. That's all you can do. I did. And fire . . . is more painful." Reflected in her eyes, fires. The wind carried the sound of screaming.

Grace frowned. Amy wanted to ask, but the look on the old woman's face destroyed her question.

"You've done a good job, with what you understand. I'm sorry. We're all in our own worlds; it's necessity. The Quarters don't cross. But—sometimes—because of how we were born and who we once were—we *can*. I heard your father call you water baby before your predecessor failed for the last time.

"There are no disasters, no elemental disasters, when we take control. We can confine them. If we were *perfect*, there wouldn't be *any*. We're not perfect. We're just as flawed, as immature, as scarred, as the rest of them. I let fire take the Northern forests. Idiots died trying to save them; the deer starved. We need new growth, sometimes, and fire's a way of clearing out the old one *fast.*"

It didn't sound like she was talking about forest anymore. "But it costs us. Me, the humanity burns away like fine layers of gauze. I forget what it's like to be you. Thank God. I forget almost all of it."

"What about the others?"

"We two pay the worst price," the fire said, as softly as she could, hissing on the *s* as if it were a coal that Amy had dropped a tear on.

"What do you mean?"

She didn't answer.

After a long pause, Amy said, "You didn't come here to see the whales, did you?"

"No."

"Why did you come?"

"To tell you that you've done well. Your predecessor didn't last through her sixteenth year; you might remember what happened then."

Amy nodded.

"Good."

"Why did she fail?"

A glimmer of light, like sympathy or even compassion, lit the fire lady's face. "For the same reasons we all fail. It's just that when *we* fail, tens, hundreds of thousands of people, die. We're not much as guardians go—we can't be, and still be heard by the elements. We've got the wildness in us. But water is the hardest."

"But you—"

"I'll be watching for her," Grace said. "Don't you worry. I'll be watching for her." She turned and walked away before Amy understood what she meant. Her successor. *"Grace!"* she shouted. The thin woman stopped, slicing ground with her ever present shadow. "What happened to her? What happened to the girl who was the water baby before me?"

"I'm sorry, Amelia," Grace said, and her voice was soft as the water's voice. It was the most frightening thing she'd ever said. "But you'll find out."

And that night, she met a man.

* * *

He was, sadly, everything she remembered about her father except old. He was patient, and indulgent in ways he probably shouldn't have been, and it was very hard for him to deny her anything. What he looked like then—hard to see it clearly, so much of the now is so real—went past her before it made sense: dark hair, dark eyes, skin the color of, well, skin. Comfortable; not the well chiseled workout look of the perfectly toned body, but lord knew she wasn't any statuesque beauty either. Her hormones didn't leap away with her and make a fool of her before she could catch them. She'd done with that. She still had scars. She could visit the graves of most of them.

"Hi," he said, "I'm diver. I'm mean, I'm Bill—and I'm a, well I—God, I'm an idiot."

He was a diver, among other things. Deep-sea diving. The first time he invited her to go down with him and fitted her with the tank and gear she had to bite her tongue—hard—to stop from laughing out loud. They went into the depths, and with every meter she descended, she felt more peaceful. Calmer. He admired the fact that she hadn't panicked at all.

But the water wasn't willing to let her go, not easily; there was an accident with the oxygen tank. She wanted him to leave her be—she *knew* it was important, suddenly—but he didn't panic. Didn't leave.

In the end, she saved his life, but only barely; the undercurrents were vicious.

"I'm sorry," he said, hours after they finally broke

water. "I—I guess you won't want to do that again. I don't know what happened—I've been down there—"

She caught his hands. "Water's unpredictable." Truth. Lie. She could feel the storm gathering in its depth, ready to launch itself, rocketlike, at some unsuspecting target.

* * *

So she worked. She accepted the responsibility of the water to the water, and of the water to the people, in this harbor, in other harbors. She wrestled with the depths and the tangled all-encompassing comfort they had always offered her. It had been enough, once.

She didn't tell Bill about the storms, of course. How could she? The loony bin was waiting, or worse: desertion. Lived with that all her life, and she didn't want to face it again.

She didn't have to. Bill McLaughlin became her husband, almost by accident. They'd been friends, and she loved that; he wanted more, and she was so afraid of the loss that came with sex that she'd pulled as far back as she could without losing him or driving him away entirely. But one night, after they'd been out drinking—or rather, after he had, as she found drinking and storms mixed a little too well—he turned to her and said, "I'd be happy if I could spend every morning of my life making breakfast for you."

And she said, "Bill, I hate it when alcohol does the speaking for *anyone.*"

"It's not the drinking," he answered.

"Tell me that tomorrow. Tell me that the day after tomorrow."

He did. And he did. They were married three days later, eloping like teenagers in a beat-up old car that barely made it across the state border.

* * *

His voice is lost to rain and water.

She should have known, the first time they ventured into the depths together, that the water would hate him. Should have known that it did; she'd thought—she didn't think—that the water was wild because she was, with excitement, with fear, with pleasure.

Fire, where fire shouldn't be, is hissing as water hits it; the water and the fire, immutable, intertwined.

You have paid the price, the fire says, and she knows, then, knows for certain, that somewhere in the storm and wilds of the storm, Bill is dead.

But she has no time to rage or grieve. Yes, she thinks. Yes, damn you, I've paid the price. And this one last time, you *will* listen to me. Like a crucifix she stands; like a religious icon; like a wall. The rain comes down.

She has always loved the rain.

* * *

Two years after the marriage, she became pregnant. It hadn't been planned, and she had agonized about whether or not she should tell her husband; a quiet abortion was a possibility. She was afraid of breaking the life that she had miraculously found out of chaos; afraid that somehow she would bring a newborn child into a world that would either devour it or adore it so completely there would, once again, be no place, no special place, for her. Except in the depth of the ocean that allowed her no other life.

But something else was stirring, some other desire, and in the end, like a penitent—as if the responsibility had always been hers—she confessed. Bill was overjoyed. Not loudly, not extravagantly, but quietly, peacefully. He watched over her, harbored her, listened to her complaints with a growing sense of happiness. Gained weight, too.

And he went to the hospital with her, she in a panic, he in a state that was a wild swing between terror and joy. He didn't drive like a maniac. Instead they took a cab driven by a man who looked decidedly relieved when they made it to the hospital without doing anything messy in the back seat of his car.

The hospital doors opened; the antiseptic smell of uncarpeted floors and poured cement walls, the uniforms, the beds and the electric equipment were the backdrops of a drama that she had never thought—not truly, not in the deeps—would involve her. She felt pain, and it was the pain of swallowing whole storms; she cried out, screamed with their voice, shouted in anger and denial, in fear, in remorse. The tears she held in for as long as she could, but they broke.

"Honey," Bill said, "Your waters have broken."

Your waters have broken.

Understanding, then. In waves, in a rhythm that matched the pain of contraction and separation.

She stayed for one day in the hospital. She brought the baby home.

She entered the home with the precious burden; Bill stayed behind to empty the car of all the things that had accumulated in one day at the hospital: infant car seat, flowers from his mother, a bassinet from his mother—because she didn't believe that the hospital wouldn't let them use it—and the requisite number of toys, from his mother, for fifty children.

And when she got to the nursery that Bill had built, the room with the window that overlooked the lake, she saw fire uncontained by grate or form, but she felt the fire lady's presence.

"The storm is coming," Grace said.

"I know."

"There is a price to pay."

"I know." She holds her child as tightly as she can; her arms move of their own volition; she has no choice. "But you—"

"Fever," the woman—and she sees this clearly, through fire and flame, the *woman*—says, voice like dry ice, obscuring more than it reveals even as it heralds all. "My three children died of fever. I couldn't hold them; it only burned them faster."

"I can't," she said.

"I know. You're the waterborn, and the waterborn by nature *must* be young. You come from the womb, and she seeks to return you to it, and there must be nothing in your life—ever—that suggests you are not a child, not her child."

"You let your children die." Not an accusation. Not quite.

She said three words. "Dresden. Nagasaki. Hiroshima." Bowed her head. "There is no death worse than fire. I can give you your names, child. But they are not those names."

"And if I don't do this thing, will I die?"

"Who can say? You will pass from my life, and I will pass from yours. That's all." Her face was grim and narrow, like the blade of an ax, like the hatchet Amy remembered from childhood. She holds out her thin arms. "Can I?"

She can't say why, rain on all sides, storm's voice raging with anger and—yes—betrayal, but she opened her arms and let Grace hold her firstborn, her only. "This is how I weep," the older woman said softly. "I have no tears.

"Good-bye, Amelia."

She kissed Amy's son and handed him back and vanished before Bill walked across the threshold.

* * *

The storms came.

First in dream, wordless, livid blue, the color of anger and isolation. She struggled out of the undertow, able, still, to speak with storm's voice.

Night terrors. Night storm.

She woke. Carried the baby to the attic.

Kissed her husband on the way back down, hoping the blankets of down would keep her sleeping child warm. Hoping that fear wouldn't drive him mad, that newborn ignorance was a shield against the primal.

Loving him. Hating herself.

Paying the price, but not *all* of the price. Just enough, she hopes. Just enough.

* * *

Bill built the pier. It creaks beneath her feet and in despair and anger she hopes it snaps. But the water won't drown her; she sees that now. It can't. It can rob her of everything that makes a life worth living, and it can rob all else of life, but she is from water, and she cannot be destroyed by it.

She loves the rain.

The rain loves her.

It descends in a flood and crashes through the windows of her living room. Her bedroom, bay window bright with light now dark with night and water. She does not scream his name because she understands *everything*. Bill.

And she shouts, now, shouts: I have paid your price!
I have paid.

Sees her father's face, her father's back, his absence, the fact of his death hidden for so many years from the place in her mind that would have made it real.

I have paid

Sees the first love, the terrible, thoughtless, cruelty

of adolescence avenged and with it her friends lying
beached like dead whales but smaller and whiter; her
mother's house, her mother, her *mother*

I have paid

Sees, in her mind's eye, Bill, hears him say, *Your
waters have broken*, understands what this means, and
knows that she will never find him, just as she never
found her father, that his absence will be worse because it is her *choice*.

I have paid.

Because in order to save her baby, she has to make
a choice, final choice. Storm whipping her face, tears
sheeting it, the child's cry, the child's single cry as it
emerges into air and life and light and, yes, fire and
earth, and she will not pay *that* price.

The storm's wild sobbing, the walls of the house
buffeted before her voice destroys the force of water,
drives it back. No! she cries, no word, but all force.
This is mine as I was yours, and I will not give it up!

Wildness, wild child, wild adult, draining from her
in an instant as the truth binds them both: water
and woman.

The moon is high and the tide is high and the water
rises with a face that she has never seen.

The water will recede, and take with it all of the childhood she has left; take the comfort, the security. Leave
her only the responsibility, terrible and profound.

Weeping. Raining.

The waters have broken.

She knows what will happen next; she knows what
will follow.

I'll watch for her. I'll watch.

Grace.

*Two men, strong of stature and kindly of counte-
nance, salute the Guardian and each other before
consuming the golden contents of their bowls. The
eagle lands next to them fanning its wings. They
follow it through the Western door where they find
themselves standing on the surface of an endless
body of water. Their winged Guide swoops and
grips each man by the shoulder. Flying upward,
darkness surrounds them, and the only sound they
can hear is the beating of the eagle's mighty wings.
At length, light appears above them, when they
reach it they will understand why it is:*

ONLY AS SAFE

by Mark A. Garland and Lawrence Schimel

ON his sixteenth birthday, the dragon boats came
back. The crazed blond-haired warriors who rushed
ashore seemed to fight even more fiercely than last
year, when they had slain his father. On the very day
he had turned fifteen, Turell, son of Lord Gerald of
Brackham, had stood on the castle wall at his father's
side throughout the night and had watched the raiders
plunder and set fire to the evacuated town. He'd seen
their pointed helms in the moonlight and had heard
their yelps among the flames as everything the people
of Brackham had built over the years was so quickly
destroyed.

Through it all, Turell's father had said almost nothing, even when his men came to stand with him and watch and listen. "It's a good place, this," Lord Gerald had said, as the night wore on and the village died.

"Are we going to leave it?" Turell had asked, near a whisper.

His father had looked over his shoulder toward the castle's keep, the yard, the parapets. Then his gaze settled on the center of everything, the place where a waist-high circle of stones surrounded the castle's wellspring. Lord Gerald had discovered the spring when he first came to this land, and had chosen it as the place where his first hill fort would stand. But the well was more than that. Growing up, Turell had seen his father go to the well many times when he did not thirst—had seen him sit on the flat-topped stones and gaze into the shimmering darkness as though it were some far horizon. Or a holy shrine. All the while rubbing at the scar on his right hand, a wound suffered in the building of the well.

Lord Gerald had looked once more to his son, then out toward the sea again as the invaders drew near the castle walls. He'd breathed a sigh and rested his hand on Turell's shoulder. "No," he had said. "Never. We will never leave this place."

But by dawn, the raiders had found a way inside the castle itself.

In the year since then, the village had been rebuilt, the damage to the castle repaired. Workmen had only just finished rebuilding one of the walls a fortnight past, and improvements inside the castle would go on throughout the summer. *If it stands this day,* Turell thought grimly.

From his high vantage, the young lord recognized the Viking leader, a massive, grizzled man who stood fearless at the base of the castle's seaward wall, shouting to his men. These were the same men who had nearly destroyed the castle a year ago, and the leader who, with his own hand, had slain Turell's father.

"Archers!" Turell ordered, and hundreds of arrows flew from the parapets. The Vikings' shields served many of them well, though not all of them. The raiders retaliated with flaming arrows, and fires began to sprout on the thatched roofs of the houses and shops that lined the castle's main bailey.

Hundreds of villagers cowered there with their livestock, hoping for the best. Turell had promised them just that, had promised the gods and himself a year ago, as he had stood over his father's dead body, that he would not leave.

Brackham Castle had been his father's dream, the key to holding one of the richest fiefdoms the true king had ever granted. Lord Gerald had paid for that dream with his life.

And there was one more reason the youthful lord would not give up, a reason he did not himself understand or even believe sometimes. . . .

"Send a squad to check the walls again," Turell told his captain, as the light of sunrise began to spill across the land.

A year ago, during the night, the raiders had managed to dig a tunnel under the wall near the northwest tower. Then they had set fire to the tunnel's wooden support beams, and collapsed a great portion of the castle wall when the ground beneath it suddenly gave way.

As the raiders had fought their way into the castle's keep, Turell's father had told him to run, to escape through the keep's little sally port, then to hide. Turell had wanted to fight at his father's side—he was ready, he thought—but his father had forbidden this, and his father's soldiers had sworn to keep the lord's only heir from harm.

He'd hidden in the blacksmith's shop until it caught fire, then among the tables and half-finished barrels in the reeve's shop after that. The fires had found him there as well. So he had moved once more, until the waiting and hiding had grown unbearable. Turell had finally ventured out into the yard—only to see his father still fighting though already wounded by the hand of the Viking leader. As Turell had watched, Lord Gerald rose up again, holding his side, and struck back, wounding the northern monarch in turn and rallying Brackham's residents. But as knights and townsmen alike rushed past Turell, armed with whatever they could find, a few of the Vikings had spotted him.

Unarmed and seeing no other choice, Turell had run again, through the smoke-filled yard, finally evading capture by lowering himself into the well. "A castle is only as safe as its well," his father had often said. It was one of the truisms of siege war, but Turell had always suspected it meant something more to his father. *Safe.* He had remembered the word well, and the feeling he'd had, sitting there with his father on the stone rim one night, watching the stars reflected in the deep pool below. The memory had seemed to warm him like a hearth fire, and it was as if the whole battle froze for a moment while Turell remembered that crystalline tranquillity.

Once again, caught up in battle, the memory of that moment was a calm focus for Turell. He listened to his captain's reports, gave new commands. Then turned his face once more to wait for his enemy, his mind traveling back again to that memory . . .

The Vikings, close behind, had thought to look for him even in the well. So Turell had lowered himself farther into the water. His breath had caught as he slid beneath the liquid, still chill despite the warmth of the air. The echo of his heart's pounding had sounded loud in his ears as he tried to hold himself just below the surface, only his face exposed to the air so he could breathe. His feet had kicked rhythmically, holding him in place.

Voices had barked in an alien tongue above him, and Turell had almost swallowed a mouthful of water as his body jerked in surprise. *They sounded so close!* He'd tried to make no sound, hoping they wouldn't think to look for him.

Suddenly, Turell had felt hands grab him as faces peered over the edge, not very far above him.

But the hands had pulled him down, deep into the water, away from the warriors. Turell remembered wanting to scream, but he had felt hands clamp over his mouth—keeping him silent, forcing him to hold his breath lest he be betrayed by the bubbling air if nothing else.

Something had slid past him through the water, slicing downward on his right. He had kicked out with his leg, which connected with the sinking object: a wooden shaft. The watery hands had grabbed his wayward leg again and pulled it close. More spears were being thrown down into the water, but the hands held him tightly, keeping his arms and legs pressed against his own body, keeping him out of the weapons' paths.

Turell had marveled even then that he was able to hold his breath for so long—he wanted to open his mouth and breathe in deeply, even knowing he would suck in a lungful of water if he did so. But the hands had not let go of him, and he could not move, not for breath or anything.

He didn't know how much time passed while he hung there, suspended in water and time and warmth, content as anyone could be while fears of what had become of his home, his father, in the world above continued to pull at the back of his mind. The hands had held him gently, still invisible in the flickering shafts of twilight that penetrated the water's surface. Then, abruptly, the invisible hands had tensed as if in agony, more powerful than any human hands Turell had ever known. He'd struggled, fearing he would be injured. The hands had loosened their grip just a bit but did not release him. Not long after he'd felt himself float free, and he'd known he was alone again. He'd kicked at the water until he'd broken the surface—and had a sudden urge to gasp for air.

It was near day's end, Turell had realized, as he emerged from the well to learn that the raiders had been driven back to the sea. He learned, too, that his father was dead.

The young lord had stood before the survivors that eve and sworn an oath in his father's name, to rebuild Brackham, to reprovision, to fulfill his father's dream. He would show the true king that this lord, Turell, son of Gerald, could be counted on as well as his father, no matter his age.

He had gone to the well that night and many nights after, as his father had, drawn there by the mystery and memory of what had happened to him beneath its waters. Surely, at some time, his father had been in those waters and felt what Turell had felt—that mystical, alien presence which had saved him, though for what reasons Turell did not know. And though he did not see or feel the presence there for many months, he felt that sense of safety surrounding him as he sat on the stone rim. And the memory of his father, which he kept pulled tight to his chest.

Some nights, with the stars shining in the water's surface, Turell couldn't help but let the tears flow as he railed against fate, as he wept for his father's death, as he felt so small in the world, too young to bear such responsibility as had been thrust upon him.

One such night, as his tears splashed into the water's surface and disrupted the image of the stars with ripples, Turell realized he was not alone. From the center of the well, rising up from the water itself, was the most beautiful woman he had ever seen.

He could not speak or think, caught up in the spell of her beauty and the magic that made her. It was as if Turell could see through her, for she was made all of water, but she had substance as well. She reached out and touched his face gently, catching a tear on her fingertip.

"I miss him, too," the creature spoke, her voice like the tinkling of water over stones as it falls from a great height.

That was all she said. Turell felt a great burden of sadness lift from his heart, although he wasn't quite sure why. Maybe it was enough simply to know that he did not grieve alone. He imagined his father's spirit up in the heavens, and lifted his face to the stars. "I will avenge your death," he whispered.

When he looked back to the well, the naiad was gone, but her presence still lingered. That feeling of safety, of warmth, of her finger against his cheek stopping his tears.

Turell thought he understood now the reason his father had come to the well so often, if not the full nature of what dwelled there or her history with his father. In fact, for the first time Turell wondered about the stories of his mother, who died in childbirth he had been told. But what if. . . .

It was all speculation, but some nights, as he sat by the well, he wondered. And he smiled at the idea that these thoughts might be true.

Turell never called for her, or requested her presence; but sometimes she would appear before him, and they would share a moment together, though she rarely spoke. Turell never asked her; it didn't matter. He was content simply to know she was there; that she existed in the world, and that sometimes she blessed their well with her presence. He understood why his father had sworn to protect this place.

But now the raiders from the sea had come again—not just a few hundred this time, more than a thousand of them.

"There has been no challenge of the walls during the night," the captain said as he returned to Turell's side. "This time, they have other plans." He pointed to the road that led to castle's main gate. Turell had already seen them. The Vikings had constructed a ram, protected by a shell framed from wood and covered with wet hides to thwart the castle's own fire arrows.

Turell and his captain watched the attackers wheel it steadily forward. When they reached the main gate, they started to pound against it, loud booms like thunderclaps, one, then another. Soon they would be through. Turell turned and made his way back into the yard, then to the well, where he spoke to the ghost of his father, and to whatever it was that dwelled in the cool, deep waters.

"We will fight them," Turell swore. "To the last man. To the last drop of blood in our veins." Silence answered him as always. He was silent in return, until his moribund trance was broken by the thick, sickening sound of heavy oak being torn apart, followed by a chorus of shouting. The Vikings were within the walls!

Turell drew his sword and rushed into the yard, his captain at his side. His men were falling back, attempting to form a line against the hordes that swept through the broken gates. The young hero joined them, fighting with a strength and fury he thought would carry him through a thousand enemy blows. But the siegers seemed unstoppable. They were wild men with the strength and daring of gods, berserk in their fury.

The Brackham line broke. "To the last!" Turell shouted to the heavens. A ragged cheer rose up, then quickly faded among the sounds of clashing steel, the howls of courage, the screams of the dying. The one battle splintered into a dozen different fights that raged throughout the castle's baileys and houses, its towers and keep, from the parapets to the cellars. Turell himself fought beneath the hot midday sun until his arms could no longer lift his sword—but the enemy who faced him did not strike him down.

"You will die as your father did," the Viking leader said, grinning far too much for a man surrounded by so much death. "But not yet."

He grabbed Turell roughly, with a strength and swiftness that the youth could not imagine, after so much time fighting. With three blows the Viking knocked him down and pried the sword from his hand, then dragged him to the castle's main bailey and across the yard, to the edge of the well.

He stood over Turell, massive chest heaving, black passion in his sky-colored eyes. "First," he said, pressing a booted heel to Turell's chest. "You will tell me what you have done to the water!"

Turell looked about, trying to see. He had a gash over his left eye that bled continuously, mixing with sweat, blinding that side. The Viking leader reached down and hauled him to his feet, then pointed. Turell looked about him. A freshly drawn and seeping bucket rested on the castle well's stone edge. All around the well, Viking warriors littered the ground, more than two dozen in all, their bodies limp.

"I have done nothing," Turell said truthfully. But

he knew who might have, and his heart leaped to think she had not abandoned them. Somehow she had known . . . Of course she had known, for the danger came from the sea.

"You knew you would lose, so you poisoned your own water!"

"No," Turell said. "I could never put poison in this well, I assure you."

"Then you will drink the water!" the Viking boomed, hauling the young lord like a sack of onions to the well's edge. He tried to dunk Turell's head into the bucket, but his face hit the edge and knocked it over, back into the well. Turell looked down into the water. A hiding place, once, but unlike the boy he had been a year before, the lord of a castle could not hide. . . .

Though he felt that same warmth envelop him now, that sense of safety.

Blood dripped from his forehead into the water below, forming little ringlets that mingled with the larger ripples from the bucket's splash. He could see nothing else.

The Viking pulled back and commanded one of his men to raise the bucket again. Holding Turell's head in large hands, he lifted the bucket to Turell's lips with the other and forced him to take many long swallows. Turell drank deeply, thirsty after fighting in the sun all day. The water was cool and sweet in his mouth, and spread strength through his body as if it contained some potent elixir.

Turell looked up and found the Viking leader glaring at him. Abruptly, he handed Turell the bucket. "Send it back to the bottom," he commanded. Turell leaned over the edge once more and looked down. The waters had stilled. He could see his own reflection on the surface, and something else, he thought, a face perhaps, looking back at him from just beneath—

"Bring it up!" the Viking leader shouted.

Turell sank and hefted the bucket. Water trickled from its seams, spattering the shimmering surface below and causing countless circular ripples to reappear. His reflection blurred, the other image faded as well. Then the Viking right-handed Turell's shoulder and the bucket fell back into the water.

When Turell had hauled the bucket up yet again, the Viking made him drink once more, and still nothing happened. Turell nodded to the stalwart invader and said, "Thank you, no more, I have slaked my thirst for now."

"What has happened to my men!" the Viking boomed, furious.

Turell only shrugged. "That is simple," he answered, loud enough for all those gathered to hear. "This land is cursed. And blessed. Only men of honor may eat of its great bounty, and drink from its pure waters. Go home, before you all die as the others have."

At this the Viking leader grabbed Turell and tossed him aside. The bucket tumbled once more, spilling its contents onto the ground. The angry king heaved the vessel into the well and hauled it back up, then plunged his hands into the bucket and sucked the waters from them. "Lies!" he said, gathering more and swallowing, splashing still more on his face. "A coward's lies!"

Then his eyes opened wide, and his lips came tightly together. Anguish swept his weathered features, and he dropped his sword. "A . . . a curse?" he gasped, before he fell to the ground clutching his gut. He moaned softly, twice, and in a moment he was still.

Turell looked up to see the other raiders backing away, glancing worriedly at one another. "There is a curse!" one of them said to those around him.

"The curse!" another shouted to men still fighting on the walls. They kept backing away.

Seeing their leader lying dead and the leader's own guard in retreat seemed to destroy the morale of the other Vikings. Turell found a sword and called to his men, rallying them as his father had, and together they chased the invaders back to their dragon boats, back to the sea.

A woman with a soft, sad face raises her bowl and sips from it. Once started, she finishes the liquid quickly. The eagle's piercing cry greets her. He lifts from the table on massive wings to sail to the Western door. Her face betraying a mix of reluctance and determination, she rises and follows to a world where ponds of steaming mineral water pock the landscape. The Seeker stirs the pool with a finger, beginning her experience of:

OUT OF HOT WATER

by Jane Lindskold

"WHY," thought Jeannette with a certain amount of despair, "doesn't anything wonderful and exciting ever happen to me?"

She was lying facedown on a massage table, a towel draped over her short, plump body, another wrapped around her mouse-brown hair. In just a few moments, her personal therapist would arrive and submit her to a "Traditional Massage," step number three in the special "Earth and Sea Grand Sampler" included in her getaway package. She'd already performed steps one and two: a soak in a private mineral tub and a Seaweed Body Facial.

"Then comes the facial massage and the eye zone rejuvenator," Jeannette muttered into the mattress. "Oh, boy."

For some crazy reason, she'd had great hopes for this holiday. She'd won the trip to the Ojo Caliente Mineral Springs spa in northern New Mexico by having the most billable hours during tax season—a truly heroic feat for a CPA in a large firm. The boss had thought, with good reason, that a chance to unwind in pleasant surroundings was a fitting reward.

So here she was on an all-expenses-paid holiday and her main response was acute dissatisfaction. It wasn't that there was anything wrong with the resort—far from it. The unhappiness was from deep within herself.

"Maybe," Jeannette said, speaking to no one in particular, a habit she'd gotten into when deciphering clients' records, "I have unrealistic expectations for my life. I have a good job, a nice place to live, even my health, but there's still something missing."

She chuckled softly, thinking she sounded like a commercial for some religious ministry.

"Maybe I should have invited someone to come along," she mused.

She'd considered it. The prize had been a luxurious trip for two or a perfectly decadent trip for one. There wasn't anyone special in Jeanette's life just now, so, out of a spirit of adventure, she'd gone alone.

Despite trail rides, fine meals, and pleasant encounters with perfectly nice people in and around the mineral pools, the experience had been curiously empty. The day after tomorrow she'd go home. The day after that she'd go back to work, and, under the boss' anxiously beaming gaze, she'd try to act like she'd had a wonderful time.

"But I haven't," she said. "I wish something would *happen.*"

"Like what, dear?" said a voice from above and behind her.

Jeannette started, trying to sit up, untangle herself from the thick towels spread over her, and keep her nudity covered all at once. A pair of thin but strong hands pressed her down.

"Relax, dear," said the voice. Female, older, but, like the hands, possessed of surprising strength. There was a faint accent, too. Not Spanish, more like one of the local Indians who had learned English as a second language.

"I didn't hear you come in," Jeannette explained, embarrassed now, letting herself be pressed into place without further struggle.

"I suspect your thoughts were elsewhere, dear," the woman agreed. "Why are you so unhappy?"

Perhaps it was feeling her muscles expertly kneaded by the probing hands, perhaps it was the curious anonymity of talking to a faceless voice, but Jeannette found herself explaining:

"I was just wishing that there was something *more,* you know." She floundered, trying to clarify. Numbers, not words, were her strong point. "More than jobs and that. Something exciting."

"Ah." Those thin, strong fingers were rolling the muscles in Jeannette's shoulders now. "This is a quiet place. The dance hall in the village has been closed for years."

"Not just here in Ojo Caliente," Jeannette went on, determined to have it out. "Anywhere, every day."

"Ah." The hands moved down her back, doing things to the edges of her spine. "Yes?"

Jeannette chuckled self-deprecatingly. "I guess I've been ruined by movies and television and stuff. I want big things. Heroics. Adventure. Excitement. Wonderful stuff."

"That's quite a large order," the massage therapist said. "I remember when my grandson was a baby. No one in the village liked me or my daughter. They liked us even less when my daughter bore a child and no one could name the father. The baby wore rags because no one would help us."

Jeannette nodded, her face rubbing against the sheet. "I guess that must have been tough for all of you," she said, trying to sound understanding. Actually, she was a little piqued that the old woman had started in on her personal problems.

"Oh." The woman laughed, a deep, rich sound. "It wasn't so bad. The villagers didn't know that my grandson's father had provided for us in his own way. We had more piñon nuts than we could eat."

"Wow!" Jeannette exclaimed. "Talk about your high-fat diets! Still, if you had so many nuts, why didn't you sell them? Piñon nuts are expensive, even unshelled."

The old woman was kneading Jeannette's buttocks in a fashion that Jeannette would have found embarrassing if the touch hadn't been so professional. She continued her narrative without answering Jeannette's question.

"But things got better. My grandson learned to hunt. At first all he caught was rats, but his mother and I taught him how to recognize the tracks of cottontails and jackrabbits. Later he learned to hunt deer."

This woman is crazy, Jeannette decided. *No one lives like that anymore. There's Welfare on the reservations, isn't there?*

"After my grandson had learned to hunt," the woman continued, "his father came and dressed him in fine buckskin, so fine that the boy's mother and I didn't recognize him at first. Oh, he was so angry at us! But later we laughed at our mistake."

Buckskin. Right. Jeannette thought she should get

up, find a polite excuse for leaving, but she wasn't certain that she could move. Under the massage therapist's hands, her muscles had turned into something like putty.

"Uh, so where is your grandson now?" she asked.

"He's gone south. That's where he went to continue his work."

"Do you ever see him?"

"Oh, yes. He comes to visit me once a year."

"That's nice."

"Roll over now, dear. Put this warm towel on your face. It will keep the muscles pliant for the facial."

Jeannette caught a brief glimpse of her therapist as she obeyed. An older woman, just as she'd guessed, dressed in a light-weight, pastel green blouse and skirt. Her iron-gray hair was gathered at either side of her head in some traditional style. Though her brown face was seamed with wrinkles, her skin was neither coarse nor tissue paper delicate. The eyes that studied Jeannette with too much wisdom were a shocking dark green, the color of some kinds of turquoise.

Jeannette was glad to pull the moist towel over her face and escape that piercing gaze. The therapist began at her feet this time.

"I've talked too much about myself," the old woman said. "You are unhappy."

Next she's going to ask me if I'm married, Jeannette thought. *If I have any children. When I say "no" she'll tell me that a man and a couple of brats are just what I need. Then I'll hear about the grandson some more.*

But the old woman surprised her.

"Real adventure isn't like what you see on television," she warned, and there was genuine tension in her voice. "Real adventure doesn't neatly end after fifty-three minutes with everything all happily ever after."

"Adventure is someone else far away in lots of trouble," Jeannette said, her voice sounding distant and distorted through the muffling towel. "Or something like that. I'd still like a shot at it."

"Be careful what you ask for," the old woman cautioned. "These hot springs have been a sacred place from long before the coming of the Spanish. There might be gods listening."

Jeannette laughed. "I wish."

"Oh, my," said the old woman. "Oh, my!"

* * *

That evening, comfortably full with some of the best green chile enchiladas she'd ever eaten, Jeannette sat on the edge of the big outdoor swimming pool. Her legs were immersed in the ninety-degree mineral water; all over her muscles still felt almost inhumanly relaxed from the massage.

Despite every reason in the world to feel about as much animation as a rubber doll, an achingly strong sense of anticipation was rising within her.

"Something," she said, to the empty pool area, "something is going to happen. I can feel it."

Above, one of New Mexico's impossibly Maxfield Parrish sunsets was unfolding. The sky was streaked with red, orange, and pink, just touched with smoke gray. The town of Ojo Caliente was located in a valley west of the Sangre de Cristo Mountains, the spa itself sheltered beneath a rhyolite cliff already black with shadows.

On top of the cliff, Jeannette knew, the evening lingered. Here below it would soon be night. She knew she should leave before the staff locked up the pool area, perhaps stop by the restaurant for a dessert to go. In her cottage, a new S.M. Stirling novel waited to waft her off to adventures in the Bronze Age. There was Earl Grey tea waiting to be brewed, mountain flower honey to sweeten it.

But she couldn't move. Didn't want to move. Lassitude impossibly mingled with exhilaration swelled within her. She felt like a young girl hoping for and yet dreading her first kiss. If she moved, the feeling would vanish just as the pinks were vanishing from the clouds above. She waited—and something stirred in the depths of the mineral pool.

Dark green, mostly solid, with lighter greens peeking through translucent bits. Swirling, like a whirlpool, though the surface of the pool remained still. Rising, lit from below or within, rising, more defined now, fountaining upward.

Jeannette gasped. A woman was erupting from beneath the warm water. Her long gray hair was loose about her, a fine mass like a storm cloud. She was naked. She was clothed in green light. She was both. She was neither.

Jerking her legs from the water, Jeannette jumped back just as the water woman burst through the surface. Droplets of spray adorned the gray hair with emeralds and diamonds as it settled about the woman's shoulders.

My hair never looks like that when it's wet, thought Jeannette in wild panic. *My hair just looks lank. Her hair looks like something from a* Sports Illustrated *swimsuit issue.*

This woman, however, would never be found in *Sports Illustrated* or in any fashion magazine. For all her vitality and unbent posture, she was clearly quite old. Her breasts sagged with the proud heritage of motherhood; her hips were broad.

Her eyes were dark green, the color of turquoise. By those eyes Jeannette knew her.

"You!" she blurted in surprise and astonishment. "You!"

"There is trouble, Jeannette," said the old woman, walking across the water to her. "Above us on the cliffs tonight thieves seek antiquities in the ruins of Pose'uinge. They have come there before and I have let them pass, but tonight they will come too close to a buried shrine to Poseyemu, the great hero who was born in this place."

Jeannette remembered hearing about Poseyemu from the guide on the Archaeological Horseback Tour she had taken the day before. Poseyemu was what the guide had called a culture hero, a semi-divine figure sacred to the Tewa Indians, whose descendants still lived in the area. The guide thought that Poseyemu might have been based on a real person who was later accorded the trimmings of mythology.

According to the Tewa stories, Poseyemu had led his people to many victories. One story said that he had even defeated Josi, the god of the Christians and Mexicans. According to others, Poseyemu's permanent return would herald a rise in power and prosperity for the Tewa people.

The time for that return, like the prophesied returns of so many heroes in so many cultures, hadn't come yet. The story of Poseyemu had an interesting twist, though. Unlike King Arthur or Ogier the Dane or Charles de Gaulle, all of whom were presumed sleeping somewhere until the time came for their returns, the stories of Poseyemu said that once a year he came back from the south to . . .

"You're Poseyemu's grandmother!" Jeanette exclaimed in astonishment. "The stories said . . . you said . . ."

Words were failing her and the old women took pity on her.

"The old stories say that Poseyemu's grandmother lives in the hot springs, and so I do. And once a year my grandson comes to visit me. If Poseyemu's shrine is destroyed, he may not visit me. Therefore, you and I must stop the pot hunters."

"Why me?" Jeannette protested. "Why not call the police or the Bureau of Land Management?"

"I might have," the old woman said, a little sadly, "but you see, you wished."

* * *

When they walked through the narrow office to leave the pool area, the woman behind the counter said a polite good night to Jeannette, then turned to the old woman (who was now wearing the same pastel green uniform she had worn earlier):

"A client has asked for a body polish before she leaves tomorrow. Can you come in early?"

"When?"

"By eight."

"Sure. See you, then."

"Good night."

Once outside on the artfully twisting paths that led between the buildings, Jeannette whispered hoarsely, "Do you really work here?"

"Why not?" Poseyemu's grandmother shrugged. "People have been coming to the hot springs for a long time, looking for healing. So now there's a spa instead of a shrine. I don't have a problem with it."

"But do they know who you are?"

"You mean that I'm Poseyemu's grandmother? Sure, I show him off every year. Some of the ladies, they think he's really cute."

"No!" Jeannette hissed in exasperation. "I mean that you're . . . you . . . that you live in the hot spring."

"No, I don't trouble their heads with such things." Poseyemu's grandmother smiled. "They think I live in the village somewhere and don't have a telephone."

"But . . ."

"Enough now," Poseyemu's grandmother said. "You need to put on better shoes. Those sandals won't do for a climb. And you need jeans, not a skirt. You have those things?"

"In my cottage," Jeannette gestured to the right.

"Good, we'll go there first. You got a flashlight?"

"In my car. Two."

"Good." The old woman glanced at the darkening sky, pushed Jeannette toward her cottage. "We'll have light enough to get to the mesa top if we hurry. Then the moon is almost full, but flashlights will help."

"What if anyone sees us?"

"Down here they will just think it's someone going to commune with the spirits of the wise Native Americans," Poseyemu's grandmother said indulgently. "Once we're near the pot hunters, well, then we need to be careful."

Inside the cottage, Poseyemu's grandmother snooped around while Jeannette changed her clothes.

"You rich, girl?"

"Jeannette. No. Not really. I mean, I do okay, but I won this trip at work."

Poseyemu's grandmother was sampling a Godiva chocolate shaped like a seashell. "These are pretty good."

"Yeah. The boss gave them to me before I left."

"Ah!" The green eyes twinkled wickedly. "He likes you, huh?"

"Like a granddaughter, maybe," Jeannette replied, lacing up her hiking shoes. "He's a little old for me."

"Ah." Poseyemu's grandmother inspected Jeannette critically, taking in her plump figure, her straight brown hair cut just above her shoulders and drawn back with a barrette, plain features too regular for either beauty or distinction.

"You look pretty good to me. Bet the boss be glad to have a granddaughter as healthy and strong as you."

Jeannette blushed and grabbed her car keys. As an afterthought, she also took a water bottle and the overstuffed fanny pack she'd been using as a purse.

"C'mon."

Heavy-duty halogen flashlights in hand, the two women hurried into the small but deep canyon behind the spa. Poseyemu's grandmother was now wearing a pair of forest green jeans, a long-sleeved shirt the color of pond scum, and hiking boots.

Determined not to seem too impressed, Jeannette commented, "I bet that trick saves on laundry."

"It does. That was a really good thing back when we had to beat our clothes against a rock in the river, let me tell you."

"I bet," Jeannette mumbled.

Poseyemu's grandmother hurried along the path at a rate that soon had Jeannette panting.

"Slow down! Slow down!" she pleaded. "I ride a desk for a living."

"You do?" Poseyemu's grandmother seemed astonished. "Why would you do that?"

"Not literally," Jeannette leaned against a fence post, catching her breath. "I'm an accountant. That means I sit behind a desk all day. I'm out of shape. I keep meaning to get to the gym, but I'm so tired after work that all I want is a good dinner and my furry slippers."

"Sounds good to me," the old woman agreed. "If I go more slowly, can you keep up? I don't want to wait too long."

"Okay." Jeannette took a long swig from her water bottle. "Lead on."

They were halfway up the steep path leading to the top of the mesa when Jeannette asked:

"I don't suppose you could enchant me or something?"

Poseyemu's grandmother glanced back at her. "What do you mean?"

Jeannette huffed the words out between breaths, "Make me stronger, faster. That way I could help you better."

The grandmother looked sad. "If I could do that, do you think I would have needed my little grandson to hunt for me and my daughter? My powers are those of the hot spring."

"Oh."

Whatever that means, Jeannette thought, concentrating on putting one foot in front of the other. *That way I will get to the top. It's simple mathematics. One plus one plus one eventually makes enough.*

At the top of the path, Jeannette leaned back against a thin, scraggly cottonwood tree to take another drink from her water bottle. As far as she could see in the failing light, the cottonwood was the only tree of its kind up there. All the other growth was scrubby juniper, piñon, and various kinds of cactus.

"I wonder how it manages," she said, trying to distract herself from the ordeal ahead. "I thought cottonwoods needed lots of water."

"Sometimes," Poseyemu's grandmother said, "a little tree can have very deep roots. Hurry now. We have a ways to go yet."

They followed a footpath through the scrub growth, carefully avoiding the cactus, especially the many-armed cane cholla that grew just about everywhere. At length, after crossing the sandy bed of a dry river and climbing a steep path along a hillside covered with rocks, they came to the ruins of Pose'uinge.

Jeannette acutely recalled her disappointment when yesterday's tour had arrived at the ruins. She'd expected something like the photos she'd seen of the Anasazi ruins at Mesa Verde or Chaco Canyon: intricately patterned walls built from small slabs of stone; buildings rising to two or more stories, their ancient, weathered wooden beams still in place; narrow doorways or windows letting light into cool interior chambers.

Pose'unige was nothing more than a series of gently sloping hills covered with scrub growth and sparse grass. That was it: not a wall, not a roof, not a hint of a kiva or shrine. Nothing.

She remembered a story their guide, Craig, had told them. Craig had been out here with a couple of friends when a young woman had come up to them. "Excuse me," she'd said. "Isn't there an Indian pueblo somewhere around here?" "You're standing right on it, Miss," the guide's friend had told her.

Most of the tour had laughed when the guide told this story, but Jeannette had felt her cheeks burn with embarrassment. *She'd* been about to ask the same question. Even after Craig had assured them that the pueblo was here, that the adobe buildings had simply melted back into the dirt, she had been reluctant to believe him and so prove herself as credulous as that unknown girl. After a while, though, she had come to believe.

The first clues were the broken pieces of pottery scattered on the ground: potsherds, the guide had called them. Most were white with complicated patterns painted on them in black, but there were gray corrugated sherds, too. In some of these, you could find faint prints of the fingers that had pressed the coils into shape.

Then there were the little chips of stone, most left over from making stone tools. Everyone looked, but no one found any arrowheads. Craig showed them how to recognize the trash middens from the greater concentration of sherds in those areas and from the grayish tint that ash from old fires had given the soil. He showed them how the little mounds which had seemed so erratically placed were actually the remnants of buildings clustered around open areas that had been plazas.

When the time had come to leave, Jeannette had paused and looked back. For a moment she could actually see the village that had once stood there, imagine women grinding corn in their stone *metates,* imagine the men bragging as they chipped out tools, imagine the shouts of the children as they rolled hoops or tossed hide balls in the plazas. Then it was just a group of hills again.

The last thing Craig had done was make everyone turn out their pockets. He'd explained that although some of the land belonged to the spa, most belonged to the Bureau of Land Management. The spa had an agreement with the Federal Government permitting limited hiking and riding on the land. In exchange, the staff worked very hard to teach appreciation of the cultural remains and to enforce Federal laws regarding theft.

"There's a hefty fine," he'd said, "and a prison term as well. So leave those sherds and bits of rock here. Maybe someday there'll be the money for a proper dig and those pieces could be the means to understanding the people who once lived here."

Everyone had agreed, though a couple of tourists had grumbled that a few sherds out of so many couldn't matter at all. However, the threat of being fined under Federal law had shaken all but the boldest.

Jeannette thought about that as she followed Poseyemu's grandmother along the twisting path. What did these pot hunters hope to gain that made taking such risks worthwhile?

She answered her own question immediately. In the last decade or so, even modern Indian pottery had become very collectible and—in some cases—very expensive. The antique stuff was almost impossible to obtain now that Federal laws made pot hunting a crime on public lands and the Native peoples appreciated the perishable nature of their heritage. The sale price of one intact bowl or pot could make even a substantial fine worth the risk. Tonight, though the pot hunters weren't aware of it yet, they were going to strike pay dirt.

Unless, Jeannette swallowed hard, *unless Poseyemu's grandmother and I can stop them.*

They located the pot hunters by their lights. These were well-shielded, but the ambient glow coming out of the ground looked eerie, almost supernatural. Jeannette shivered, but she could no more pull herself away than a moth could ignore a candle flame.

"They've found a kiva," Poseyemu's grandmother whispered. "The very kiva where Poseyemu taught the people to hide their sacred dances from prying eyes. This is very bad."

Jeannette knew that kivas were the subterranean rooms used for ceremonies by the Pueblo Indians even today, but she had no idea what the pot hunters might find in one. Pottery, she guessed, since that seemed to be everywhere, maybe masks or figurines or beads.

"But what do we do?" she whispered back.

Poseyemu's grandmother shrugged. "I don't know. You were the one who dreamed wonderful dreams. What do you think we should do?"

Jeannette didn't think that this was particularly fair, but she didn't have the courage to say so to the strange old lady. Instead, she crept a little closer, moving to where she could get a look at what the pot hunters were doing.

She managed to get quite close by crawling up one of the mounds. The kiva was just below. Quite possibly it originally had been dug in or near one of the plazas. When its roof had collapsed, it had become nothing more than a deep hole that had gradually filled with windblown matter and rocks.

The pot hunters had cleared out a lot of the fill dirt, detecting the walls of the kiva by some mysterious art at which Jeannette could only guess. There were three: one digging, one shifting the dirt through a screen, and one standing guard. Despite the guard, they didn't seem at all nervous. The man screening had a cigarette smoldering in one corner of his mouth.

"This is a waste of time," he grumbled.

The guard replied, "If this is a kiva, like I think it is, there might be more here than pots. We don't want to miss beads or anything, do we?"

"Guess not," the screener replied. He paused to look down into the pit where the digger was grubbing about with a trowel. "What you got, Tom?"

The digger rose, cradling something reverently in his hands. "A bowl. Nearly hit it with the shovel, but something made me slow down."

When he lifted his find into the light, Jeannette could see that he held a small, shallow bowl only slightly larger than his cupped hands.

"Biscuit B Black-on-white," he said in satisfaction, "and a nice example, too. Box it for me, Bud. I want to see what else might be down here."

"Right." The guard accepted the bowl and crouched to wrap it in old newspapers.

Jeannette watched Tom start digging again, her thoughts in turmoil. The voice of Bud, the man on guard, was terribly familiar. In a moment she placed it. He'd been the guide on the horseback tour the day before! They hadn't called him Bud, though. . . .

She suddenly remembered his name. Craig! Craig Hillsen. He'd been an undergraduate archaeology student, he'd told them, but he hadn't been able to get work as anything other than a skilled laborer, so he'd taken a job giving these tours.

A strange fury burned in Jeannette's heart. This was worse than just pot hunting. What Craig was doing was akin the betrayal, because he *knew* better. If these men had just been poor farmers from the Ojo Caliente Valley, the theft would have been bad enough, but this!

She wondered if both of the other men were trained as well, decided that at least the man in the pit probably was. He handled his tools with too much delicacy to be otherwise.

"You have learned something?" Poseyemu's grandmother whispered in her ear.

Jeannette jumped. The old woman had glided close as quietly as the steam lifting from her hot springs. A small exclamation, swallowed at once, escaped Jeannette's lips.

"Someone's out there!" Bud/Craig said, flashing his light across the mounds.

"Shut up, dickhead!" Tom growled softly. "Probably just a cow. If you keep shouting like that, one of these New Agers might come looking."

"I heard something," Craig insisted sullenly, but he let his light drop and Jeannette thanked whatever impulse had made her freeze rather than run.

She knew from that moment, however, that there was no way she could capture these three men. As much as she wanted to leap from concealment, shrieking like her favorite television heroine, she had to face the knowledge that she was nothing more than a short, overweight accountant. The facts depressed her, but they also gave her an idea.

Slowly, carefully, she began to retreat down the edge of the mound.

"Where are you going?" Poseyemu's grandmother hissed softly, sliding after her. "We must stop them!"

"We will," Jeannette promised. "And not just for tonight, but for good!"

* * *

The first thing she did was find the men's four-wheel drive truck parked alongside the trail used for the horses. Quickly, she unscrewed the cap from the gas tank and then dug into her purse.

"Here," she said, pulling out brown packets of organic sugar and handing them to Poseyemu's grandmother. "Pour this into the gas tank. That'll keep them from getting away."

"They could walk down by the trail to the spa," the old woman said, obeying nonetheless, a wicked smile on her wrinkled face.

"They could," Jeannette agreed, "but they won't want to carry shovels and screens and—most of all—looted pottery out that way. They'll either have to leave the stuff or take an even longer way around. Either way, it'll slow them."

All the truck's doors and windows were locked, and Jeannette didn't know whether to be relieved or disappointed. She wasn't certain if she'd be committing a burglary if she went into the truck without the owner's permission. However, she carefully copied the license number, model, and make onto the pad she always carried for recording deductible business expenses.

"Are you done?" she asked Poseyemu's grandmother.

"Yes. What are you going to do next?" Poseyemu's grandmother asked.

"Go back to the spa."

"But the shrine!"

"If your grandson is such a twit that he won't visit you because some men have been digging in his cellar, then he's due for a tongue-lashing from Granny," Jeannette replied, more confidently than she felt.

"I'm no hero," she continued. "It's time to call in the police and the BLM. I should have done that in the first place. I just got muddled about who I am . . . or maybe I was hoping that you could make me into someone else."

"No, I can't do that." The old woman's green eyes were shining in the pale moonlight. "But then I can't understand why you would want to be anyone else."

* * *

Walking down to the spa took time and convincing the local police took even more, but Jeannette and Poseyemu's grandmother were so persistent that a junior officer was sent out to check on their story just to shut them up.

The three of them arrived shortly before dawn to find the truck where they had left it, though shovels and such that Jeannette was prepared to swear had not been there before had been tossed into the back.

Then they made the wearisome climb up to Pose'-uinge. The kiva had been abandoned, but, even by the dawn's pale light, fresh digging was evident.

"They must have left," Poseyemu's grandmother said, inspecting the damage, "soon after we did. I don't think much more has been disturbed."

"I apologize," the officer said graciously, "for doubting you, ladies. You were onto something, but we're too late to catch them."

"Just a little late," Jeannette insisted. "One of the men who was here gives archaeological trail rides. We can get his address from the spa. Certainly you can get another of the men's names from the vehicle registration. In any case, they can't have gone far, not without their truck and if you bring them in, we can identify them."

"They still could have gotten away," the officer reminded her, but the fire of the chase was in his eyes. "I'll radio in your suggestions. That way we won't lose more time."

Jeannette pulled out her notepad. "I have the license number of the truck right here."

The officer nodded approvingly. "You have a very organized mind, Miss."

"Thanks. It goes with the job."

Much to Jeannette's disappointment, the officer dropped both of them off at the hot springs before driving off to join in the hunt for the fugitives.

"I guess," Jeannette said wistfully to the old woman, "that it's only in the movies that civilians get to be in at the capture."

"Those men may be desperate. They certainly have guns," Poseyemu's grandmother said. "I think it is better you are here."

"I *am* beat," Jeannette admitted, rubbing her eyes against a grubby sleeve.

"Go. Rest. Later this morning there will be news. They will probably want us to come identify the pot hunters."

"Right." Jeannette turned to walk to her cottage. "Do you need a bed?"

The old woman laughed. "You forget. I live here."

Then, right before Jeannette's eyes, she walked over to one of the arroyos, stepped in, and vanished.

Jeannette gaped, then grinned, imagining she could hear the old woman's laughter bubbling from the ground.

"Cute trick," she said. "Really cute."

* * *

A few months later, Jeannette sat at her desk doing a bit of recreational number crunching. In the weeks since her return, she had become something of a local hero.

Needless to say, there had been footprint evidence and other nifty forensic facts that tied the three men to the looted site, but it had been Jeannette's dramatic account of how she had watched the little bowl taken from the earth that had convinced the ordinary folks of the jury. That her description had precisely matched a bowl in the possession of the men when they were taken by the police hadn't hurt one bit.

Poseyemu's grandmother had confirmed Jeannette's testimony, but it had been the dramatic image of a young woman spying on thieves by night that had caught people's imagination. The fact that Jeannette was so ordinary that everyone had a sister or friend just like her had made Jeannette's bravery something people identified with.

"I didn't think I was brave at the time," she admitted over and over again. "I still don't think I was brave. I went. I saw. I ran away."

And she still didn't believe she had been brave, but if other people wanted to believe she had been, well, secretly she was rather pleased.

The experience had changed her—that she was more than willing to admit. Looting of archaeological sites would continue as long as there was a market for the stolen items. Quietly drawing on information the attorney for the prosecution had leaked to her, she began looking for evidence of where antiquities were being bought and sold.

This time she didn't do her lurking in ruined pueblos by night, but followed the paper trails that she was an expert at tracing. Already she had tracked down enough damaging information to force one prestigious gallery to quietly close its doors forever. A second gallery had donated a handsome collection of prehistoric pottery to the Museum of Indian Arts rather than face further investigation.

So that if she didn't get to do somersaults through the air and wave a sword? The villains were defeated nonetheless.

*   *   *

A tap on Jeannette's door made her pause in her contemplation of a very interesting column of figures. Putting her finger next to the important numbers, she looked up.

"Yes?"

The door opened and Poseyemu's grandmother walked in. Today she was wearing a green velvet broomstick skirt and a matching blouse with tarnished silver buttons. A thick necklace of rough turquoise beads that just happened to match her eyes hung around her neck.

"Grandma!" Jeannette greeted her happily, leaping to her feet. "Come in! What brings you to Santa Fe?"

"A little shopping, visiting some relatives." The old woman gave a sly grin. "My grandson is visiting, and I really want him to meet you."

"Grandma!" In the months of their acquaintance, Jeannette had learned that, water spirit or not, the old woman was a determined meddler.

The old woman only laughed and beckoned a handsome young Tewa man into the office. Poseyemu looked nothing like the heroes portrayed on the covers of popular romances. Indeed, he was hardly taller than Jeannette herself, but there was something likeable in his solid bearing and in the expression in his warm brown eyes.

He smiled shyly at Jeannette, then turned to his grandmother. "You're right. She's as fine a woman as you said."

"Grandma!" Jeannette protested.

The only answer she got was the old woman's laughter, bubbling up as warm and as healing as the waters of her spring.

*The eagle turns its attention to a golden-haired
woman who is staring thoughtfully into her bowl.
He flutters his wings, drawing her attention. She
nods in acceptance of the summons and drinks. At
the Western door the Seeker hears the roar of the
ocean and the creaking of moored fishing vessels.
Following a wharf to the water, she steps onto a
seaworthy craft embarking on the journey of:*

STRANGE CREATURES
by Kristine Kathryn Rusch

DAN Restler sat on the hull of a half-submerged boat,
the mud thick around his thigh-high fishing waders. In
his right hand, he held an industrial quality flashlight;
in his left a pocketknife. He was filthy and wet and
exhausted. Night was coming and there were still
hours of work to do, buildings to search, items to
move. He had managed to send the warning out early
enough to evacuate most of the homes along the river,
but the destruction was still heartrending, the loss almost unimaginable.

The trailers were the worst. The water had knocked
them about like Tonka Toys, ripping them in half,
crushing them, scattering them all over the low-lying
valley as if they weighed little more than matchsticks.

They were worth about that much now.

He ran a hand through his hair, feeling the thick

silt that seemed to have become a part of him. The foul stench of the mud might never come out of his nostrils.

The river looked so tame, a narrow trickle through the valley. He had seen the Dee flood before: once after a particularly wet December, and during the 1996 February storms, dubbed The Storm of the Century by commentators who felt it was pretty safe to apply that label when the century was nearly done. But he had never seen anything like this, so sudden, so furious, and so severe.

The Dee was a tidal river that opened into Hoover Bay just south of Whale Rock. High tides and too much rain often caused the Dee to flood her banks, but the floods were low and fairly predictable. Until 1996, no water had ever touched the trailer park, dubbed Hoover Village by some wag, and until that morning, had never touched the highway winding its way along the valley and into the Coastal Mountain Range.

The sun was going down, turning the sky a brilliant orange-red, with shades of deep blue where the clouds appeared. The Pacific reflected the colors. Retsler stared at it, knowing that any other day, he would have stopped, appreciated the beautiful sunset, and called someone else's attention to it.

A hand touched his shoulder. He looked up and saw the coroner, Hamilton Denne, standing beside him. Denne had a streak of river mud on the left side of his face, and his blond hair was spiked with dirt. His silk suit had splotches and watermarks, and his Gucci loafers were ruined.

Denne's wife would probably have a fit—she came from one of Oregon's richest families, and despised the fact that Denne still insisted on doing his job even though they didn't need the money. If anyone asked her what Denne did, she would tell them he was a doctor, or if they pushed, a pathologist. She never admitted to the fact that he worked best with corpses. He was able to keep the secret because the coroner's position was an appointed one in Seavy County, and no one ever printed his name in the papers.

In his left hand, Denne balanced a clean McDonald's bag and a cardboard tray with two Styrofoam cups of coffee. He nodded toward the sunset. "This looks like the best seat in the house. Mind if I share it? I'll pay my way with food."

Retsler didn't reply. Any other time, he would have bantered back, said something about bribing a public official, or teased Denne about whether or not he could have afforded the food. But Retsler didn't feel like banter. He didn't feel like company either, although he didn't say so.

Denne handed him the coffee tray, then sat beside him. Retsler took out a cup and wrapped his hand around it, letting the warmth sink through him.

"Didn't know what you liked, so I got everything," Denne said. "Whopper, Fish something or other, Biggie Fry—"

"Whopper's from Burger King," Retsler said.

"Well, you know me," Denne said. "It was my first time at a drive-through window. The wonders of technology."

Retsler was too exhausted to smile. He knew it wasn't Denne's first time in a fast-food joint, since he'd dragged the coroner to them countless times. Denne always protested, and then ate like a thirteen-year-old at a basketball game.

Denne was holding the bag open. Retsler reached inside, and pulled out a Big Mac and fries. The smell of grease and sugar made his stomach cramp, but he knew he had to eat. He pulled back the wrapper and took a bite, tasting mustard, catsup, pickles, and mayonnaise long before he got to the meat.

With the lining of his silk suit, Denne wiped mud off the boat's aluminum hull. Then he set the bag down, and rooted inside of it, pulling out a Fillet O' Fish. Denne had a penchant for the things, which Retsler always found odd, considering they lived in a place where they could get the freshest fish in the world.

"At the Club," Denne said, peeling the wrapper from his fish sandwich—he was referring to the Club at Glen Ellyn Cove, Whale Rock's gated community—"they have old maps of this coastline, some dating from the turn of the century. The last century."

Half of Retsler's Big Mac was gone. He was hungrier than he thought. He took a sip of coffee, waiting for Denne to finish. It was always easier to ignore Denne when the man was talking.

"Up until 1925 or so, this river wasn't the Dee at all. It was the Devil's River."

That didn't surprise Retsler. The Devil, in his opinion, had once dwelt on the Oregon Coast, eventually leaving behind his Punchbowl, his Churn, and oddly, his Elbow.

"When folks decided they wanted to bring tourism into Whale Rock, they shortened the name of the river." Denne took a bit of the sandwich and talked while he chewed. "Know why it was called the Devil's River?"

"Sea monster?" Retsler said. The food must have helped him feel slightly better. He answered Denne this time.

"No," Denne said. "That's Lincoln City. Devil's Lake."

Retsler wadded up the sandwich wrapper and shoved it in the bag. He sipped his coffee. It was black and burned. He drank it anyway.

"They called it Devil's River," Denne said, "because it flooded unexpectedly fourteen times between 1899 and 1919. On clear nights, they said, the river would rise and fill the valley until this place looked like a lake."

In the distance, cars swooshed across the Dee River Bridge, oblivious to the destruction hundreds of feet below them. The sun was gone now, leaving traces of orange against the night sky.

"You're saying this is not my fault," Retsler said.

"Acts of God happen," Denne said.

Retsler drained the Styrofoam cup. "You don't believe that."

"Of course I do."

Retsler turned to him. "Hamilton, you and I've seen some strange things in Whale Rock."

Denne's eyes were hidden by the growing darkness. "It was a freak storm."

"You've never lied to me before, Hamilton. Don't start now." Retsler stood, grabbed his flashlight, and flicked it on. The beam made the mud glisten. "Thanks for the comfort food."

Denne had his elbows on his knees, his right hand holding the cup by the lip. "Dan," he said. "You didn't start this thing."

Retsler paused, wondering why that didn't make him feel better. Then he said, "And I didn't end it either."

* * *

It had begun a few days earlier, on the first day of the new year. Retsler had answered the call about a suspicious smell on the beach.

The woman who obviously had made the call sat in the loose sand near the concrete cinder blocks lining the beach access. Her black hair flowed down her back. The constant ocean breeze stirred a few strands, but she didn't seem to notice. Her legs were spread in front of her, her toes buried in the sand. She wore a light jacket despite the day's chill. Retsler had a sense that she had been crying, but she wasn't now. Instead, she was staring out to sea, as if the frothy brown surface—filled with dirt from the rainstorms of the last few days—held the answers to questions he hadn't even heard yet.

Retsler stood on the concrete slab above the beach access and watched her for a moment. She didn't seem to know she was being observed. Cool mist pelted his face. The moisture felt good. He hadn't gotten much sleep last night: fifteen drunk and disorderlies; dozens of drunk driving stops; illegal fireworks on the beach. By the time he had turned in, about four a.m., he was praying that the Y2K bug would hit on Christmas so that no one could travel to the coast for New Year's Eve. Vain hope, he knew, but it was the only one he had.

He walked down the sand-covered ramp. Driftwood littered the beach, a testament to the rough surf of the last month. The air stank of charred wood and something else, something he didn't want to think about.

When he reached her, he crouched. "Maria Selvado?"

She raised luminous brown eyes to his. Her eyes were so dark they seemed to have no pupils. The whites were stunningly clear. There was moisture on her lower lashes, but he couldn't tell if it was from the mist or from tears. "Yes?"

"I'm Dan Retsler. I'm the chief of police here in Whale Rock." As if that meant something. He ran a department of ten, double what they'd had two years ago. Whale Rock was big enough to keep them busy, but not big enough to pay the salaries of more officers.

"Thanks for coming. I didn't know who to call."

Probably Fish and Game, he thought. Or the State Department of Natural Resources. Half a dozen agencies probably had jurisdiction over this one.

"Where?"

She waved a hand toward the surf. "That one."

He followed her gaze. The remains of a bonfire, piled high on a dune. He swallowed hard, thankful that he hadn't partied the night before, and stood.

The stench was intermittent, whenever the breeze happened to blow in his direction. Otherwise, he smelled only the salty ocean freshness and knew it could lull him into thinking nothing was wrong.

He slogged through deep sand as he walked up the dune, then crossed to a driftwood log the color of long abandoned houses. On the other side of the log was a pile of charred wood half covered in sand, and about two dozen beer cans, scattered in a semicircle. The odor was strong here, and mixed with the smell of Budweiser and old vomit.

The carcass lay half in the fire, flesh burned and bubbled, but still recognizable by shape: a seal pup, skinned. Bile rose in his throat and he swallowed it down, reminding himself that he had seen worse and not too long ago: the cats in the bag by the river, the dog the vet said had been tortured for days, the horse, still alive, and half-crazed by knife wounds all along its flank.

Retsler had read the studies, been to schools, knew the psychiatric lingo. Serial killers started like this—usually as teenagers, practicing on bigger or more difficult targets, needing a greater thrill each time to duplicate that same sick feeling of pleasure.

Seal pups. Jesus.

He looked away, stared at the ocean just as the woman had been doing. The sun peeked through a break in the clouds, falling on the white caps, adding a golden hue to the ocean's brown and blue surface. He reached into his pocket and pulled out his cell phone, flipping it open and hitting his speed dial.

After two rings, he got an answer. "Hamilton," he said, "sorry to disturb your holiday, but I've got something I need you to see."

* * *

The woman chose to wait beside him. When he told her he could take her statement, if she wanted, and then she could go, she shook her head. She seemed to think her actions warranted an explanation because, after a few moments, she told him that she worked at the Hatfield Marine Science Center in Newport. Her speciality was seals.

Denne saved him from answering. Retsler heard the rumble of Denne's rusted Ford truck, the one he'd bought in November against his wife's wishes, because he was tired, he said, of showing up at crime scenes in his silver Mercedes. Not that there were that many murders in Seavy County, which was Denne's jurisdiction, but Denne had an eye for detail and a knowledge of the obscure that made him useful to all the police departments in the county. For a job that was supposed to be part-time, a job that should have taken very little of his precious social time, it seemed to be a major preoccupation for him, one that was growing more and more of late.

The door slammed and Denne made his way down the beach. Retsler led him to the carcass, and watched as Denne's face went white.

"This is how someone chose to ring in the New Year?" he asked.

Retsler stuck his hands in the back pockets of his

jeans. "I want you to treat this like a human murder scene. And then we'll—"

"Compare it to that dog, I know." Denne glanced at the ocean, then at the bonfire. "They wanted us to find this. It's above the high-waterline."

"Or maybe they were just careless," Retsler said. "That's a lot of beer."

"Looks like it was some party," Denne said. "I'll bet there're one or two people who aren't happy about how it ended."

"Thought of that," Retsler said.

"You know you'll have to call the state. These pups are protected. Hell, you could get slapped with a gigantic fine if you move a live one. I have no idea what happens if you kill one."

"It's the same thing," Retsler said. Tourists came across seal pups alone on the beach all the time, then picked the poor things up and hauled them to a vet, thinking they were orphans. The act of kindness always doomed the pup, whose mother had left it on the beach on purpose and would have been back for it. Very few pups were ever safely returned to the wild; most died after being separated from the mother.

"It's not quite the same," Denne said, and went to work.

* * *

After he'd collected the beer cans and all the other evidence he could find, Retsler offered to drive Maria Selvado back to Newport, but she refused. She said she was staying in Whale Rock for her work. She had told him, as if it were more a threat than a promise, that she would drop in his office on Monday to find out how his work was progressing.

He had left Denne to the mess, and had driven back to the station. It was in the center of downtown, with a display window that overlooked Highway 101. The station had once been prime retail space, but Retsler's predecessor had demanded, and received, the building because, he said, most crimes were committed just outside its doors.

That was true enough. One most days, the police log was something Jay Leno might read as a joke: two people pulled over for running red lights; *Slow Children* sign vandalized (for the eighth time) on South Jetty Road; lost puppy found in front of Safeway store, identified, and returned to owner.

It was the other days that were difficult: the spur-of-the moment kidnapping outside the local Dairy Queen; the Fourth of July gang war that featured rival gangs imported from Portland; the drownings, search-and-rescue operations, all caused by the stupid things tourists did on the beach. If someone asked him how hard his job could get, those were the things he mentioned. He never brought up Whale Rock's secret side.

Denne was familiar with it, and Retsler's dispatcher, Lucy Wexel, was a firm believer that there was some sort of vortex here that brought out the magic in the world. Retsler's introduction to it had come two years ago when intact and seemingly recently deceased bodies appeared on the beach, all from the same sixty-year-old shipwreck. Then there were the three so-called women who seduced people to their deaths in the sea; Retsler had seen them, and narrowly escaped. Denne called them mermaids, but they weren't. They were sirens, perhaps, or sea hags, and they were something Retsler never ever talked about.

Eddie was working dispatch today with Retsler on call. New Year's Eve was always a nightmare, but New Year's Day was usually as quiet as a church—people were either too hung over or too tired to get out of the house. Even though the sun was peaking through the clouds, the beach was empty, something Retsler was grateful for.

Eddie was sitting with his feet on Lucy's desk, a *Car and Driver* magazine on his lap, and three Hershey's candy wrappers littering the floor around him. When Retsler entered, Eddie sat up, and immediately started cleaning.

"Sorry, Boss. Didn't expect you."

Retsler waved a hand. "You're fine."

"Figure out what died on the beach?" Eddie, of course, had taken Selvado's call.

"Seal pup. Skinned and burned."

"Je-zus." Eddie whistled, then shook his head. He'd seen a lot of the strange things around Whale Rock as well, but they never ceased to surprise him either. "What the hell would anyone do that for?"

"Kicks, it looks like." He took one of Eddie's candy bars. "Mind?"

Eddie shook his head.

"Do me a favor. Look through the files, see if you can find more animal killings, anything that predates that spate of them we had last year."

"You got it."

"And do a location map for me, too, would you?"

"Sure." Eddie actually looked relieved. He was usually patrolling because he liked to be busy. He wasn't suited for dispatch.

Retsler went through the open door into his tiny office. He didn't pull the blinds on the glass windows—another feature left over from the retail days—but he sat down hard at his desk. Incident reports from the night before littered the left corner. He stared at them for a moment, as if they were the enemy, then he frowned.

He might find something in them as well.

He slid them over to the center of his desk, and began to scan. He had to sign off on them anyway—

a departmental policy as old as Whale Rock and one
he saw no need to change—and he might as well do
so now while he was waiting for Denne. Retsler had
a few incident reports of his own to file from the night
before, as well as the one this afternoon, but he wasn't
ready to put anything down on paper.

Fifteen reports later, almost all of them drunk and
disorderlies, almost all of them depressing in their
sameness, Retsler stood and stretched his cramping
hand.

"Hey!" Eddie said from the front. "Got something weird."

Retsler left his desk and walked to the dispatch
area. Eddie had files scattered around him—both of
them would pay dearly for that when Lucy came in
on Monday morning—and at the center of it all, a
map of Whale Rock. There were multicolored dots all
over the village. Retsler had forgotten how good
Eddie was at details. Usually he didn't have to focus
on them when he was on the street.

"I used red for this year," Eddie said. "I mean, last
year. You know, '98. Green's for '97, and blue's for
'96. I put the seal pup in last year's because the poor
thing probably died before sundown."

"How do you figure?" Retsler asked.

"It takes a lot of work to skin an animal, don't care
how good you are at it. It's harder if you can't see
too good."

"They had a bonfire."

"And found a seal pup at night? I don't think so."

He had a good point. Retsler made a mental note
of it. He leaned over the map and saw, while there
were a few dots all over the city, the biggest concentration of them was around Hoover Bay.

"That's odd," Retsler said.

"That's what I thought," Eddie said, pointing to
them. "And they're mostly from the last year or so.

The rest're what you'd expect, and if I'd had time, I'd've marked 'em by month, too. Outside the bay, most of the animals died between May and September."

"Tourists."

"Sicko, psycho kids, probably brought to the beach because there's nothing for them to tear up, or so the parents think."

That was one of the things Retsler hated the most about summer, the teenagers who invaded from other towns. After they saw the single movie playing at the Bijou, shopped at all the stores, and found out that the casino just outside of town really did enforce its eighteen and above rule, they turned to vandalism or small acts of terror to take up their time.

"What about the others?" Retsler asked.

"Late '96, spaced about a month apart. Been escalating since October. That dog you found tied to the river piling was only two weeks ago, and the cats a week before that."

"You forgot the horse," Retsler said.

"Horse?"

"You know, Drayton's new mare, the one they'd bought their daughter for Christmas."

"Oh, yeah," Eddie said, and grimaced in distaste. "It's not down here as a killing."

"It should have been," Retsler said. "The vet had to put her down." The little girl had been heartbroken, and convinced, somehow, that it was her fault. The parents had promised her a new horse, but she had refused, saying she couldn't be sure it would be safe. The parents had looked at Retsler then, perhaps wanting him to reassure her, but he said nothing. He wasn't sure the family would be safe on their hillside retreat, with its two-mile long road and 360-degree view of the ocean and the river. He'd felt the horse incident was particularly cruel and had thought perhaps it had been directed at the Draytons.

Now he wasn't so sure. They lived awfully close to Hoover Bay, and a horse wasn't a dog or a seal pup. Horses had an amazing amount of strength.

Had the horse been the killer's attempt to ratchet up the pleasure, only to be thwarted? Maybe that's why the killer went after something like a seal pup, something so helpless and vulnerable and cute that it would be easy to kill.

A shiver ran through Retsler. He didn't like what was loose in his little town.

* * *

Denne showed up three hours later. He was wearing a Harvard sweatshirt over a pair of chinos. His deck shoes were mottled and ruined, and he wore no socks. Retsler had seen the outfit before. It was the one Denne kept at his office and used only when something at a crime scene made him leave his regular clothes behind.

Denne's blond hair was ruffled and his mouth a thin line. He pulled open the door, nodded to Eddie, and then came into Retsler's office without knocking.

Retsler had just finished going through the reports. Nothing from the area of the beach where they had found the seal pup. He would have expected something to come from the nearby hotels, perhaps, someone seeing the skinning of the pup or getting upset by the conduct of the beer drinkers. He was surprised no one had complained about the smell until that afternoon.

Denne sat in the chair before Retsler's desk. Even though he was wearing his grubbiest clothes, Denne's pants still had a crease, and even his sweatshirt looked pressed.

"If you can call two a pattern," Denne said without preamble. "We've got one."

"Looks like a different m.o. to me," Retsler said. He'd had all afternoon to think about it. "Dog tortured to death, left on a stake beneath the Dee River Bridge. Pup's skinned and burned on the beach. All those beer cans. I'm thinking a bunch of drunk kids got carried away—"

"Whoever skinned that pup was an expert," Denne said. "The flesh was clean in the unburned areas. And the pup bled. It was alive, at least for part of it. But that isn't the clincher."

Retsler folded his hands over the report. He hadn't wanted to hear that the pup was alive. He hated some of the things this profession made him think about.

"The clincher is the knife itself. It's one of those thin serrated knives, made especially for that sort of work. Around here, folks usually use knives like that on deer or elk. It's got a slick nick in the blade. It leaves an identifiable mark. The dog and the pup had it. If I'd thought to keep those cats, I bet they'd have had it, too."

Retsler sighed. Apparently Denne took that for disappointment because he added, "If I were dealing with human deaths here, I could make a case for a serial killer based on the knife evidence alone."

"What else have you got?"

"Some fibers. A pretty good print, in blood, on the body itself."

"Good," Retsler said. "That's a start. With that, and the cans, we might be able to find something."

"Hope so." Denne stood, then paused as if he had a thought. "There's one more thing. It may be nothing, or it might be everything."

"What?" Retsler asked.

"Did you find the pelt?"

Retsler shook his head. "I assumed it got burned."

"No. There was no fur in the fire at all, and they were too far from the waterline for it to have been swept away with the tide."

"I'd better get someone to comb the beach, then," Retsler said.

"Yeah," Denne said. "But I don't think you'll find anything."

Retsler met his gaze. "You think our friend is selling the pelts?"

"Probably not. I have a hunch we're dealing with someone young here."

Retsler felt himself go cold. "Trophy hunter."

Denne nodded. "I suspected it with the dog, and I bet, if I looked at your report on the cats, I could find something, too."

"The horse's mane," Retsler murmured.

"Hmm?"

"Nothing," Retsler said.

"If you don't find that pelt," Denne said, "I'd bet every dime I've got that our killer still has it."

"Should make it easier to convict someone."

"On what? Animal cruelty?" Denne said. "Seems minor for this kind of offense."

Retsler agreed, but felt the day's frustration fill him. "What am I supposed to charge him with? Prospective serial killing?"

"Wish you could," Denne said.

"We'll get the state involved," Retsler said. "Maybe they'll have ideas."

"They'll think we're a small town with too much time on our hands."

"Maybe they would have with the dog or the horse," Retsler said. "But we're dealing with a seal pup. That makes TV news reporters sit up and beg."

"Think twice before you invite those vultures here," Denne said. "They'll mess up the entire case."

"I'll wait," Retsler said, "until I have something that'll stick."

Denne nodded. "I'll give you all the help I can."

Retsler smiled. "You've already given me plenty."

* * *

The weekend wasn't as calm as Retsler would have liked. Two major traffic accidents on 101 backed up traffic for hours and caused several more citations. A suspicious fire downtown in one of Whale Rock's failing seasonal businesses had Retsler calling in a state arson team. A Saturday night bar fight got out of control and spilled into the street, forcing Retsler to call his entire team to help quell the violence. He wasn't able to think about seal pups and animal mutilations until he arrived at work at 8 a.m. Monday morning, sleep deprived, bruised, and more thankful than he cared to admit that all the tourists had finally gone home.

Lucy was already at her desk, an unlit cigar in her mouth. She had curly gray hair and a military manner that her grandmotherly face somehow softened. Retsler had known her since he was a boy, and sometimes she still made him feel like that boy. He really didn't want to cross her.

She had two tall cups from Java Joe's on her desk. As he passed, she handed him one. He turned to her in surprise. She had made it clear, when he became chief, that she didn't do windows or coffee.

"What's this for?"

"I figure you haven't gotten no rest since New Year's Eve. Caffeine won't cure it, but it'll cover it up."

He grinned at her. "You're a lifesaver, Lucy."

She frowned. "Don't go ruining my reputation."

"I won't tell a soul."

"Good," she said. Then she leaned back in her chair. "You got a woman in your office."

He glanced over, surprised he had missed it. Maria Selvado was sitting primly in the chair in front of his desk, a vinyl purse clutched to her white sweater. Her coat hung over the back of the chair, and she wore what appeared to be a very cheap pair of boots beneath her faded jeans.

"How long's she been here?"

"Half hour or so. I told her you don't normally come in until ten."

"Lucy!"

Lucy chuckled. "Well, I figured if you got in any earlier than ten, she'd think you were good at your job."

"I am good at my job."

"Just goes to show," Lucy said. Then she raised an eyebrow at him. "And if you let that Eddie dig in my files again, so help me God, I'll pour that coffee down your back."

"Yes, ma'am."

This time it was Retsler who chuckled as he headed to his office. Maria Selvado turned her face toward him. She looked even more exotic in the artificial light. "Chief," she said in greeting.

"Dan," he corrected.

She nodded. He sat behind his desk. She leaned forward, still clutching that purse. "I came for an update."

"I can't tell you much," he said. "We know that the pup's death is part of a pattern, and we are working on that angle. We have some leads—"

"A pattern?" she muttered.

He stopped, frowning. She seemed disturbed by his words. "Yes. There have been other animals killed in the same area—"

"But not other pups."

"Not that we know of."

She let out a small breath. The news seemed to relieve her. "But you have nothing on the killer."

"Not yet."

She raised those liquid eyes to his, and he thought he saw accusation in them. He parted his hands defensively, and then shook his head a little. He didn't have to defend himself to anyone.

But he did say, because he felt she needed to know, "We don't have much of a lab facility here. We've sent several items to the State Crime Lab. We should hear later today."

She bit her lower lip. "You'll keep me informed."

"If I know where I can find you."

"I'm at the Sandcastle."

He shuddered. He couldn't help it. Someone bought the land a year ago, and in that time tore down the old hotel. The new one had the look of the old—once one of the coast's premier resorts—and people from all over the world had flocked to it in the last few days of the summer. But he had memories of the Sandcastle, memories of finding intact bodies in front of it, memories of unusual goings-on that dated to his boyhood—talk of ghosts and kelpies and strange creatures that emerged from the sea.

She looked amused. His reaction must have been visible. "They've remodeled," she said. "It's quite nice."

"I have no doubt."

She smiled and stood, her movements fluid and graceful. "Thank you for cooperating with me, Chief."

"You're welcome," he said, and waited for her to leave before he shut his office door.

* * *

That night, Lucy chose the dinner spot and, as always, she picked the False Colors. It was a pirate-themed bar just off 101, but more locals went there than tourists. The sea chanties played low, the fireplace that burned real wood, the ropes and life rings that came from real ships played to the out-of-towners, but most people who came to the coast brought their families. The skull and crossbones that decorated most corners, the human skulls on the mantel, the tales of death and murder framed on the walls were not the best atmosphere for children, so tourists usually came once and left, allowing the locals to enjoy the excellent food and the even better bar.

Retsler ordered his usual, a cutely named fish and chips entree that came with a large salad and a double order of bread. He got a Rogue Ale with that, and planned to get a huge dessert, thinking that the combination might allow him to go home and go to sleep at 9 p.m.

Lucy had the fisherman's platter, a meal three times the size of Retsler's, and he knew by the end of the evening, she would have eaten all of it. After a few minutes, Eddie joined them.

He was still in uniform, and as he sat down, June, the waitress, scurried over. "You know Jeff don't like it when you guys come in your blues," she said in a half-whisper.

"What's he going to do, call the cops?" Lucy asked and then smiled, a grandmother with fangs.

"It's just he doesn't think the presence of police adds to the atmosphere."

"He's afraid the real pirates will stop patronizing the place," Lucy said and chuckled.

"It's okay," Eddie said. "I won't do it again. It's just I had to talk to Dan, and I didn't have time to change."

"Tell Jeff it's January fourth and the tourists went home, not that they're going to be in here anyway," Dan said. "And tell him he can chase his regulars away if he wants, but this is the slow season and it probably wouldn't be wise."

June bobbed her head. "It wasn't from me, you know. It's just that Jeff—"

"Is delusional." Lucy picked up a crab leg and broke it in half. "We know."

June flushed. "You want something, Eddie?"

"Burger and fries and a diet."

June left and Eddie leaned forward. "I've got a couple of things on that seal pup killing," he said softly, even though there were no other patrons within hearing range. "Okay to tell you here?"

Sometimes Retsler frowned on discussing work at the False Colors. But that was usually in the summer, when the place was packed with first-timers who really didn't need tales of car crashes and children crushed by driftwood logs as an accompaniment to their meals.

Retsler picked up a fry. "Let's hear it."

Any news would be good news. Retsler expected a visit the next morning from Maria Selvado, and he hadn't heard from the crime lab yet. He supposed he could give her some information from Denne's autopsy of the pup, but even someone as involved as Selvado probably didn't want to hear about knife serrations and the fact that the pup had been skinned alive.

Retsler winced at the memory.

"You okay?" Eddie asked.

Retsler nodded. Then the main door opened, and Denne walked in. Retsler looked up. Denne's wife had expressly forbidden him to come here. She had discovered, through small-town gossip probably, that twice before he had turned up here to discuss a case, and had demanded that he not disgrace the family by showing his face in the False Colors again.

Yet there he was, in a charcoal-colored silk suit with a sterling silver pocket watch attached to a fob on the outside. His blond hair had been slicked back, and his aesthetic face looked almost haunted.

"She's pushing him too hard," Lucy murmured. "He's drifting over to the other side."

Retsler started, then considered the evidence: the truck, the clothes Denne had worn home on New

Years, and now the appearance at the False Colors. Denne was abandoning his gated community for the peasants who ran this small town.

Eddie sighed. "You want to hear this or not?"

"Let's wait for Hamilton," Retsler said as he waved. Denne smiled—he never quite grinned—and walked down the worn stairs into the main dining area. As he did, he stopped June and ordered, then took the only empty chair at the table.

"Eddie," Retsler said, "was about to tell us news on our seal pup."

"Really?" Denne removed his suit coat and hung it on the back of the chair.

Then he rolled up the sleeves of his white button-down shirt, revealing muscular forearms. With his left hand, he loosened his tie, and pulled it off. The entire group was watching him with astonishment. Retsler could feel his own mouth open in surprise.

Denne raised his eyebrows. "Don't let me stop you, Eddie."

"Um, yeah." Eddie shot Denne a slightly perplexed look, then said, "I been having conversations all day, casual ones, you know."

Retsler did know. One of the strengths of Whale Rock was its citizens' willingness to discuss anything if approached properly by someone they knew. A glance at the ocean, a mention of the dead pup, and a softly worded query about something related often got a glut of information.

"And I didn't get nothing on anyone selling pelts."

"I called fifteen different departments," Lucy said as she stabbed a scallop with her fork, "and no one in the entire state of Oregon has heard of anyone poaching seals."

"I asked her to. Hope you don't mind, Boss," Eddie said.

A year ago, Eddie never would have taken that kind of initiative. "I gave you the legwork of the investigation," Retsler said. "You can divide it up how you want."

June brought Eddie's soda and an Alaskan Amber for Denne. Retsler looked at him in surprise, but Denne didn't seem to notice. Lucy did, however, and winked.

"Then what did you need to tell me?" Retsler asked when June left.

"You remember when they tore down the Sandcastle to make way for the new version?"

"A mistake if there ever was one," Denne said. "You do realize the hotel is on the beach."

They all looked at him. Building on the beaches—on the sand—was against the law in Oregon.

"How'd that happen?" Retsler said.

"You know the Planning Commission." Denne took a sip of the Amber and looked like a man who had just had the most sublime experience of his life.

"It's a state law," Lucy said.

Denne raised his eyebrows. "The Sandcastle Hotel predates the law. The Commission claimed they couldn't do anything because it grandfathers in."

"How much did Roman Taylor pay them?" Retsler asked.

"Pay them? Kickbacks, in our small town? Impossible." Denne leaned back. "Just a sidebar. Didn't mean to derail you, Eddie."

Eddie grunted, and took a sip of his drink. "Anyway," he said, "when they were bulldozing the Sandcastle, they found an open area underneath it. There was all kinds of junk under there, old watches, gold coins, shiny stuff. Some of it wasn't worth much, but some of it was worth a lot, and Taylor said he got it, because he bought the property. Nobody fought him about it and nobody tried to trace it."

"And, not surprisingly, nobody thought to call us," Retsler said.

Eddie nodded, meeting his gaze. "Ain't it amazing how some things just don't make it to our attention until we can't do nothing about them."

"So what do the shiny things have to do with this investigation?" Lucy asked.

"Well, in there was a pile of fur, all sleek and shiny. Turns out it was seal pelts—about twenty of them. Just beautiful things. I guess Taylor's the kind of guy who hangs deer heads on the walls and he was really excited about them pelts. He took them home."

Retsler whistled. "This was what? Last January?"

"Yep," Eddie said. "And that's not all. Various folks have come up asking for them seal pelts, even though the only people who knew about them were the digging crew and Taylor. Taylor won't talk to anybody about them."

"Curioser and curiouser," Lucy said.

June set down Eddie's hamburger, and placed a double cheeseburger—an item the False Colors proudly called its Gut Blaster—in front of Denne. Retsler couldn't resist.

"Your wife isn't going to be too happy when you come home smelling of hot sauce, jalepeños, and onions."

Denne shrugged. "The woman's got to learn to calm down."

This time, Eddie was the one who raised his eyebrows. He picked up the catsup and proceeded to pour it all over his food. "I got one more thing to tell you about them pelts," he said. "The latest person who's come to inquire about them is Maria Selvado. She's been after Taylor since the first of December, and she's got the Marine Science Center behind her. Guess they're doing some sort of seal study or something, and the pelts would be really useful. They're even offering to pay him. But he won't meet with her. She says she's not leaving until he does."

"Our Miss Selvado gets around," Lucy said.

"Yeah," Eddie said. "She even went up to his house on the Dee. Got real mad when she saw how he's displaying the pelts. Guess he's got them in one of those wall-sized glass cases beside his fireplace. He came to the door and she was yelling something about pins ruining the fur, or something. Anyway, he threw her off the porch, damn near landed her in the river. She hasn't been up there since."

"But there was a break-in," Retsler said.

"Thwarted break-in," Lucy said. "The alarm kicked on with the sirens and all the lights, remember?"

"And tiny footprints, woman-sized, in the mud beside the window on the fireplace side of the house. Passionate woman," Retsler said.

"Mystery woman," Denne said. "She called me, asking if she could have the pup's body when I was through with it, said she wanted it for the Science Center. I offered to drive it over there for her—I mean, who wants a corpse in your car if you can help it?—and she turned me down. That made me suspicious, so I called the Science Center."

"And they'd never heard of her," Lucy said, her eyes sparkling as they always did when the story started getting juicy.

"Oh, they'd heard of her all right. But she hadn't worked for them for six months. Seems that she broke into the Oregon Coast Aquarium last summer, and was going to liberate the seals. Security stopped her before she made it to the outdoor pen, but the Aquarium offered not to press charges—which would have embarrassed the Science Center—if she promised to leave Newport. She did."

"And came here?" Retsler asked. "That seems odd to me. We're not that far from Newport."

Denne nodded. "The Science Center is none too happy that she's still representing herself as part of their staff. Not that she was ever staff-staff anyway. She was one of the student projects, interns or whatever, that they get coming through. But they still don't want their name connected to hers."

"And they have no interest in the seal pelts?" Retsler asked.

"None," Denne said.

Lucy nodded. "Selkies," she said.

All three of them turned to her. She grinned and shrugged. "Come on," she said. "We have no secrets between us. We are talking Whale Rock, aren't we?"

"Silkies?" Eddie asked.

"Selkies," Retsler said. He'd been boning up on his seafaring lore since the last strange encounter. "They look like seals in the sea, but when they come on shore and shed their skin, they look human."

"Oh, God," Eddie said.

"But don't they usually come looking for love?" Denne asked. "Aren't they supposed to mate with human women, leave them pregnant, and return to the sea?"

"You've been reading too many Celtic stories," Lucy said. "That may have been true hundreds of years ago, but I think selkies are more sophisticated than that."

"Sophisticated?" Denne placed his chin on the palm of his hand and looked at her. "Do you mean they're sending their children ashore in search of a better education?"

"You may mock me, young man, but think about it. What better way to find out about the things that threaten your people than to study those things?"

Retsler was silent. A lot threatened the seal population, which had been thinning in recent years. Some blamed oil spills farther up the coast, others blamed changes in commercial fishing laws, and still others blamed things like tourists taking pups off the beaches. Whatever the cause, there were fewer seals in the last few years than there had been in a long time.

"That seal pup," Denne said, "was one hundred percent seal. There was nothing magical about it."

"The myths say that the smaller seals—like the common seal—belong entirely to the animal world, but the larger seals, like the gray, the great, and the crested, can be selkie folk." Lucy pushed her plate aside. "How else do you explain the clean, unrotted pelts found among all that shiny stuff, as Eddie calls it? It was a nest, a place to hide wealth that enabled them to trade in Whale Rock."

Retsler put aside the remains of his fish and chips. "So?" he asked. "We have a bunch of selkies in human form walking around Whale Rock?"

"Or in the sea without their pelts. It's probably hazardous to their health." Lucy shook her head. "A year's a long time."

"What does this have to do with our dead pup?" Denne asked.

"Maybe nothing," Lucy said, "but selkies do have a kinship with seals. They're probably not happy about this."

"You think Maria Selvado is a selkie?" Retsler asked.

"I didn't say that." Lucy sniffed loudly. Of course she hadn't said that. She had implied it, like she often did, and Retsler could ignore her at his peril.

"Selkies," Denne mused. "I thought selkies were dangerous."

"Only if you're a man in lust," Retsler said.

"No," Lucy said. "They are dangerous, if you kill one."

"What?" Eddie asked, setting down the soda. "All the other selkies toss their pelts at you?"

"No," Lucy said. "If you kill one, don't get its blood in the ocean."

"Or?" Denne asked.

"Or a storm'll come up the likes of which you've never seen."

Retsler sighed. "Do you actually believe that, Lucy?"

She met his gaze. There was no twinkle in her gray eyes. "I've seen a lot of things, Dan. I don't disbelieve anything."

"But you don't actually believe it."

"Let me put it this way," Lucy said. "That myth is not one I'd want to test."

* * *

"The language is plain, Retsler," Roman Taylor was a large man, made to seem even larger by the low ceilings in the second story of his riverside home. He hunched over a rough-hewn log table, made to match the rough edges on the outer walls. The inner walls were smooth and painted white. It was on one of those that huge case with the pelts gleamed in the morning sunshine. "I brought the Sandcastle Hotel and all its contents. The pelts and the treasures around them in that room were inside the Sandcastle. No one disputes that."

Retsler stared at the deed before him. Apparently he stared too long because Taylor shifted from one foot to another.

The language was clear. Taylor did own the pelts and there was nothing Retsler could do about it.

"Maybe you should show this to the city attorney," Taylor said. "Then maybe people'll leave me alone."

"They'll leave you alone now," Retsler said. "Sorry to bother you."

Taylor nodded once at the apology. Then he glanced at the case. "That woman's crazy, you know. If I could find a way to get her out of my hotel, I would. If you could think of something, I'd be forever in your debt."

"Has she broken any laws, Mr. Taylor?"

"I'd be the first to scream if she did." He walked over to the case. "She says the seals that had these pelts are still alive, and they need them. Isn't that nuts? You can't skin an animal like this and have the animal live."

"Can I see one?" Retsler asked.

Taylor opened the case. The glass swung open, and the scent of fur and an animal musk filled the room. "Come here."

Retsler obliged. The pelts glistened as if they were still wet, but there was a dullness that was starting to appear around their edges.

Taylor picked up a corner of the nearest fur. "See that?" he asked. "Best work I've ever seen. Not a trace of flesh, no knife marks. Just the fur. Isn't it beautiful?"

Beautiful wasn't a word that Retsler would have used, but he nodded anyway.

"Hey, Dad!"

Both men turned. A teenage boy stood in the stairwell, face flushing when he saw Retsler.

"Didn't know you had company," the boy said.

"The chief's just leaving."

The boy grunted. He stood perfectly still as if movement weren't allowed. "Why're you showing him the pelts?"

Something in the question made Retsler look at the boy. The boy's eyes were bright, almost too bright. And cold. So cold that Retsler felt a chill run through him.

"He'd heard about them, that's all," Taylor said.

"Dad thinks those pelts are the real thing," the boy said, his chin raised in something of a challenge.

Retsler became completely still. "You don't?"

"I think they're fake. I think he should get them checked."

"Why?" Retsler asked.

"Because I don't care how good you are, you can't remove a pelt making a single cut."

"Hmm," Retsler said. "Have you tried?"

"He hunts with me sometimes," Taylor said too fast. "Don't you, Michael?"

"We've never hunted together in our lives. My father never pays attention to me." The boy tilted his head, eyeing Retsler speculatively. "You ever spend New Year's Eve on the beach, Chief?"

Retsler didn't answer. Taylor's face flushed.

"It's amazing what people'll burn—"

"Michael!" Taylor said.

The boy grinned and shrugged, as if he had just been making conversation. "Nice seeing you. *Chief.*"

And then he walked down the stairs. Retsler's entire body had turned numb. He had expected a teenager, but not one who would challenge him, although he had heard stories about Michael Taylor for the last year. A teacher at the high school had asked how to deal with a boy who seemed to love violence. A female student filed a complaint, only to withdraw it a day later.

Retsler debated for a moment whether or not he should follow, whether or not he should search the boy's room, and then decided the boy wouldn't issue a challenge like that if he expected to get caught. Better to take it slow, build a case the right way. Maybe Retsler could even talk to Taylor, convince him to send the boy to a hospital where he could get help.

"Sorry about that," Taylor was saying. "He's at that age when no adult is worth his time."

Retsler stared at him. Taylor's flush deepened. "You know we found a skinned pup on the beach New Year's Day."

"No," Taylor said. "I hadn't. It's amazing what people will do."

"Isn't it?" Retsler asked. He looked at the case again. "How many of these did you find?"

"Twenty," Taylor said. "And that's how many are there."

Retsler silently countered to himself. Twenty. If the other pelt were here, it was somewhere else. "Maybe I should take a peek at your son's room."

"Not without a warrant," Taylor said.

Retsler nodded. It played out just as he expected. He shrugged, like the boy had, then he thanked Taylor for his time, and left the house.

The river was low here, sixty feet down the bank, and sparkling in the bright sunshine. Taylor had bought the land and built the house the year before he had bought the Sandcastle. Lucy said that Taylor had spent that year getting on the good side of the Planning Commission. Lucy would know.

The pelts were disturbing, the boy more so. But Taylor had a legal right to the pelts, and Retsler would have to work hard to make anything more than a misdemeanor stick on the boy. Taylor had more money than God, which meant that he could afford the biggest lawyers in the country.

Retsler was suddenly walking into the big leagues, and he wasn't even sure he wanted to play the game.

* * *

The State Crime Lab could find no match on the fingerprints, nor did they have anything to say about the requests from Whale Rock. They apologized profusely, but perfunctorily, and probably, when they got off the phone, chuckled at the things that passed for important in small towns.

Retsler didn't care. He had other things to check. Lucy had called Seavy County Deeds and Records, and had found the date of Taylor's home purchase. It was one month before the animal mutilations started near Hoover Bay. Now she was checking with the local police department in Taylor's previous home in San Jose, hoping to find another pattern.

It wasn't much, but it was a start. He also had a call in to an old friend at the FBI who might have a few ideas on how to proceed in a case as delicate, and insubstantial, as this one. Animal deaths and mutilations were bad enough, but, truth be told, they weren't what Retsler was really worried about. What worried him the most were the coldness of that boy's eyes, and the possibility—make that the probability—of what the boy would become.

Retsler had all that on his mind as he drove to the Sandcastle. He wasn't sure why he wanted to see Maria Selvado, but he knew he probably should.

Her room was on the top floor of the Sandcastle Hotel. Like all of the rooms, it had double glass doors on the ocean side that opened onto an extra long balcony. When she led Retsler onto it, it made him feel as if he were standing over the water. He supposed, in high tide, that he would be. The balconies hung over the concrete breaker that protected the hotel from high surf—another illegal measure grandfathered in by the Planning Commission. Retsler had hated the look from the ground, but he had to admit that, from the balconies themselves, the view was spectacular.

Selvado had let him in, no questions asked. That she had been in her room on such a beautiful afternoon, neither of them mentioned. The room itself was spectacular. The door opened into a hallway which led to a large bathroom, passed a king-sized bedroom, and opened into a well-apportioned sitting room filled with antiques and facing a marble fireplace. The ubiquitous television was hidden in a wall unit that still looked suspiciously out of place. It was also covered with dust.

The ocean breeze had a trace of mist. Selvado raised her face to it as if it gave her life. She was obviously waiting for him to speak.

He cleared his throat. "I spoke to Roman Taylor today about the pelts."

She turned, stunned.

"He showed me the deed. They're clearly his."

"They have nothing to do with him," she said fiercely. "They don't belong to him."

"By law they do."

She bit her lip and turned away. "The law is wrong."

"The law is what we have, Ms. Selvado. It may not be right all the time, it may not make things easy, but it's what we have."

She shook her head. "It's not enough."

He knew that. He leaned on the balcony railing, and dangled his arms over the edge. This next part he did partly because he knew he had made her angry, and he agreed with Taylor: she had to leave Whale Rock. She was too unpredictable. Retsler was afraid she would try to break into Taylor's house again. If she got near that teenage boy, her own life might be in danger.

"I've also learned that you're presenting yourself as an employee of the Marine Science Center, and asking for privileges due to your position."

"I am—"

"You were," he said. "I found out about the dismissal. You're bordering on fraud, Ms. Selvado. I'll look at your actions as a simple misunderstanding right now, but any more of it, and I'll have to inform the Newport police."

She whirled toward him, her liquid eyes full of fire. There was a power to her, like the sea the day before a storm. "You wouldn't."

"I have to, Ms. Selvado."

"Taylor put you up to this."

"No." Retsler sighed. He would give her this next because he had to give her something, and then he would ask her to leave. "I'm dealing with Taylor in my own fashion. I'm trying to make a case against his son. I'm pretty sure the boy is the one who slaughtered that pup."

"Pretty sure?"

He held out his hands. "Meaning I'm convinced the boy's the one we want. I simply have to prove it. So if you'll leave me to my work, maybe I'll be able to help you."

"Bargain the boy's freedom for the pelts?"

"No," Retsler said. "I think the boy's too dangerous for that."

"Then what?"

"I'm not sure yet," he said, and felt the emptiness of his promise. "But I'll do the best I can."

"By asking me to leave town?" she asked.

"It's a start," he said.

"For you, perhaps." Then she paused. The ocean was a deep clear blue. The sunshine this early in January was unusual, and welcome. She stared at it as if it gave her an idea. "And maybe for me as well."

* * *

The next morning brought a spate of strange calls: boats all over the coastline and up the river had been damaged, not badly enough to ruin them, but enough to prevent anyone from going on the ocean that day. At a dock near Hoover Village, one old fisherman claimed he saw a group of seals nudging a hole in the hull of his boat, then moving to his neighbor's boat at the next mooring. Retsler had to call his entire staff in to meet the workload of examining each and every boat, and Lucy had the volunteer firemen help as well.

Retsler was so busy, he missed what later turned out to be the most important calls of the day.

Hotel patrons of the Sandcastle lit up the emergency lines with a gruesome tale: a dark-haired woman, bleeding from both arms, dove off her balcony into the sea.

When Retsler finally got the page, he knew at once who had died. Maria Selvado. And he had felt a chill. He went over to the Sandcastle, and demanded to be let into her room.

The door was locked from the inside. A bloody knife sat on the back of the toilet. The bathroom floor was covered with blood. The trail led to the balcony. There was only one set of footprints—women's size six, flat-footed (no arch) with webs between the toes. They ended at the railing, although there were bloody handprints on the iron, and another splotch of blood on the top of the concrete breaker.

The body below was gone, taken by the rising tide, returned to the sea.

On the fireplace mantel was a note addressed to Retsler. It said, simply: *When the laws of man fail, we rely on the laws of God.* And it was signed with an M.

* * *

The storm came an hour later, at high tide. Intense and furious, it concentrated on Hoover Bay, the Dee River, and Whale Rock. The rest of the coast had delicious sun and a perfect January day. In Whale

Rock, sustained winds of one hundred miles per hour ripped the roof off a gas station, tore down several signs, and knocked out power to half the town. Waves crossed the concrete breaker and smashed into the Sandcastle Hotel, destroying it as if it were made of paper.

Retsler had ordered an emergency evacuation of all low-lying areas, even though the National Weather Service swore that the satellite pictures showed no storm system in the vicinity. He had the radio and TV stations broadcast warnings, ordering everyone to high ground, to places that could survive winds, to places of safety. And because he was trusted, the town listened.

Someone later said that the storm would have caused a lot more destruction if it weren't for Retsler's clear thinking. Later they would call him a hero because he had saved hundreds of lives. That only two were lost in a freak storm, the governor would say, was miraculous. But Retsler knew better. He knew, the moment he saw the blood, how he failed.

* * *

Denne stood, a shadow in the growing darkness. He picked up the McDonald's bag and shoved his Styrofoam cup into it. Then he walked around the boat to Retsler.

"You've ruined those clothes," Retsler said, avoiding, knowing what he was avoiding. He shut off his flashlight, listening to the calm ocean in the distance, the gurgle of the river behind him. In the darkness, the cloying stink of the mud was almost overpowering. "The wife'll be mad."

"The wife isn't entitled to an opinion anymore," Denne said. "New Year's resolution."

"You can't stop a woman from having an opinion."

"You can when you move out." Denne turned on his own flashlight. The beam illuminated the mud before them, and the footprints that led up to the Taylors' log house. He put a hand on Retsler's back. "You can't avoid this forever, Danny."

"I'm not sure I want to see this in the dark."

"It won't be any better in the light."

Denne led the way down the path that, twenty-four hours before, had been covered with greenery and winter flowers. He mounted the stairs to the main level.

The windows were gone, the door off its hinges. The water damage was so severe that the rough-hewn logs looked as if they'd been polished smooth.

Denne ducked inside. He shone light toward the fireplace. It took a moment for Retsler's eyes to adjust. The light was reflecting off the glass on the case. He stepped away from the beam and peered inside.

Roman Taylor had been crammed into the square space, his arms and legs held in place by some wickedly tight knots. It didn't take a degree in forensic medicine to know that the man had been alive when he had been tied down. The watermark was two inches below the ceiling, and there was mud in the bottom of the case.

Mercifully, Denne moved the light. Retsler didn't use his.

"I'll photograph all of this tomorrow," Denne said.

"Three's no need," Retsler said. "He drowned."

Denne looked sharply at him.

Retsler shrugged. "Who am I going to charge?"

"You might want to wait until you see the rest." Denne led him down the stairs into the daylight basement. In the corner, someone had stuck a log into the floor. It looked like one of the mooring posts that littered the river. On it, Taylor's son Michael—or what was left of him—stared balefully at them.

Retsler swallowed hard to keep down the bile. He recognized the position—recognized everything, in fact, right down to the expression on Michael's face.

The dog. That was how they had found the dog.

Denne raised his flashlight beam. It caught on a knife stuck into the pole. The knife was serrated and used for gutting animals. The handle was ivory, and engraved on it, was this: *Michael Taylor, Happy 13th Birthday, Love, Dad.*

"Is it our knife?" Retsler asked.

"No doubt about it," Denne said.

Retsler closed his eyes. He would have had the proof he needed after all. Damn him for talking to Selvado. Damn him and his worries about a conviction. Damn him, and the lack of respect he had for his own abilities.

"Of course," Denne said slowly, "any good lawyer could make hash of a case based on one single knife."

"Really?" Retsler asked.

"I think so," Denne said. He took one more glance at the body. "And I don't think I was alone in that belief."

"Millions of dollars in damage," Retsler said. "Lives ruined. Two deaths. Because of me and my mouth."

"You didn't start this," Denne said.

"But I should have ended it," Retsler said. He sighed and sloshed his way back to the stairs. "Next time, I trust Lucy."

"Next time?" Denne asked, following him. "Let's hope to God there is no next time."

But there would be, Retsler knew. As long as Whale Rock was here, as long as strange things happened, there would be another clash between the humans and the strange creatures that lived in the sea. He only hoped that the next time, he would try some cooperation, maybe learn how to bend the laws of man, so that no one had to rely on the laws of God.

The Guardian turns to the Seeker seated at the Arm of Air. You have chosen to seek things that are not always seen or touched, but can be known. Your choice can lead you to places beyond your present experience. If it is still your desire to learn, drink and your Guide shall come.

The man at the table considers only briefly before drinking. He has worked hard and waited long to fulfill his quest. At the end of the Arm of Air, the Guide appears. It is the Winged Aeon. Some might think him an angel, this winged creature, yet others an evolved human. The Aeon beckons to the Seeker. Together, they pass through the threshold of the Eastern door. Here, the man finds himself supported by the wind. Clouds drift by him as he gently descends, and as one is shaped into words, he reads:

SONS OF THUNDER

by Edward Carmien

"LET Jesus by your savior."

The line, crisp, clean, professionally delivered, struck like a lance. A citified wind-devil erupted on the quiet street, throwing hot dog wrappers and bits of dirty cellophane into a mad dance. The missionary blinked in the sudden gust, her skirt spiraling tight against her trim legs.

"Jehua Mashiah," I said with a flat and hollow voice, "killed my brother and many others, and nearly killed me." How easily my anger returned, boosting detritus 'round and 'round in a miniature tornado. I turned my back on her and walked into traffic. Horns blared, and the sound was like a certain horn—

* * *

—which blared from a middle distance, difficult to tell how far in the desert heat.

"They who once wandered in Kadesh," said my brother, "are stirring now in Nazareth."

"What stirs the Jews?"

"A man, a teacher they say."

"I am not fond of the man places," I said, whisking my brother down a dune and stirring sand as we went. The horn-blower deserved bedeviling for troubling our quiet afternoon in the sky. Blown sand could sting. "And I do not like taking the form of a man, even for an hour."

"A day, grant me a day," laughed my brother, and we topped a rise and rushed down it, to a boy with a shell horn out in the sun for no good reason.

After we left the boy blinking and sneezing, my brother cajoled me again. "Come. We'll play at being fishermen, stand in the crowd, smell the cooking food, and listen to the teacher's speech. It is too long since we have played at being men."

I allowed myself to be convinced. And when the teacher pointed us out in the crowd I said, "Look, here are the Sons of Thunder come to join me in my journey." What arrow wounded me then, that a mere man knew me for what I was?

"He picked us out of the crowd," I said—

* * *

—"That isn't what's written," the missionary stated.

I blinked, and found myself almost two thousand years from that time. Memory took me like that. I would discover myself in some random place, alone or in chance-met company. Darkness cloaked the windows, making them a blank wall. We sat in a coffeehouse, one of the new big ones with plastic made to look like intimate wood and not a furnishing out of place.

Had she pursued me across the street? How did she come to be here now? Time left me, time came back. I often found one or more following me, caught up in some eddy, walking, a bit dazed, in my wake.

"Why are you here?" I asked. My employees awaited my arrival at the studio. Today they would have to wait a bit longer for me. My manager, the thief, no doubt sweated the most. I meant to replace him, abruptly and finally.

She shifted, and I saw her for the first time as separate and individual from all the busy millions that hived in and about the concrete towers. Asian, tall, with black hair and a wide, friendly face. The figure beneath her clothing would sell well.

"Because you were so angry," she said patiently, as if repeating herself. She probably was. "And . . ." her voice edged to silence.

I had that effect at times. Hypnotic was the word they used. Sometimes they came after me because they could do nothing else, caught as blown flotsam in the sucking lee of a tornado. Eventually they came to rest, always some distance from here I'd picked them up.

"Will you finish the story? Please?"

I shrugged. "Jehua pointed to us in the crowd, named us Sons of Thunder. He knew us with a look, and that was enough to make us follow him, we who scarcely knew ourselves. He named us James and

John, after fishermen he'd known in Galilee . . ." She gasped, and I slipped back into memory—

* * *

—Where I sat with my back to a stone and my chest to a fire. It was the desert, and I should have felt the night's chill, but did not. Jehua, not yet named Mashiah by those who had wandered in Kadesh, was gaunt. He had gone many days without food, taking only a little wine in his water, for health.

"I do not understand why you will not eat," I said to Jehua. My talkative brother was silent, as he had been silent much during these long desert nights.

Jehua, as was often his habit, did not answer directly. "My fasting is not for you, but for my eyes that I might see. Our stay has nearly come to an end in any case. Remain here, by the fire. I shall return by morning."

My brother nodded meekly as the man rose and left the fire. I turned to him with amazement. "Why do you accept his word so easily? Are we not of the wind, taking this form for but a time, in jest?"

To my dismay, he shook his head and stared into the fire. I could not stand his thoughtful quietness, so unlike his former self. I teased our distant cousin the fire with a quick breeze, then left. I found Jehua some distance away, sitting in the dark. I whisked sand about to let him know I was there. It was delicious, having a man know my true self, for usually we are unknowable except to our brothers.

"Son of Thunder," he acknowledged, "you have come to ask me what I am, so I tell you now, I am the son of God, and with my words I am to lead my people out of a great darkness."

"If you are a god," I whispered into his ears, "make yourself a meal from these stones."

"Bread alone is not what feeds me," he said with a smile that stretched the skin tight over his cheekbones, thin as he was.

This made me angry, and I howled in a great circle around him, feeling strong after so long a time confined in the shell of a man. After a moment I snatched him up, a thing I could not always do, but he was wasted and light from all his starving days. In a matter of moments I carried him to a city much prized by men and there to a temple, on a high roof. "If you are a god," I whispered, "leap, and save yourself. Does not some scrap of learning you have tell you your father shall keep you safe?

"I am nothing but the son of man," he said, "and my learning tells me not to test God."

I left him there and roared through the city streets, dousing lanterns and raising dirt with a caterwaul of pent-up anger. I did not understand this man, did not understand how he had muted my brother, did not understand why I was unable to sway him with either silken words or displays of power.

"Come!" I shouted then, and took him high where the air is cold. It was a clear night. Below, the land dwindled. The city lights became like a single candle seen from afar. All the lands I roamed could be seen beneath us. Jehua gasped and choked in my feathery grasp. At any moment I might weaken and drop him. Let him die, I thought, by such an accident, let Jehua die and grant me my brother back from manlike silence!

"Look below, Jehua. Look below at all the lands of Samaria, of Judaea, Idumaea. Look there, to the sea, to the human places of Joppa, Caesarea, Jamnia, Azotus. Admit you are nothing but a man with a fast tongue, and I will help you rule these places. I am much more a god than any you have ever seen. Give me your worship, and all these places are yours."

"Djinn," he gasped, and he named me by the name given to my brothers by the people of the desert, by the people who never came to the places of men but stayed instead in the sands with their flocks. "Djinn, I reject thee! Take me down!"

I brought him low again, near the place where I had snatched him up. Nearby burned the fire where my silent brother sat. Jehua collapsed on the ground at my feet. He rolled onto his back. I made a semblance of a man to speak to him, but he spoke first.

"I told you our time here in the desert would soon end," and with that, blood came from his nose. The heights of the air are not for men. I picked him up in my false man-arms and carried—

* * *

—"I don't believe you," she said. We stood in a pool of light, on a dark street hellishly lit by electrical lamps. "You can't have lived during the time of Christ. You can't be . . . the devil."

"The devil?" I said, and forced a smile to my wooden face.

"It was the devil who tempted Christ in the desert, and he went alone—" she began. She still clutched a Bible in one hand. She lifted it now.

"I am not responsible for the poor telling of the tale," I snapped. We were at the foot of a tall building. Inside, at the very top, my business was housed. My employees had waited many hours, for the sun had long fled.

"But—" She brandished her Bible.

"But nothing," I said, making my voice harsh. "You choose to follow me? You dog my steps? Come, then!"

Her eyes went wide as I became what I truly am and picked her bodily up and high into the air. The glass squares of the building blurred past as she struggled against my grasp. Soon we streaked past the roof.

"Look down. Know me as more real than your God. You need no faith for this miracle to work. Name me as your deity, and I will make you rich." I spoke in jest, I had no interest in making her rich, and there was nothing I wanted from her, not even a renunciation of her God. I'd wrung enough such statements in a hundred different languages during a thousand different years to satisfy me. Now I pursued a different agenda.

"No," she said, no longer struggling against my grasp.

So she was one of the strong ones. I liked her better for that, and brought her gently down to the rooftop. It would cause gossip among my employees when we came down from the roof as if out of the air. I didn't care. Their mewling meant nothing to me.

"This way," I said, a man again, and descended a few steps to a door that was never locked, by my order. The missionary followed.

My employees lounged in the studio, weary of waiting. The banks of machines hummed a tone which always made me wish to lash out in anger. I did not understand them, only what they were: a window into millions of souls.

"Why are we here? What is this place?" she said, very matter of fact for a woman who had just flown through the air. She asked this, surrounded by beds covered with sumptuous pillows and satin sheets, walls of scenery, cameras, cheap metal shelves lined with intimate toys, racks holding wispy bits of cloth.

"I am here to fire my manager," I announced, answering her first question.

"No!" the man cried. "You can't fire me! What will you do . . .?" I cut him off with a gesture.

"Do not presume. You have stolen from me. Keep

the money. Your weakness is punishment enough. Tomorrow or tomorrow or tomorrow you will steal again, and you will pay. Go." I was well satisfied. He was now a ruined man, no Jehua to refuse temptation. He stood, ready to argue. "GO!" I shouted, and took pleasure in seeing him jump. Within moments he was out of the studio.

"But what will we . . ." begin my photographer.

"Hire a new manager," I said to my remaining employees. I knew what they said about me, that I came to the studio infrequently, never collected the profits, paid them well, urged them on to new and more creative ways to do what they did with their cameras and lights and computers and credit card company accounts. I did not care, so long as their work went on.

"What is this place?" asked my guest, her voice trembling.

"This is my business. My employees take pictures. They sell them. We make quite a bit of money."

"But you, you . . ." her eyes were round, and dark brown.

"I don't need money," I stated quietly. Best to keep the employees guessing.

"Then why do you do . . . all this?"

I felt a guilty pleasure in her interest. During the years I had told few the answer to that question. If she wanted answers, I thought wickedly, she would have to pay.

"Let them photograph you."

"No," she said.

"Yes."

Tense silence fell between us. I heard the young woman who took care of the machines mutter, "Check it out. The boss' new model has a Bible."

"Shut up," said the photographer, who had worked for me longest. He knew I could hear them, no matter that they whispered half a room away.

"No," the missionary declared. "I won't help you . . ."

How close she came to knowing everything. I answered her in a soft but grating voice. "Yes. You believe I have seen what I describe. Say no. Leave. And never sleep again, knowing you could have learned more about your faith, your savior."

She bit her lip, a fetching gesture. Her eyes bored into me, then closed. "There's no point looking at you, is there? You're not there. Not the real you." She swayed on her feet, clearly tired. Probably hungry. She had been following me for hours. People did that, if I let them. She would agree, even if she did so with some clever motive in mind.

Finally, she hung her head. Some of her black hair escaping a plain clip, fell around her face on each side. "Yes," she said. Then she looked up, and her chin was set firmly, her eyes open and clear. "Yes," she said again. "And then the rest of your story."

I gestured to the photographer, who stepped forward to do his business. "Never done this before?" he asked, but it wasn't really a question. He led her away to a changing area, a square of movable wall panels that hid a corner of the wide-open space my business occupied. When he brought her back, she was naked and tried to cover herself with her hands. Completely unbound now, her hair trailed past her shoulders.

The photographer left her, moved a tall panel of glass that provided a dim reflection. He posed her in front of a false wall, stepped back. "Hair," he said critically. "Can't hide those pretty shoulders. Can you hold it up?"

I silently applauded his ruse. Slowly, her right hand left her full breasts, gathered up her hair. "Can I have my hair clip?" she asked. Her left still cupped her groin. The photographer didn't answer. Instead, he took her picture. She jumped, startled.

"Sorry," said the photographer tonelessly. That was the image to keep, I knew. He continued to pose her and shoot. I watched the images take life on screens out of her view. Yes, the first was by far the best image. Knowing for certain she was going to be photographed, her grin was forced in one shot, absent in another. No. It had to be that first image, taken by surprise. It captured her innocence. It would serve well in the machines, go forth over the wires and out into similar screens, wherever men made their computers show them such images.

"Give her a check," I said finally, bringing the session to a halt.

"I don't want to be paid," she said. "Not with a check."

I made myself nod, and following her to the changing area. Somewhere, deep down, she knew I was not a man. She relaxed as she dressed and began breathing more regularly. The flush left her face.

"Tell me the rest," she said—

* * *

—And there I was, shadowing Jehua and his followers in yet another dusty place made by men. I looked with longing on the shape of my brother, now called James, walking with his human brother, John. I had seen John called forth from his father's fishing boat: people now said my brother and John were the sons of Zebedee. Later, the man James would join his brother John, and people would say Jehua had named them the Sons of Thunder.

Jehua, now called Mashiah by many who heard him preach, stopped by a small stream. His followers walked round about, gathering a crowd to hear Jehua's words. A messenger came. I hovered close.

"The Baptist has been arrested. He is in Herod's prison, Mashiah. What shall you do?"

By this I knew the messenger to be a Zealot, one of many who buzzed around Jehua's camp and carried tales of his preaching for their own purposes.

Jehua said, "Then I shall preach, and I shall baptize, in honor of the man who baptized me." And later that day it came to pass that my brother stepped forward for this ritual. I was frantic. Why would a spirit of air wish to be immersed in a stream? Such could offend the water spirits. In my panic, I could not take the guise of a man, but watched as a zephyr above the water as Jehua spoke to my brother, James, already waist-deep in the quiet stream.

"You know what your faith may bring, Son of Thunder?"

By this I knew Jehua had not forgotten our true form. My brother nodded. As Jehua dipped him beneath the water, he spoke in a clear voice: "Reform all that you are! The kingdom of human spirit is at hand!"

When my brother rose from the water, he was no longer my brother. His flesh softened. He breathed because he must. His eyes were full of water. He sputtered. His skin became hot. I would have raged into storm and killed Jehua where he stood, with a crowd of men and women standing witness, but my brother spoke.

"Be calm, my brother. This great faith is my choice. Be free of your anger. Go."—

* * *

—"But . . ."

Her question brought me back from the dead past. "But what?"

"Your brother . . . accepted what he became. Why are you angry? How can you be so angry today, thousands of years later?" She had finished dressing while I spoke and once again clutched her Bible. The way she held it told me this was her weapon, this was her reason for remaining with me. She meant to do battle. Her hair was still free, unclipped and wild against her conservative white shirt.

I was silent. I remembered what else had happened during those years of tumult.

"And why run this. . . *business?*"

"Jehua killed them all," I said, voice toneless. "My brother was only the first. He went among my tribe in the desert and spread the Mashiah's faith. One by one they came to the cities of men and were baptized. One by one they became men. And no matter what storms I brought against them, no matter what I whispered in the ears of those who might listen, no matter . . ."

Wind stirred and whistled throughout the suite. Beyond the screens came a shout of alarm. Lights flickered. Great anger returned to me, the tremendous pain that had sustained me through all the years I had worn the face of a man.

"Anything," I said. "Anything to tarnish your faith. To quench your spirit, the light behind human eyes. To make you all pay."

Somewhere, glass broke. The photographer shouted. A stiff breeze lifted the missionary's hair and made it stand out straight behind her, yet she was not afraid.

"I am the only one left of my tribe!" I wanted desperately to shake her confidence. I did not know what I wanted of her, but I would discover it, if I had to throw her from a high place and chase her to the street to do so.

Not fear, but confusion wrinkled her brow.

"You fool, my tribe turned into men, into men. There are no more of us. Men die!"

A hand flew to her mouth. Beyond the screen, shards of glass would be plummeting earthward and shattering into pea-sized fragments. By now, my staff had no doubt fled.

Her hand reached out for me, and I could only imagine what she saw: a ragged facsimile of a man, face intact, limbs streaming away in ribbons with my anger, raising winds that screamed. "You must forgive," she said quietly, but I could hear her well despite the din. "You must forgive yourself, you must forgive!"

"I do not believe!" I shouted, and took pleasure in her recoil. But she leaned toward me once again.

"It is not a matter of faith!" she cried. Looking to the Bible in her hands, she cast it loose into the wind. It immediately swept aloft. The screening panels lifted free and joined the tornado in the center of the suite. Bare concrete and girders lay exposed. Even the heavy computers, in their headstone-sized cases, were stirred by the shrieking winds.

"I don't understand what you are, but you're not the devil. Whatever you are, I forgive you!" she yelled. Reaching forward, she grasped the shell of my face and kissed my brittle lips. "I forgive you," she whispered, her face tight against mine.

I brought hands into being and held her close. Then I took us into the air through a shattered window. High up we went, but no so high as I had once taken Jehua Mashiah. "You don't know the things I've done. I've fanned the fires of ovens that burned human flesh. I have sold human children into slavery. I have made these craft crash," I pointed at a nearby set of quick-moving lights in the sky, "Killing hundreds at a stroke. I have devoted hundreds of your lifetimes to my revenge."

"Then consider it complete!" she shouted into the wind of our passage. "Will you kill and torture us forever? Do you enjoy taking the form of a man? So your tribe has passed. Aren't there other tribes you can find, and make them your brothers?"

She was nothing, a shivering young woman who had angered me with a few words. I could drop her and not give her another thought. Or could I? Unbidden, her nakedness came to mind. Her eyes wide, she stood tall and proud, knowing what the photographer was about to do, yet determined to make her nakedness mean nothing.

Her nakedness. I began to understand by what human magic Jehua had stolen my brothers from me. Her beauty was not Jehua's. His had been a charisma of words and ideas. Her flesh almost made me want to be a man. Yet not only her flesh. Her innocent spirit as well. But there was more I had to know.

I set us motionless in the air. "Why did you let me take your image? You know what I would have done with it? Adolescent boys would steal credit card numbers in order to make your picture appear on their computers. Older men would sit in front of their screens, view your nakedness with lust."

She was silent. Then she said "My naked body is not evil. And after you showed me . . . showed me what you are, I knew I had been sent to touch your anger."

"You knew?" I asked, ridicule in my tone.

She shrugged. "I knew. I thought maybe my faith would be enough, but it wasn't." She looked at her empty hands. "So I threw away my Bible. But I still believe." Not so far above, a jet began to rumble as it approached. Below, the lights of the city burned, a monument to the cleverness of humanity.

I thought long on this, that a woman who knew

what I was risked so much. Far off, I thought I heard a joyful shout from high in the air. I felt a twinge of shame, knowing now my yearning for revenge had kept me from hearing my foreign brothers of the air.

Change, change is our essence. How long I had fought to keep my ravening anger, my great hate. And now, after hearing a chance phrase on the street, after seeing an innocent face offered up for faith and nothing else, change had come to me.

"Name a wish," I said, the ancient ritual for blessing a service done one of my kind. I was done speaking with this woman. She smiled nonetheless, as if she knew my thoughts well.

She told me a wish, a paltry thing. After naming my conditions, I set her down on the street, amidst the rubble, to welcome the wailing sirens come to salve the injured. "Freak storm," I heard the rescuers say over and over. "Freak storm."

I do not know the count of years between that time and when she finally called me to a green field, to a man and a boy with a kite. But I made the kite fly high and well, and it did not tangle in trees that day. I knew when she waved into the sky that she waved to me, and to my new brothers, whom I had brought for a day of whispering amongst green leaves and dancing birds.

EPILOGUE

The Guardian looks at the Seekers seated around the table. They are the dreamers, the bearers of knowledge. They are his chosen. He looks at each directly. "The time has come for you to return to your world. Remember what you have seen and share it with those around you. We enter the time for new knowledge to be given to the world. You may always return here: simply call and I will hear you."

One by one, they take their leave of him, each leaving by the path between the worlds that he opens for them. When the last Seeker has departed, the Walker of Two Worlds dissolves the semblance of the Hall. Surrounded now only by the gray mist of the ether, he releases the form he assumed for their convenience and returns to eternity.

ABOUT THE AUTHORS

Born in the Maritimes, **Tanya Huff** now lives and writes in rural Ontario. On her way there, she spent three years in the Canadian Naval Reserve and got a degree in Radio and Television Arts which the cat threw up on. Recent books include the novel *The Quartered Sea* and a single author collection entitled *What Ho, Magic!*

Linda P. Baker is the author of two fantasy novels, *The Irda* and *Tears of the Night Sky* (with Nancy Berberick). Her short fiction also appears in *First Contact*, *Wizard Fantastic*, and several *Dragonlance* anthologies. She and her husband, Larry, live in Mobile, Alabama.

Carrie Channell lives in Chicago, Illinois, where she pursues freelance work as a writer, editor, proofreader, and anything else relating to books and magazines. She is the assistant editor for both *Filmfax* and *Outre* magazines, and writes reviews of videos, books, and CDs for anyone willing to print them. She has published one horror story in issue 3, entitled *Strange Creatures,* of the acclaimed *Twilight Tales* chapbook series.

Bruce Holland Rogers has won numerous awards for his short fiction, including several Nebula Awards. He has written excellent fantasy stories for such collections as *The Fortune Teller, Black Cats and Broken Mirrors, Alien Pets*, and *Warrior Princesses.*

Nina Kiriki Hoffman has been nominated for several awards for her fiction, including the World Fantasy Award for her novella "Home for Christmas." She also has stories in *Tarot Fantastic, Enchanted Forests,* and *Wizard Fantastic.*

Creator and developer of the *Tales from the Eternal Archives* series, **Robyn McGrew** is a writer and editor currently living in the southeast. Her fiction has appeared in the anthologies *Sword and Sorceress X* and *Relics and Omens* among others, and in various fantasy magazines. When not writing short stories and novels or working as an administrative assistant, Robyn studies the Western Mysteries. As a lifelong student, Robyn believes one of the greastest joys is to learn and share her discoveries.

Nancy Varian Berberick is the author of seven fantasy novels and numerous short stories in the fantasy genre, with a few short fiction forays into children's literature. Her fiction, steeped in folklore, mythology, legend, and history, has been variously described as epic fantasy and historical fantasy. Nancy's latest novel is *Tears of the Night Sky* (with Linda Baker). Her newest work, *Dalamar the Dark,* will be published early in 2000. Nancy lives with her husband, architect Bruce A. Berberick, and their two dogs in a fascinating and flourishing inner city neighborhood in Charlotte, North Carolina. There she writes her fiction, *Dragonlance* and original, translates Old English poetry for fun, and gardens when she needs to come up for air.

Donald J. Bingle, a corporate attorney, has written a wide variety of material for science fiction and fantasy role-playing games, as well as authoring movie reviews, short stories, and an action/comedy screenplay. He is also the world's top-ranked player of sanctioned role-playing tournaments. When not gaming or writing, he spends large quantities of time with his wife, Linda, and their puppies, Smoosh and Sara. Sometimes he immerses himself in the abstract and largely fictional theories of neo-psychophysics, but more often he just immerses himself in the hot tub.

Michelle West is the author of *The Sacred Hunter* duology, *The Broken Crown, The Uncrowned King,* and *The Shining Court,* all published by DAW books. She reviews books for the on-line column *First Contacts,* and less frequently for *The Magazine of Fantasy & Science Fiction.* Other short fiction by her appears in *Black Cats and Broken Mirrors, Elf Magic,* and *Olympus.*

Mark Garland is the author of several novels, including *Dorella, Demon Blade,* and *The Sword of the Prophets.* His short fiction has appeared in *Xanadu III, Monster Brigade 3000,* and various other publications.

Lawrence Schimel is the coeditor of *Tarot Fantastic, The Fortune Teller,* and *Camelot Fantastic,* among other projects. His stories appear in *Dragon Fantastic, Catfantastic III, Weird Tales from Shakespeare, Phantoms of the Night, Return to Avalon,* the *Sword & Sorceress* series, and many other anthologies. He lives in New York City, where he writes and edits full-time.

Jane Lindskold spent many pleasant days in the Ojo Caliente valley while working as an archeological volunteer on the excavation of Anasazi cobble and gravel mulched fields. The author of over thirty short stories and several novels—including *Changer* and *Legends Walking*—she lives in Albuquerque, New Mexico with her husband, archaeologist Jim Moore. She is currently at work on another novel.

Kristine Kathryn Rusch is an award-winning writer whose novels have also been on several bestseller lists. Her most recent novels are *The Fey: Victory* and *Hitler's Angel*. She has also coauthored *Star Wars: The New Rebellion* and several *Star Trek* novels with her husband, Dean Wesley Smith.

Edward Carmien writes and teaches in New Jersey. He had published short fiction in a number of magazines and anthologies (but dares anyone to track them down—and checking his web page would be cheating). He hikes when he has the time, motorcycles when he can afford a bike, adds to his library because he can't help it, and knows how to say "there are eels in my hovercraft" in German.

Don't Miss These Exciting DAW Anthologies